BULLET COUNTRY

THE HOLLY LIN SERIES

BULLET COUNTRY

A NOVA BARTKOWSKI NOVEL

ROBERT SWARTWOOD

RMS PRESS

ISBN: 978-1-945819-29-2

www.robertswartwood.com

Dedicated to my father-in-law, Norman Sargent
April 16, 1946 — September 29, 2022

ONE

By the time she arrived at the scene, the ambulances had already left and only two police SUVs remained, their roof flashers and other LED lights still strobing dully in the midafternoon sun.

Sheriff Veronica Chapman eased her unmarked F-150 into the Yellow Bird Cafe's parking lot, the bug-splattered grille aimed so she had a good view of Main Street and the mechanic shop across the way. That's where the two SUVs were parked right now, blocking off the inside of the open bay to anyone trying to peer inside.

Stepping out of the pickup, Veronica felt the tightness in her muscles and once again promised herself she would take a stab at yoga even though she knew it was never going to happen, not with her schedule.

She slammed the door shut, adjusted her Ray-Ban sunglasses, and scanned this portion of Main Street. Besides a score of lookie-loos milling about on the sidewalk, nothing appeared out of place.

Except, no, that wasn't right.

A man Veronica didn't recognize was sitting on a bench in front of the cafe. Jeans, Timberland boots, green Carhartt jacket. He almost looked like he fit in the scene except his face wasn't familiar, and as somebody who had been born and raised in this town—and who would probably die here, just like her parents—Veronica knew every person in town by face and name.

This man was an outsider.

"Sheriff!"

Deputy Jamie Bennett jogged across the street to meet her. He was one of her younger deputies, having just turned twenty-five last year. Tall and athletic with a pretty-boy face that got him much more action than he probably deserved with his bland personality, he was a solid cop, who wasn't one to slack off.

"What do we have, Jamie?"

"To put it bluntly, Sheriff, it's a fucking mess."

"How so? I thought there were no fatalities."

"Not yet, but that could change."

Veronica followed the quiet scrape of her deputy's boots as he led her across the street, purposefully ignoring the lookie-loos watching them.

Wednesday afternoon, almost two o'clock. The sky a deep blue with a patch of cumulus clouds off on the horizon, looking like the cotton candy you'd find at the county fair. The temperature a comfortable sixty-five degrees, which for early September was about as nice as you were going to get it around these parts.

Usually town was quiet for the most part. That was the nice thing about Remington—it was so tiny it didn't get too many outsiders passing through. Sure, it was right off the interstate, and sure, it had a motel, but this portion of the state wasn't as breathtakingly gorgeous as the western portion. No rolling fields or snow-capped peaks here.

Two of her other deputies were waiting by the SUVs.

George Murphy, who worked for Ed Schaffer, was sitting on a stool just inside the bay, his knee bouncing like a pent-up jackrabbit. He lifted his tired, bloodshot eyes as Veronica joined the others but didn't nod or wave or give her even the slightest notice.

Veronica noted the socket wrench on the garage floor and the blood splatter on the wall and pavement and offered up a silent prayer of gratitude that what happened here hadn't been any worse.

"Tell me what happened."

Before any of her deputies could answer, George Murphy grunted from his place on the stool.

"What do you think? Blake Hogan's boys are what happened."

He hopped off the stool and strode right over to them, his steel-toed Wolverines stomping across the concrete floor, his weathered face pinched in anger.

"They been coming around here for the past couple of weeks, causing trouble. I kept telling Ed to call the police, and he kept waving it off because he knew it would be a waste of time."

"Why's that, George?"

Those bloodshot eyes stayed steady on hers.

"Because when it comes to Blake Hogan and his old man, this town has a particular fondness for looking the other way."

George Murphy hadn't been born and raised in Remington like most others in town. He'd ended up here five years ago, looking for a place to lay low for a while. (It wasn't for any nefarious reason, at least as far as Veronica could tell, having done a background check on George and finding only a decade-old DUI and two citations for speeding.) He'd stopped by Ed's looking for work, and Ed had hired him with the idea the man might only be around for a few months. But then those months started piling up until they became years, and now here he was, practically running the garage with Ed.

Veronica said, "I'm not sure I appreciate the insinuation, George."

"Well, shit, Sheriff, I didn't mean to *insinuate* anything. I meant to say it flat out: Blake Hogan and his boys are a public threat, and your office won't do fuck-all about it."

Jamie Bennett, clearing his throat: "George, we understand that you're upset after what happened—"

"Upset? *Upset*? You mean nearly seeing my boss beat to death isn't supposed to be upsetting?"

Veronica glanced at her two other deputies, who immediately moved in tandem to direct George back into the garage. Jamie watched the three of them as they drifted away, George mumbling a string of curses under his breath, and then tilted his face down as he lowered his voice.

"He's not wrong, you know."

"About what?"

"Blake's guys have been harassing Ed for the past couple of weeks."

"Why is this the first I'm hearing about it?"

"Because like George said, Ed never called to make a formal complaint."

"Then how do you know about it?"

Jamie Bennett offered up a helpless shrug.

"It's a small town, Sheriff. Fact is, I'm surprised you didn't hear about it too."

She turned away from him and pointed at the ground.

"Whose blood is that?"

"From what we can tell, some of it's Ed's blood, some of it's BJ's, and some of it's Finlay's."

"Christ," Veronica whispered, staring again at the socket wrench and blood spatter. "And BJ and Finlay both were taken to the hospital?"

Jamie nodded.

"BJ with a broken arm, Finlay with a broken leg. But Ed" —Jamie issued a heavy sigh—"Ed was unresponsive when the EMTs left. I got a call from the hospital right before you arrived."

"And?"

"They had to intubate him because they're worried about brain swelling. He's still out, and it's not clear if and when he'll wake up."

She tried picturing Ed Schaffer. A large man in his early fifties. Fairly good-looking for his age, though his face had become worn and he was starting to lose his hair around his temples. He'd been living in town for nearly fifteen years, running the town's only mechanic shop and trying his best not to get undercut by Hogan Auto.

"BJ and Finlay are both, what, in their thirties?"

Jamie flipped through his notepad.

"BJ's thirty-four. Finlay's thirty-two."

"Either way, they're young guys. Strong and competent. I'm having a hard time picturing Ed Schaffer getting the upper hand on either man to the point he puts any kind of hurt on them."

"He didn't," Jamie said, and pointed across the street at the man sitting on the bench. The outsider in the jeans and Timberland boots and Carhartt jacket. "He did."

"And who the hell is he?"

Jamie only grinned.

"What's so funny?"

"Well, the guy says he's just passing through, and maybe he is. But his first name? You're never gonna guess it. Fact is, I thought it was a joke at first, but I confirmed it with the DMV."

Veronica regarded the outsider again—the man was leaning

forward, staring down at his phone—before she turned back to her deputy.

"What's his first name?"

"Casanova."

TWO

Nova watched the woman wait for a truck to pass before crossing the street. Even though she'd parked on this side next to the cafe, he knew by her purposeful stride she was headed straight for him.

"Casanova Bartkowski? I'm Sheriff Veronica Chapman."

Late thirties, tall and fit. Strong cheekbones and brown hair pulled back into a tight bun. She wore sunglasses and a shit-brown uniform, just like the other deputies, only the star-shaped badge over her left breast prominently proclaimed SHERIFF.

He shook the woman's hand and offered up a smile but didn't stand from the bench.

"People call me Nova. What can I do for you, Sheriff?"

"I understand you were involved in a situation earlier."

"If you want to call it that."

"Mind telling me what happened?"

"I've already told your deputies."

"I know. I'd like to hear it from the horse's mouth, if that's okay."

She was smiling, trying to butter him up. But Nova had

been sitting on this bench for nearly two hours, and he was irritated and grumpy and just wanted to get the hell out of this place.

Taking a breath, he said, "What do you want to know?"

"For starters, what brings you to Remington?"

"The town sits right along the Yellowstone. I read online it's one of the best for fishing."

"Oh, it certainly is, though I guess it depends on what you're fishing for. Most people typically go to the Missouri or the Bighorn or the Clarks Fork or practically any other river in this state."

"I plan on getting to them too. Been working my way west. I started up north and came down I-94. This place looked nice enough, so I decided to give it a try."

"You got a fishing license?"

"Of course I do. I already showed it to your deputy. Why— would you like to see it for yourself?"

"That's all right. So how long have you been in town?"

Something told Nova the woman already knew the answer. That she already knew almost all the answers to the questions she was asking as he had already given his statement to the deputies, who had no doubt already filled her in. This was just part of the dance, an elaborate tango of carefully considered and strategic questions that cops were trained to ask witnesses and suspects and pretty much anyone else unfortunate enough to cross their paths.

Nova didn't blame her. He had intended to come and go without much notice. And now three men were in the hospital, two of which he'd had a hand in placing there himself.

"This is my second day."

"Where are you staying?"

"The Millport."

"How are you liking it so far?"

"It's a motel, that's for sure."

Now the smile turned into a genuine grin. It looked cute on her.

"Like many towns in this state, Remington is a bedroom community. Last census taken had us at just under eight hundred residents. We don't have that many outsiders coming and going, which is why you won't find a Holiday Inn or Motel 8 anywhere nearby. We don't even have a McDonald's. And if you want gas, your choices are either the Kwik Stop or the Cenex Zip Trip. So is the Millport the best motel in the state? I'm sorry to say it's not."

"That's okay. And I apologize—did you want to sit down?"

Nova started to slide toward one corner, but the sheriff raised a hand to wave him off.

"Thanks, but I've been driving around most of the day and need to stretch my legs. Now, how was the fishing this morning?"

Again, Nova sensed that the woman already knew the answer.

"I didn't go."

"No? But didn't you say the whole reason you came to town was to fish?"

"I wasn't feeling well this morning. Probably something I ate last night."

"Where'd you eat?"

"Stacey's."

The only steakhouse in a twenty-mile radius. He'd eaten there last night, in a booth tucked in the far corner, so it wasn't a lie, but the food hadn't made him sick. In fact, it was some of the best food he'd had in quite a while.

This woman was testing him, though, something the deputies hadn't done earlier. Nova had already gotten his story straight, knew what he needed to say and how to say it, and now here was the sheriff seeing if she could catch him in a lie.

"That's a shame," she said, shifting on her feet as she

glanced down the street, her profile cutting right in the sunlight. "Stacey's usually has great food."

"Yeah, well, it tasted good at the time."

"So then what did you do this morning?"

"I came here for breakfast."

"Did you? I thought you said you weren't feeling well."

"Not feeling well enough to go fishing, but well enough to try to put something in my stomach."

"And so then after breakfast?"

"Went back to my room and lay down for a bit because I still didn't feel great. Then I decided to come back here for lunch. Wasn't going to go back to Stacey's, not after last night."

The grin again.

"I don't blame you. And so then you were here having lunch."

"That's right."

"And then?"

"And then what?"

"Well, Mr. Bartkowski, I've currently got three men in the hospital, two of which I understand you put there. I'm just trying to assess what took place so that I don't have to place you under arrest."

This was new. None of the deputies had made this threat, and it almost caught him off guard, but he smiled back at her, staring at his reflection in her Ray-Bans.

"While I was sitting inside eating my burger, I happened to look up and saw two men start pushing the mechanic around."

He looked left and right, at the two separate clusters of townies that hadn't yet dispersed. Earlier, there had been more —mostly older folk whispering to each other as they threw furtive glances his way—but now there was only a handful, still hanging out because most likely there was nothing else for them to do.

"I saw your deputies interviewing everybody here. They all saw what happened too."

"That's true—they did. But what I don't understand is what made you decide to leave your table and hurry across the street to get in the middle of the ruckus."

Ruckus, he thought. Did she really just call it a ruckus?

"I'm not sure what to tell you, Sheriff. I've always believed that if you see somebody in trouble you help them out."

"But you could have gotten hurt. In fact, from what I see, you *did* get hurt."

She touched the side of her temple, where in the same spot Nova had gotten punched. It was tender but nothing compared to what he'd sustained over the years.

"The EMTs checked me out. They said I was okay."

"I'm glad to hear it. But you could. have gotten yourself hurt even more."

"That's true."

"It's my understanding you broke one of the men's arms. The other man has a broken leg."

"I didn't purposefully try to hurt either of them, if that's what you're asking. When I stepped into the ruckus, as you call it, those men came at me. I was protecting myself."

"I'm not accusing you of anything, Mr. Bartkowski, and I apologize if you get that impression. But the simple truth is you're an outsider, and I have three people from this town in the hospital."

"They looked like they were going to kill him."

Sheriff Chapman was quiet, gazing back across the street at the garage.

Nova said, "I apologize if I caused any trouble, but again, I couldn't stand by and watch the man get hurt."

"I understand that. What do you do for work, by the way?"

"I'm between jobs right now."

"What did you do previously?"

"I worked for the government."

"Doing what?"

"IRS auditor."

He knew the moment the answer left his mouth that he'd screwed up. He'd wanted to come up with a job so inane and boring nobody would bother asking any follow-up questions, but clearly the woman didn't buy it.

"An auditor," she said flatly. "You're a big guy, Mr. Bartkowski. And based on the fact you put two men in the hospital while you barely sustained a scratch, you seem to know how to defend yourself pretty well."

Nova offered up another smile.

"Auditors are people too, Sheriff. I go to the gym just like everybody else. And I've taken some self-defense courses. Nowadays, it doesn't seem safe anywhere you go."

The woman stared back at him, her face expressionless. Nova hated that she was still wearing the shades; he couldn't easily read her eyes, which made this whole situation even more difficult.

Finally she said, "How much longer do you intend on staying in town?"

"Not much longer. Probably just another couple of days."

"If I were you, I'd consider leaving tonight."

"Why's that?"

"As I said before, Mr. Bartkowski, you're an outsider. You may not have come to this town intending to hurt two of the men who live here, but that's what happened. Remington is a nice place to live, but the people here are rather close-knit, and I don't imagine some of them will look kindly on an outsider hurting two of their own."

"Sheriff, back in middle school I once had a teacher tell me, don't use a dozen words when a half-dozen words will do."

Those strong cheekbones twitched as the sheriff smiled again.

"Fair enough. Those men you hurt? They're not the most upstanding citizens this town has. And when their friends learn what happened to them, they might not take it very well. Do you get what I'm saying now?"

"Won't they be charged?"

"Of course they'll be charged. The question I'm wrestling with is whether charges should be brought against you."

Nova held her gaze as he said, "I was just defending the guy who couldn't defend himself."

Sheriff Chapman bit her lip as she nodded and gazed across the street again. She stared for a beat, and then asked, "How many days are you booked for at the motel?"

"At least two."

"I know the manager of the Millport. I'll call him and make sure he refunds you the difference."

"Is it okay if I think about it?"

"It's a free country, Mr. Bartkowski. You can do whatever you'd like. I'm just giving you my recommendation as the sheriff of this county."

Nova stood, deciding he'd had enough of the verbal tango. He intended to thank the sheriff for her help and go on his way, though he had zero intention of checking out of the motel tonight despite the place being a piece of shit.

But then he found himself pausing, clearing his throat.

"The mechanic those men attacked—is he going to be all right?"

Hands on her hips, the sheriff sighed.

"Honestly, I'm not sure."

"Does he have anybody who cares for him?"

"His employee certainly does. And his family, of course. From what I'm told, they're already at the hospital."

Suddenly Nova found his mouth dry. He licked his lips, cleared his throat again.

"His family?"

"Yes. I imagine they're out of their minds sick worrying about him."

"So he has a wife?"

As soon as he voiced the question, Nova regretted it. He kicked himself for being so impetuous, but what was done was done.

Despite her sunglasses, Nova knew the sheriff was giving him a particular gaze. Tilting her head just slightly, assessing him in a different light. No doubt trying to determine what it was he was hiding.

"Yes," she said in a measured tone. "And a son."

THREE

Four weeks ago Nova was living just outside Washington, D.C., working a job that didn't exist, at least not on paper.

In essence, he killed people for the United States government. People who deserved to die but whom the government couldn't have any connection to in any way.

When a person like this needed to be eliminated, Nova was sent in, him and what was left of his team—Holly Lin and Scooter.

Only in Las Vegas they'd lost Scooter during a shootout in the desert, and then later … a lot of shit went down, shit that introduced Nova and Holly to a man named Atticus Caine. It turned out Atticus had preceded Nova's and Holly's boss, Walter Hayden, who to Congress was just another general in the US Army, but who also secretly ran the covert-op team.

Nova loved his job, but after everything that went down—much of it still difficult to believe—he decided to walk away from everything.

Because the truth was he was starting to become disillusioned. And, well, bored. But the disillusionment was more of the reason—that feeling that he was simply a tool, being used for a particular skill, and while he was one of the best at performing that skill, he still didn't like what was going on behind the scenes.

And then he'd ended up in Parrot Spur, Nevada, simply passing through in a 1966 Mustang Shelby GT 350, and if his two wheels hadn't blown out—what he would later learn was from the barrel of a sniper rifle—he probably would have never had to deal with the shit that went down in that town.

Not long after that he'd ended up in California. A nice, cozy spot a quarter mile from the ocean, the sun warm and bright and the air so saturated with salt you could taste it in the air and feel it on your skin. But before he could start enjoying himself, he'd gotten a call from Atticus telling him that Holly was in Mexico and needed his help.

And so to Mexico he went, arriving just in time to help Holly save a town from a cartel—while also saving a family from a man hell-bent on revenge.

That was, what, two weeks ago? And then after coming back from Mexico, he'd contacted Atticus with a simple request, something that had been bugging him ever since a young woman named Jessica Hirsch had asked him about his family in the desert just outside Parrot Spur.

Nova's true skill was having suppressed his childhood for most of his adult life. It's never a young boy's dream to have to watch your mother wither away from cancer by yourself because your old man decided he was too much of a chicken-shit to stick around.

For a good decade or more Nova had managed to forget all about his father, relegating the bastard to the part of his brain where thoughts and memories were hidden away to never see the light of day again. But then ... well, he was asked about his family and it brought up that old wound, and to be honest, maybe he hadn't forgotten about his father after all, even though he hated the man's guts.

So Nova had asked Atticus if he or anyone he knew could track down where his old man had gone, whether he was even still alive, and a few days later Atticus emailed him an address.

For days Nova wasn't sure what to do with the address. He'd considered deleting the email and doing his best to forget it existed, but the more he forced himself to forget the more he kept remembering, and no matter where he went or what he did, all he thought about was the address, a place in a small town in Montana.

Remington.

And so that's why he'd come here. To confront the man he once called his father. To look him in his eyes and tell him what it was like to watch his mother die, the woman his father had promised to stay with in sickness and health and then had abandoned.

But before Nova could decide on his next step, he saw the two men out the cafe window.

Tall, broad-shouldered, Stetson cowboy hats bobbing as they advanced toward the garage. They looked like everyone else in town, and if Nova hadn't been paying attention, he probably would have just dismissed them as another pair of locals.

Except for when one of the two men got into the mechanic's face.

He watched as one of the men started gesturing wildly, his voice gaining in pitch loud enough to be heard across the street and through the thin windowpane.

As soon as the man pushed his father, Nova had slid out of the booth.

But a lot can happen in only a few seconds, and by the time Nova crossed the street the man who had once been his father was already on the ground, his eyes closed, his face slack, a nasty gash on the side of his head.

And the two men?

When they turned to him, smug smiles on their faces, they had no idea what was coming.

———

Sunlight filtering through window shades. A constellation of dust motes suspended in the faint glow.

The clock in the corner ticking away the seconds.

His mother in bed. Slender and frail. Her skin shriveled like a raisin. Her eyelids lifting ever so slightly, sensing him nearby.

Her hand shifting on the bed. Pencil-thin fingers reaching toward him.

Her dry lips parting.

A soft wheeze that may or may not be his name.

His eyes snapping open, Nova sucked in a deep breath.

He'd been sitting here now for almost an hour. In his pickup right outside the county hospital, in the parking lot with a slew of other vehicles. The late-afternoon sun was already starting to set, its fading glow skimming the horizon.

Again he thought about driving across the country only a few weeks ago, following the sun toward the Pacific Ocean. Before his tires had blown out. Before he met Jessica Hirsch and she'd asked him about his family and opened the door he'd tried so hard to keep shut.

Just as he often wondered about Holly Lin—where she had ended up, whether she was okay—Nova now wondered the same about Jessica. A young woman, still in college, who didn't look any more threatening than a newborn puppy. But she was much tougher than she looked, and she'd gone to Parrot Spur looking for her brother because, well, he was her brother and she loved him.

Family, Nova knew, could be a funny thing.

When Nova walked through the hospital entrance, he still wasn't sure what he was doing there.

He eyed the signs directing guests toward the ER and thought maybe he should head in that direction but then realized there was a chance the man who had once been his father had been moved to another wing.

There was a desk at the entrance, manned by two employees, and right now they were dealing with three people ahead of him. Nova waited, hating the bright lights and the antiseptic odor that permeated every corner of the place, and before he knew it one of the employees called to him.

"Hello, how can I help you?"

The man behind the desk was smiling expectantly. The bright lights in the ceiling glinted off his wire-rimmed glasses, reminding Nova about how the man who had once been his father had worn glasses too, only for reading, though his father hadn't been one to read much besides the box scores in the paper every morning.

"Sir?"

What was he even doing here? Did he really want to see the man who had once been his father? To maybe spy on the man's wife and … and his … his son?

Nova swallowed. Cleared his throat. Opened his mouth but nothing came out. Which was odd because he wasn't typically the kind of person who wasn't able to form words.

"Sir, are you okay?"

Genuine concern in the man's tone. A worried expression crossing his face as he noted the bruise on Nova's temple.

"What happened there?"

When Nova didn't answer, the man reached for the phone.

"Let me call a nurse, and—"

Nova turned away and strode back out through the automatic glass doors. The sun having dipped down even lower behind the horizon, the sky a watercolor of orange and pink and indigo. He beelined straight for his truck. Breathing in the air that was so clean and fresh it didn't even seem real.

He didn't realize his heart was pounding until he heard the blood thumping in his ears.

When he was kicking the shit out of those two assholes back at the garage, he didn't think his heart rate had gone up more than a dozen beats per minute.

So those men you hurt? They're not the most upstanding citizens this town has. And when their friends learn what happened to them, they might not take it too well.

He knew Sheriff Chapman—whose eyes he never got a chance to see because of her sunglasses but whose color he suspected was brown—meant well enough. Remington was a small, quiet town. They probably didn't have situations like the one earlier today, at least not that often. Especially situations that involved an outsider.

Maybe he should return to the motel and grab his things and hightail it out of town. There was no longer any reason to stick around. He'd seen his father, so there was that. Did he honestly expect to get anything out of confronting the man? Was that going to solve anything?

Yes, maybe he should leave. Head back toward the Pacific coast, which had been his intention weeks ago when he purchased the vintage Mustang and started west on his road trip.

Before he'd ended up in Parrot Spur.

Before he'd met Jessica Hirsch and she asked him about his family.

Before he'd beat the shit out of the Mustang with a crowbar and left the remains in a gas station parking lot.

As Nova steered his pickup out of the hospital parking lot toward the highway back to Remington, he realized he wasn't going anywhere.

FOUR

Tripp Hogan had always valued his privacy. At least one hour out of the day where he could take time for himself and not think and worry about his family or his job or the state of the country. At least one hour where he could lock himself in the peaceful quiet of his den and tinker with one of his favorite hobbies.

"Dad, are you listening to me?"

Yes, he was listening. How could he not? How could he possibly ignore the fact that his son had barged into his den only minutes ago, trailed by Marc and Keith, both men who knew better and lingered by the door while Blake rambled on and on?

"Dad"—Blake pounded his fist on the desk—"look at me."

Tripp's grandfather was the one who had started him on collecting antique guns. He'd already started a small collection featuring pieces from the American Revolutionary War to the Civil War to both World Wars, as well as pieces from other countries' wars. He'd taught Tripp how to properly handle the pieces, how to disassemble and reassemble, how to store them, how to display them.

Blake, not having elicited any reaction from his father, lowered his voice.

"Dad."

Today he was disassembling a recent acquisition: a Charleville musket, one of the very first French infantry muskets produced in 1717. Despite how much he'd paid for it the musket hadn't arrived in tip-top shape, so today he was cleaning it. He'd already separated the wooden parts from the metal parts, as they needed to be cleaned and coated differently.

He'd been in his den now for only forty-five minutes (give or take, as evidenced by the hourglass sitting on the corner of his desk, the fine grains of sand on the bottom half of the hourglass already three-quarters full), and he was owed another fifteen minutes but knew that ignoring his son was only going to irritate him more.

Stripping off his nitrile gloves, he raised his eyes to his son. Blake so closely resembled Tripp's late wife that sometimes it was startling to look at him. The same brown eyes, the same narrow slope of the nose, and Blake had this habit of squishing up his brow that his mother had often done when she was losing her patience.

Blake waited for Tripp to say something, and when he didn't, he lifted his hands.

"Well?"

"Well what?"

The brow squished, a motion so subtle Blake probably didn't even know he was doing it.

"I just told you about what happened to two of our men, and you're sitting there staring back at me like a—"

Tripp raised a finger. A simple gesture, but it was enough to silence his son. Blake might only be thirty-four years old, and it might have taken him longer during his boyhood to understand to respect his elders, especially his father, but eventually he'd gotten there.

Letting the blessed silence fill the room, Tripp waited a few seconds before tilting his finger to point at Marc and Keith standing near the door.

"Are you sure you want them in here for this?"

Blake's gaze didn't waver as he stared back at his father.

"I don't see why not."

Tripp took a deep breath. Even now, after all these years, his son wasn't always the shiniest bullet in the box.

"All right, then." Tripp leaned back in his wheelchair, gaze fixed squarely on his son. "What do you want?"

Again with the brow squishing.

"Are you shitting me? Didn't you hear anything I said?"

"I did. BJ and Finlay are both in the hospital. BJ with a broken arm and Finlay with a broken leg."

Blake stared at him, his eyes slightly widened as if to say, *Isn't that enough?*

Tripp said, "What were they doing there?"

"What?"

"The incident you described happened at Ed Schaffer's garage, yes?"

It took a moment longer than it should have, but understanding dawned across his son's face. His mouth dropped open, and his eyes started to widen, but before Blake could say anything, Tripp addressed Marc and Keith.

"Fellas, please give us the room."

Both men were more than eager to please, hustling out of the room without any hesitation. As soon as the door latched shut, the silence grew so palpable Tripp thought he could hear the individual grains of sand in the hourglass.

Blake's lips were moving, though no words were coming out. This was something he'd done ever since he was a boy.

Trying out the words before voicing them. It had irritated Tripp then and it still did now.

"Spit it out, Son."

"You … you already knew?"

"Of course I did. Nothing happens in this town without my knowing it."

"But then … why did … why didn't you say anything?"

"Because this is my hour, Son. My one hour a day to myself. You should know that better than anyone."

Once, when Blake was nine years old, he'd barged into the den with fourteen minutes left to spare. Their maid at the time had refused to give him a treat, and Blake had felt so incensed and wronged by this egregious slight that he believed bringing it to his father's attention would work out in his favor. Instead, he's gotten the stick.

Blake said, "If you know what happened, then you know something needs to be done."

"You didn't answer me, Son. What were they doing there?"

"Finlay's *leg* is broken. He's going to have to wear a cast for weeks. The same with BJ and his arm."

"And what about Ed Schaffer?"

A pause.

"What about him?"

"What is his condition?"

"I don't know what that has to do with—"

"He's in the neuro ICU. Still unconscious. Because of two of your men. Because they couldn't leave well enough alone."

Blake's expression had begun to harden the moment he realized his father wasn't going to take his side.

"Ed Schaffer isn't the problem here."

"Oh really," Tripp said, amused. "Then why did BJ and Finlay go there today to rough him up?"

Blake opened his mouth but then promptly shut it. His brow once again squished.

Tripp asked, "Are you a retard?"

"What?"

"A retard. I'm asking if my beloved late wife gave birth to a retard. If my one and only son is retarded."

Anger now radiated from Blake's face, as hot and intense as the sun. When he spoke, his voice was tremulous.

"You ... you can't talk to me like that."

"The reason I'm asking, Son, is because only a retard would fuck things up when we're so close to our goal. We're only days away. But instead of remaining focused you okayed your men to go mess with Ed Schaffer for whatever asinine purpose, and now both of them are no longer any good to us."

"I didn't okay anything. They did all that on their own."

"Then I'm even more ashamed to have a son whose men don't respect him enough to at least give him the courtesy of a heads-up."

"You don't understand, Dad. There was a man there. An outsider—"

"What about him?"

"Well, like I said, he's an outsider. He could be anybody. ATF. FBI."

"From what I understand, he works for the IRS. So for the government, yes, but not for a department you or I need to worry about. Unless you also have been messing up with your taxes."

"How ... how do you already know that?"

"God, you are retarded, aren't you? Nothing in this town happens without me knowing it. I probably heard what happened before you did. And do you know what I thought as soon as I did hear what happened? Thank the Lord my wife is no longer breathing to see what a retard her son has become."

Blake, fuming now, took a step forward. His pinched gaze shifting down at the disassembled musket on the desk.

"Go ahead, Son. Touch one of those pieces and see what happens."

Blake gave it an extra moment, his brow squishing again, before releasing a breath and shaking his head.

"We don't know who this guy is, Dad."

"It doesn't matter who he is. He saw somebody in need and stepped in to help them. To be honest, we could use more men like him in this country."

"He's a Jew."

"God, you are stupid. His last name is Bartkowski. That's Polish."

"It doesn't matter. He messed with two of our own. We need to make an example out of him."

A knock at the door, two solid raps. Carson stepped in without being summoned. He didn't look at all surprised to find Blake standing in front of the desk.

"Is everything all right, sir?"

"Everything's fine," Tripp said. "My son was just leaving."

His brow bunching up, Blake said, "Dad—"

"Now."

Blake stood motionless, his face set. Shoulders back. Like he was as tough as he believed himself to be. But then those shoulders slumped forward, just a bit, and he turned and started for the door.

Tripp said, "Nothing better happen to the outsider. Understand me?"

Blake didn't turn back but he mumbled a yes before slipping out into the hallway. As soon as he was gone, Carson turned to Tripp.

"I told him and his men not to bother you during your private time."

Tripp leaned forward in his chair, steepling his fingers in front of his face as he stared down at the pieces of the musket.

"Sometimes I don't know what's going through that boy's

head. He knows what's at stake, but now he won't let this go, no matter what I tell him."

Tripp slid his eyes up to his oldest friend and confidant.

"Keep an eye on him. Make sure nothing happens to the outsider."

"You don't believe he's a threat, do you?"

"I'm not sure. I put a few calls out to our friends in Washington. We'll see what they say. Meanwhile, how is our guest?"

"He's doing quite well. I'd just returned from delivering his dinner when I saw your son heading to your office."

"The girls are still arriving later tonight, correct?"

"Yes."

"Good. As long as our guest is happy, that's all that matters. Now, give me fifteen more minutes."

Tripp waited until the door latched behind Carson before slipping on a new pair of nitrile gloves and returning to work.

FIVE

Nova's meal had just arrived—a 12-ounce New York Strip, medium rare—when the men entered the restaurant.

It was just past seven and Stacey's was packed for a week-night. Though, after some reflection, Nova figured this was probably how business typically was for the place, as it was the only steak joint in the area.

The lights were low and the conversations loud. They had to be loud because the country music hammering from the speakers set up around the place was close to ear-splitting. A stage sat off toward one end of the restaurant, the kind that hosted local bands, but tonight the stage was empty and every-body was going about their business like it was any other night.

Then the men walked through the front doors.

Nova noted them the same way he'd noted every person who came not just through the front doors but also through the swinging kitchen door and the hallway that led back to the bathrooms and exit door. Blame it on his training, though Nova had been doing it most of his life, ever since he was a boy. Even then there was no actual reason for it other than mere curiosity, but he always made sure to sit with his back against the wall with a good view of the entire room. It was only later, as he grew older, that he began to clock every person coming and going from a room, immediately analyzing them for any potential threats and pinpointing potential weaknesses.

The three men who entered the restaurant tonight were of the same breed as the two he had confronted at the mechanic shop earlier today.

Well, no, that wasn't quite right.

Two of them were, yes—tall, muscular, hard eyes and stoic faces—but the third was different. He was tall like the others, and he looked to be in good shape, but there was a softness to him just underneath the surface, one Nova could spot even from this distance.

A man who acted tough but who didn't get his hands dirty.

Nova pegged this man as the one in charge.

One of the foot soldiers—Nova couldn't think of the two men as anything else—scanned one side of the restaurant while his counterpart scanned the other. Almost immediately the one spotted Nova. He turned back to the boss and whispered something in his ear, and the boss nodded and started in Nova's direction.

Nova sawed off a slice of steak as he watched the boss make his approach. White, mid-thirties. Expensive jeans, button-up shirt, light jacket, cowboy hat. His face looked innocuous enough, like he wasn't any threat. The face looked familiar too, though Nova couldn't put his finger on the reason why.

"Evening."

Without bothering for an invitation, the boss slipped into the other side of the booth.

Silent, Nova chewed his dinner. The steak was tender and juicy, just like the one he'd ordered last night. Steak two nights in a row probably wasn't great for his health, but hot damn they were tasty.

He gripped the steak knife in his right hand, the fork in his left hand. Both could be easily used as a weapon if need be. Though push come to shove, Nova had a Glock 36 strapped to his ankle. Six rounds of .45 ACP, it would take less than two seconds to pull it free from the holster if either of the two men standing off to the side made a move.

The boss said, "I hope I'm not interrupting anything."

Nova sawed off another slice of steak, began chewing it silently.

The boss nodded at Nova's plate.

"Is that the New York Strip? Probably my favorite steak on the menu, if you ask me."

Nova, of course, hadn't asked the man anything. He swallowed his bite of steak, and then stabbed at one of the asparagus with his fork.

The boss, making a face: "I'm not a fan of asparagus, though. Always makes my pee smell weird."

"You might want to see a doctor about that. For all you know, it's not the asparagus."

The boss looked momentarily stunned that Nova had said anything, let alone given him medical advice. He allowed a slight grin.

"I just might have to do that. I'm Blake Hogan, by the way. I'd shake your hand, but I see you're currently otherwise preoccupied. Can't say I blame you. Stacey's is perhaps the best steakhouse in the state."

"Can I help you with something, Mr. Hogan?"

"Call me Blake."

Nova forked another slice of steak into his mouth. He wasn't sure where the boss was going with this and already didn't like it.

The sliver of a grin faded when the man realized Nova wasn't in any mood for niceties. He cleared his throat, looked around at the other tables nearby, and then leaned in slightly.

"I understand you were in a tussle earlier today."

Nova couldn't decide which word was more ridiculous to describe what had taken place at the mechanic shop, tussle or ruckus.

"Don't worry about it," he said. "I'm not a litigious person."

Blake Hogan blinked, clearly not having expected this.

"Excuse me?"

"I'm assuming the two men at the mechanic shop work for you, or are at the very least associates of yours. And I'm saying that I'm not the kind of person to press charges or seek any civil restitution. The mechanic, however ..."

Nova scooped up some of the baked potato. Enjoying the mixture of emotions passing over Blake Hogan's face. Before the man could say anything, though (his lips already moving slightly as if preparing to speak), Nova pointed his fork at him.

"You're on a billboard."

Again, this caught the man off guard.

"What?"

"Yeah, that's it. I knew you looked familiar. You're on a billboard off the highway. You a car salesman or something?"

It was slight, almost imperceptible, especially with the low lighting, but the man's face had begun to flush.

"I'm the owner."

"Good for you," Nova said. Then, because he never knew when to stop: "Must be a family business, I bet. Your old man do all the work and then hand it off to you?"

Blake Hogan's brow started to ripple. His face went even darker. He leaned forward, opened his mouth to say something, when suddenly Sheriff Chapman appeared at the table.

"Blake, I think you're in my seat."

The man started, just a bit. He looked around at the nearby tables again, then up at the sheriff.

"My apologies."

Glaring once more at Nova, Blake slid out of the booth and headed back toward the front of the restaurant, his men coalescing behind him.

Veronica Chapman watched them go. She was wearing jeans and a checkered shirt, her brown hair pulled back in a ponytail. She waited until all three men had exited through the front doors before sliding into the seat Blake Hogan had occupied only seconds earlier.

Nova said, "I didn't know we had a date, Sheriff."

No expression on her pretty face.

"What are you doing here?"

Nova forked another spear of asparagus, made a mental note to double-check his urine later tonight.

"I'm having dinner. What are you doing here?"

"I thought the food last night made you sick."

"It did. But that doesn't mean it wasn't good. And besides, I feel like everybody deserves a second chance, including steakhouses. Don't you?"

Veronica Chapman eyed Nova warily. She was a woman who could read people easily enough, which was probably how she'd been elected sheriff, but she was having a hard time reading Nova.

She said, "Why are you smiling?"

"Your eyes."

"What about them?

"They're brown."

"So?"

"I just had a feeling they were brown when we spoke earlier today."

She let out a measured breath.

"Did you drive here?"

"I walked. It's a nice evening and the motel's only a mile down the road."

"Are you planning on getting any dessert?"

Smiling again as he noted her ringless fingers: "Why—you want to split something?"

"No, I want you to finish your meal so you can pay your bill and we can leave. I need to show you something."

SIX

The clouds from earlier in the day had dispersed, the night sky now a glittering bowl filled with the bright moon and a distant jet on the horizon, flashing white and red like a beacon.

Nova stared out the passenger-side window at the jet as Veronica Chapman steered them down the highway, the F-150 chasing its headlights. Past the Millport Motel and the Thirsty Moose Tavern and a hardware store. Then onto Main Street past the cafe and mechanic shop and laundromat and bank and hair salon, all the businesses closed and dark for the evening.

"When I was a little girl, about seven or eight years old, there was a circus that set up right outside Bozeman. It's a two-hour drive but my parents wanted to do something extra special for me, so we loaded up in my dad's truck early one morning and hit the road."

Veronica made a turn at an intersection and headed south, toward the river.

"I'd never been to the circus before. Had heard of it, of course. I mean, what kid hasn't? Especially a kid who grew up on a steady diet of Disney movies. *Dumbo* was a personal favorite. Made me fall in love with elephants."

Leaving the town proper, they passed houses and trees and fields, the pickup the only vehicle on the road.

"When my parents told me to get in the truck, I had no idea where we were going, so when we got close and I saw all the tents in the distance … I can't even describe the excitement. I think I might have squealed."

The glow from the truck's dash made it easy to see the grin on her face.

"I still remember that day vividly. The smell of the popcorn. The stench of the hay and all those animals in one place. Other kids with their parents. My parents had gotten me cotton candy. It was the first time I'd ever had any. My mom was strict when it came to sweets. She was honest-to-God worried about my teeth rotting out, because I think one of her cousins had had that happen to him once. But because this was a special trip my mom relented."

As the road straightened, Veronica's foot grew heavy on the gas pedal. The truck's six-cylinder engine growled and soon they were speeding at eighty miles per hour, the dark empty fields whipping past.

"Did your parents ever take you to the circus?"

Nova didn't want to talk about his parents. He didn't even want to think about them, despite the fact his parents were the only reason he'd come to this town. He made no reply, and after several seconds Veronica continued.

"I only ever went to the circus the one time, and I still remember everything about it. The crazy mustache the ring-leader had. How he shouted so loud his voice cracked. How hot it got in the tent. All the animals, the clowns, the trapeze artists. And then … there was her."

The highway began to curve toward the interstate. Bright lights appeared on the horizon. Nova knew what they were because he'd passed through here just the other day.

Veronica, seeming to remember she wasn't alone, nodded toward the lights as she slowed to make a turn.

"The Hogans own a half-dozen car dealerships across the state, but that there is the original one. Around here, anyone who wants a vehicle purchases it from Tripp Hogan and his son."

"His son being Blake."

Veronica nodded.

"Now that his dad's older, Blake oversees the day-to-day operation."

"He's the one you warned me about earlier today."

She didn't say anything for a minute or so as they drove. One hand on the steering wheel, her other hand in her lap. The F-150's headlights cutting through the darkness like a scythe. When she spoke again, her voice took on the tone of someone who thinks she's alone.

"So at the circus, they'd had this net set up so that none of the trapeze artists would hurt themselves badly if they fell. But then they took the netting down. The ringleader announced how the one and only Petra Kovačević would now perform her death-defying tightrope act. I still remember her name. I remember everything about her. You could barely see her up at the top, but she was the most beautiful woman I'd ever seen. Her hair was pulled back in a bun, and she wore a sparkly leotard, and the ringmaster warned us to be silent because the slightest noise might break her concentration and send her to her death. Still, the drummer started going, that low du-du-du-du-du, and without any netting at all—without anything keeping her from falling to the ground—Petra began to walk across the tightrope."

The fields had faded away and trees had started to take up most of the area. A lone deer stood between the trees, its glassy eyes glowing in the moonlight as it watched them speed past.

"She looked so fearless up there. Like nothing could stop

her. Everyone was stunned silent. Except when she did a cart-wheel on the tightrope. That's when everyone gasped. A few people even screamed. And the ringmaster had to shout again for everyone to be quiet, but still that drum kept going and Petra continued back and forth across the tightrope like it wasn't a hundred feet above the hard ground. And then ... that was it. She finished, and everyone in the tent went crazy with applause, and that was how the show ended."

The trees fell away again. Off in the distance, after a stretch of nearly a half mile of open field, a large house glowed at the base of a hill.

Veronica Chapman flicked off the headlights and slowed to a crawl.

"That's where Tripp Hogan lives. Him and his son. The family owns most of the land in Remington. Their family goes back generations, and some say that a Hogan was there when Remington was founded."

She looked at him, intensity in her brown eyes.

"These are powerful people with powerful friends, and you attacked two of their men."

"*Attacked* seems a bit strong."

"I told you it would be in your best interest to pack up and move on. But you didn't listen, so I thought maybe you're the type of person who needs to see a thing with his own eyes before it gets through his thick, stupid skull."

"Hey," Nova said. "My skull isn't that thick."

"I never wanted to be the sheriff of this town. My daddy was the sheriff, and his daddy before him. I come from a long line of lawmen, but that was never what I wanted to do. In fact, for a spell I wanted to move to Africa to work with elephants. But there was a time, a short time, when I wanted to learn to walk a tightrope just like Petra Kovačević. A time when I wanted to join the circus. Can you imagine how well that went over at home? Even if I was just a girl who made up stupid fairy tales for herself, my father wasn't going to let me waste my time on such stupid aspirations. He made sure to drill it into my head how he and my mother expected me to do much more with my life. It wasn't his lifelong goal to see his only child become a cop just like him, but he wasn't unhappy to see it either. And then he passed away, only a couple of years after my mother, and suddenly I found myself wearing the same badge he had worn."

The truck was still coasting forward. Nova kept his gaze on the house lit up at the base of the hill. A large barn was positioned slightly behind it. He only blinked when the sheriff jerked the wheel to perform a hasty three-point U-turn.

"She died, you know. Petra Kovačević. I looked it up when I was in high school. It was a show just like any other show, but this time she wasn't so lucky. And she of course didn't have the netting in place. She broke her neck. It practically shut down the entire circus. I have to admit, I got a little teary-eyed when I read about it. Because I remember her being so beautiful. And so fearless. But even now after all this time I often find myself thinking about her. Because this job I do, it's like walking a tightrope. I have to deal with the Hogans and all of their shit, and I have to deal with everybody else in this town and every other town in the county, and sometimes I even have to deal with outsiders who happen to show up in the wrong place at the wrong time."

She glanced at him as she slowed the truck to turn back out onto the highway leading into town.

"I've gotten pretty good at walking the tightrope. Even without a net. I'm not a political person by nature, but this job is a political one, and I've learned how to play the game to keep everyone in this county, myself included, safe. That's why I'm not bothering to make it seem like I'm asking you, Mr. Bartkowski. I'm telling you. For your own good, you're going to leave and never step foot in this town again."

SEVEN

The guy working behind the counter at the Millport Motel looked to be in his fifties. Stoop-shouldered, thinning hair, pockmarked face, with eyes beady like a weasel. And now, shifting between the sheriff and Nova, those beady eyes were full of confusion.

"I don't get it. Why check him out? He's booked for two more days."

Veronica Chapman issued a calm, practiced sigh.

"I understand that, Wayne, but Mr. Bartkowski will be leaving tonight. So however many days are left, refund him the difference."

"But—"

"Wayne"—she placed her hands square on the counter to lean forward—"I'm not going to say it again. Mr. Bartkowski is checking out tonight, and you will refund him the difference."

Wayne nervously eyed Nova standing just behind the sheriff. The man hadn't been working the counter when Nova had arrived the other day, and he didn't think he'd spotted him at all during his brief time in town. So this was the first time Wayne was laying eyes on him, and he no doubt wondered what the hell Nova had done to make the sheriff run him out of town like this.

"Wayne?" Veronica's voice was gentle, calm. "I understand this doesn't make sense to you, but that's okay. People come and go all the time, don't they?"

Swallowing, the man nodded silently.

"Exactly. So check Mr. Bartkowski out of his room, and we'll be good to go."

In the end Nova had to sign a refund slip and was promised that the remaining balance would show up on his credit card. Nova typically didn't like using credit cards but had one for emergencies, such as motels that didn't want to accept cash.

He wasn't sure how long the sheriff planned to babysit him, but she followed him to his room and waited on the walkway while he went inside and grabbed his stuff. Which didn't take long because he hadn't brought much to begin with. It took him less than a minute before he was back outside in the cool night air, noting the gravel parking lot and the two other vehicles and the field across the highway with ponderosa pines lined up fifty yards out like shadowed sentinels.

"I just realized something," Nova said.

Veronica Chapman was staring at her phone, her finger swiping up and down the screen, and paused to glance up at him.

"What's that?"

"This is the second time in only a few weeks a sheriff is running me out of town. I'm hoping it's not the start of a trend."

She stared at him for a moment.

"You're not being run out of town, Mr. Bartkowski. Remember: this is for your own safety."

"My own safety."

"That's right."

Nova didn't want to engage any further with the woman.

He was already on shaky ground and didn't want to say or do the wrong thing. Like Petra Kovačević, he was walking a tightrope and had to be careful.

Still, he had to ask.

"How is he, by the way?"

A slight frown crossed her face.

"Who?"

"The mechanic."

She glanced down at her phone again, sucked in a heavy breath.

"Still unresponsive, last I heard. Why?"

Nova thought about sitting in the cafe booth, watching the two men head toward the garage, violence in their stride.

"Just wondering."

His bag strapped over his shoulder, he started for his truck.

Veronica followed him.

"Mind if I ask you a question?"

Tossing his bag inside the truck, Nova said, "Boxers."

The sheriff didn't react for a beat, and then she did her best to bite back a grin.

"That's not what I was going to ask."

"Sure it wasn't."

"What I wanted to ask is if Casanova is really your first name."

"Sadly, it is."

"Why do you say sadly?'

"Why do you think?"

"Can I ask how that came about?"

"It's a long story."

Veronica Chapman lifted her hands, indicating the deserted parking lot and the empty moonlit sky above them.

"I think we have the time, don't you?"

"Sorry, Sheriff," Nova said, stepping into his truck. "From

what I'm told, I need to get out of Dodge as soon as possible. You know, for my safety."

She followed him through the heart of town, which was what he'd expected, but then she followed him the fourteen miles to the interstate, which was something he hadn't.

Interesting.

What was it about Blake Hogan and his goons that would put such a scare into the county's head of law enforcement?

For that matter, what had brought two of Blake Hogan's men to the mechanic shop earlier in the day to rough up an old man?

"Just let it go," Nova murmured as he came to a stop sign. It was here that he would take a left and continue down the interstate. It was here, presumably, where the sheriff would finally turn around and head back to town.

He checked the rearview mirror. Veronica Chapman's F-150 was sitting right behind him, only a few yards back, waiting for him to make his move.

The interstate was quiet for this time of night, and in no time at all an eighteen-wheeler tore by and there was enough space for him to pull out to follow it.

He watched the rearview mirror, wondering if the sheriff would surprise him. She didn't. The Ford pulled a wide U-ey and started back toward Remington.

Within seconds, the pickup's taillights had disappeared.

The bell above the entrance door caused Wayne to glance up from the newspaper, but it was the person who walked through that kept his attention. The man's beady eyes widened, and his mouth fell open, and he swallowed a few times before finding the words.

"But I … I thought the sheriff … didn't she—"

Nova scanned the counter. Computer, phone, haphazard stack of papers. He glanced out the window at the parking lot before clearing his throat.

"I decided I wasn't quite ready to leave."

"But the sheriff—"

"Yes?"

Wayne paused, looking flummoxed. Under the bright ceiling lights Nova noted the broken capillaries on the man's nose and understood why he smelled the faint odor of brandy.

"Well, didn't the sheriff—"

"Wayne, what country is this?"

The man paused again.

"Wh-What?"

"What country do we live in?"

"Um … well, the United States of America."

"Correct. And if I'm not mistaken, the great thing about this country is the freedom it allows its citizens. Isn't that right?"

"Well, yes, but—"

"Is there another motel nearby?"

"Huh?"

"I'm seriously asking. If I could stay anywhere else but here, I would. I get the sense you guys don't wash the linens too often."

"Well now, that's just not true. We certainly—"

"Wayne, look at me."

The man blinked, his mouth slightly askew.

Nova said, "Is my room still available?"

Swallowing, the man nodded.

Nova slapped his credit card on the counter.

"Then check me back in."

He set his bag on the chair in the corner and took out the FNX-45 from the small of his back and once again checked the load before turning on all the lamps and the TV.

He used the remote to cycle through the limited number of channels—the Millport hadn't bothered to splurge for premium cable, for shame—until he came to the White Sox game. He left it there and turned up the volume loud enough to be heard outside but not so loud that anybody in any adjoining rooms might complain.

Nova tossed the remote aside and sat on the bed so that his back was against the headboard.

He checked the time on his phone.

Five minutes after nine o'clock. He'd driven for almost twenty miles, debating the pros and cons, before getting off at an exit and looping back toward Remington. And now here he sat on a stiff mattress, having willfully returned to the lion's den.

He opened his phone, dialed a number, but didn't press the green button to connect the call. Not yet.

Closing his eyes, Nova leaned his head back against the headboard and waited.

EIGHT

Just after eleven o'clock they pulled into the motel's parking lot, Blake Hogan's Range Rover Defender trailed by Dominic's Ford Raptor, the light from the Millport's neon sign shimmering off their hoods.

Wayne was standing outside the office, having himself a smoke, and as soon as he saw the two trucks—as soon as he realized who those trucks belonged to—he dropped the cigarette and stamped it under his boot and straightened his posture so that he looked more presentable.

The Defender's window dropped, and Blake Hogan peered out at him with pure distaste.

"Which room?"

Wayne's beady eyes shifted back and forth between the two trucks and the rooms beside the office.

"Room four," he whispered.

"And he hasn't left since he came back?"

Wayne shook his head, a quick back and forth. He dug into his pocket and withdrew a key.

"Here," he said, hesitantly holding the key out.

Blake said, "What do I want that for?"

"Well"—Wayne shrugged nervously—"to let yourself into the room."

Blake grinned and asked, "What fun is that?" Then he nodded toward the office. "Head back inside, Wayne. We'll take care of this."

As Wayne disappeared inside the office, the two trucks drifted forward at a crawl, their heavy tires crunching over the gravel.

Blake halted the Defender just past the outsider's pickup, while Dominic stopped his Raptor only a few feet behind, boxing in the outsider in case he tried to make a run for it.

They all climbed out of their respective vehicles—Blake and Marc and Keith from the Defender, Dominic and Gary and BJ from the Raptor.

Marc and Keith immediately went to the back of the Defender, where they opened the rear door and pulled out two HK416 assault rifles. Keith and Gary each strapped one over their shoulder while Dominic hefted the Mossberg shotgun he'd pulled out from under the seat of his truck. Marc grabbed a tire iron. Even though BJ's casted arm was in a sling, he gripped a pistol with his right hand.

Blake carried his own piece, a SIG P226 just like the other men, but he didn't intend on using it. Still, he held the pistol at his side, the 4.4-inch barrel pointed toward the ground.

The plan wasn't to kill the man. Just rough him up a bit. They'd break his arm for sure—that much they'd already determined—though whether they would break his leg depended on just how much fight he put up.

Blake stood with BJ beside the outsider's pickup as they watched the four men quietly step up onto the walkway, Keith and Gary now holding the HKs in port arms position, Dominic gripping the shotgun as he squared his shoulders at the door.

Tire iron squeezed tightly in hand, Marc stepped close to

Room 4's window. He cocked his ear and listened for a few seconds—the TV's volume so loud they could all hear the local news—before glancing back at the others and giving them a quick nod.

Dominic raised his boot.

NINE

The moment the door splintered open, the four men rushed in, weapons raised, shouting like they were playing real-life *Call of Duty*.

Since the room wasn't large it didn't take them long to determine that nobody was inside.

Nova watched as the four men streamed back out onto the walkway. Barrels dipped low. Shoulders slumped.

The night was quiet enough to hear Blake Hogan ask, "Well?"

One of the men, shaking his head: "Empty."

Blake stormed up onto the walkway, shouldering past one of the men to peer inside. He spun around, asking to no one in particular, "Where the hell is he?"

Positioned behind one of the trees across the highway, FNX-45 in hand, Nova smiled.

He hadn't been one hundred percent certain Blake Hogan and his goons would try to take retribution if he were to stay in town, but it was a safe bet. Nova had his guns, yes, but this was Montana, a red state where practically everybody carried a gun, so he didn't like his chances against a group of heavily armed men, especially when he was in a motel room that only had one exit.

Earlier, when he'd returned to the Millport, he'd noted the phone on the office counter. It sat off to the right, which meant that when the person manning the counter went to answer the phone, their back was momentarily to the window which over-looked the main parking lot.

Two hours ago, Nova had dialed the number to the motel —making it so that his number wouldn't show up on any caller ID—and he kept the phone on mute while he opened his door, peeked outside, and then slipped around to the back of the building.

He ended up hiking a good half mile through the woods before crossing the highway and looping back through the trees. He took his time, knowing Blake Hogan and his men wouldn't come immediately. They no doubt had gotten word that Nova had checked out of the motel and left town. What-ever plan they'd had before would have immediately been discarded. But when they received word that Nova had returned? Game on.

The office door opened and Wayne reemerged. Blake Hogan strode straight over to him, his voice low enough that Nova couldn't make it out from this distance, though by the wild gesturing it was clear he was upset.

Nova got the gist: Wayne had probably told them Nova hadn't left his room since he arrived, so how the hell was he not in the room right now?

One of the men maybe got the sense they were being watched. He separated himself from the rest of the group to step close to the highway. He looked up and down the deserted strip and then out toward the tree line where Nova was hiding.

Nova stayed stock-still, holding his breathing, grip on the FNX-45 tightening.

The man turned away and headed back to the others. More

talking, more gesturing. Then the one with the tire iron marched straight for Nova's truck. The man swung the tire iron and shattered the back window. The men all laughed, including Wayne.

Another man dug into his pocket for a knife. He started at the back of the truck, plunging the blade into the rear tires, then into the front ones.

The men all laughed again.

After that Blake Hogan said something else to Wayne, jabbing his finger at the man's face, before he and his men loaded up into their vehicles and took off, the Raptor's tires kicking up gravel in its wake.

Wayne flicked his cigarette away and headed back into the office.

Interesting, Nova thought. The men didn't even bother with masks. Armed with guns and a tire iron, they'd intended to storm into his room, maybe catch him asleep on the bed or with his pants down on the toilet, and they intended on beating the shit out of him—or worse.

Veronica Chapman was right to try to run him out of town. These men had no fear of local law enforcement.

Nova waited a good fifteen minutes before he emerged from the trees. He trudged through the field under the soft moonlight and then crossed over the highway and went directly to his room.

The doorframe was splintered, just as Nova had suspected. The door wouldn't shut properly, not even when he tried to force it and use the chain.

Nova regarded his bag on the floor. Its contents were strewn everywhere. That was fine—in fact, it had been expected. That's why he had removed anything valuable before returning to the motel. All that the men had gone through were clothes—unwashed clothes at that.

Gathering the clothes and stuffing them into the bag, Nova

turned off the TV and stepped back out onto the walkway. He stared at his truck, surprised the men hadn't done more damage, and then started toward the office.

He wasn't sure how it was possible, but Wayne's beady eyes seemed to grow twice their size as they watched Nova enter.

"Hello, Wayne. There seems to be something wrong with the door to my room. Any chance you can help me with that?"

TEN

They parked behind the dealership, out of view from anyone passing by on the interstate.

Despite the bright moon it was dark back here—just the dumpsters and a few cars besides their own trucks—and they climbed out of the Defender and Raptor in angry silence.

Keith grumbled as he opened his door, "We should have fucking stayed."

Blake stepped out too, stretching his back as he surveyed his men.

"Wayne said he'll call when our guy shows back up. Besides, he won't be going anywhere any time soon."

The men chuckled at this, remembering how the truck lowered a few inches as its tires deflated.

Then Blake's smile faded as something occurred to him. He turned to BJ.

"How's the arm?"

BJ shrugged, glancing down at his sling.

"Hurts like hell, though the Oxy helps."

"I should break your other arm after what you pulled."

The grin dropped off BJ's face. The other men went quiet, sensing the mood shift.

"Boss, we didn't mean to—"

"We are *this* close to our goal." Blake holding up his thumb and index finger barely an inch apart. "A nice payday for everyone here, and you almost fucked it up."

"Boss, I'm sorry—"

"Why were you at the garage today anyhow?"

"Finlay wanted to—"

"Goddamn it," Blake said. "I get that Finlay has a beef with Ed Schaffer—everyone here understands that—but you should have been smart enough to talk him out of it. Especially when it turns out the two of you have been stopping by there the past couple of weeks to harass him."

BJ, eyes downcast, merely nodded.

Blake looked around at the other men, his jaw tight, feeling electricity in his blood. Because it was his fault, in a way—he'd become too lax, had let his men forget who was in charge.

Clearing his throat, he addressed the others, his voice low despite the fact there wasn't anybody around within a mile.

"We have to be careful moving forward. I understand what happened today pisses the rest of you off, as it should, but the simple fact is BJ and Finlay put themselves in that situation. Will the man who hurt them be taken care of? At some point, yes. But right now we need to focus on the bigger picture as we're only three days away. That means I need you all to focus on the job at hand. Got it?"

The men nodded, mumbled that they understood, and one by one they turned away and headed to their vehicles—even BJ, who had driven here in his pickup, saying that he was okay to drive even with the cast.

Blake arrived home twenty minutes later. The sky was still clear and full of stars with just a light breeze in the air, and as he stepped out of the Defender he paused to note the hill standing behind the house. He cocked his ear, listening, and could make out the distant sound of rock music.

"Enjoy yourself," he murmured, smiling. "You deserve it."

He headed inside, through the side door leading into the kitchen. The light above the sink was still on. The whole place still smelled of the meatloaf from earlier in the evening.

His stomach growling, he thought he might warm up a piece as he opened the fridge to grab a beer. But before he could reach inside, something heavy struck him in the back of the knees, sending him sprawling to the floor.

Carson stood over him, a baseball bat in his hands. Emotionless, no anger or rage painted on his face. He was simply doing his job, what he'd been told to do, and there were no mixed feelings, no remorse.

"Thank you, Carson."

Tripp Hogan wheeled himself into the kitchen. He gazed down at his son on the floor, and slowly shook his head.

"What a pathetic sight you make."

Blake bit the inside of his cheek. This was his father's house —his father's town—and while one day it would all be Blake's, Blake still had to adhere to his father's rules.

"What did I tell you, boy?"

Gritting his teeth against the pain, doing everything he could not to show emotion, Blake said nothing.

"Do you want Carson to hit you again, this time on the side of your head?"

Blake glared up at his father, ignoring his father's right-hand man standing off to the side with the Louisville Slugger primed for another swing.

"You told me to leave the outsider alone."

"Yes, I did. And what did you do?"

Again he bit the inside of his cheek, hard enough to taste blood.

His father said, "You not only confronted the man tonight

at Stacey's, but you and your boys decided to pay him a visit at the Millport."

Blake didn't bother disputing this. For starters, it was true. And not only that, his father knew everything that happened in town. No reason to deny it.

"Do you understand what's going to happen in the next few days, boy?"

Blake closed his eyes, tried to steady his breathing.

"I do, yes."

"And do you understand just how significant it will be?"

"Of course."

"Then start acting like it. I'm sorry that two of your men had their asses handed to them—and by an outsider, no less—but that's on them. What you should be doing besides the normal work is making sure our guest is happy."

"He is, Dad. I met with him earlier tonight before I left—"

Tripp Hogan lifted his hand, and Carson stepped forward, swinging the bat over his shoulder with his left elbow dipped low so the swing would come straight for Blake's face.

Blake couldn't help himself—his entire body spasmed, every muscle tensing up in anticipation.

A second later, as it registered that no blow had come, his father's chuckling inched its way past the blood thumping in his ears.

"Pathetic."

He started to wheel away but paused, glaring back down at his son.

"You want to take over someday? You have to be stronger. You have to be smarter. I failed you, Son. I thought I did everything I could to make you a man. But right now from where I'm sitting, you're still just a scared little boy."

ELEVEN

Wednesday morning, bright and early, Nova found himself back at the Yellow Bird Cafe. In the same booth he sat in yesterday. The booth in the corner so that his back was against the wall which afforded him an open view of Main Street and the empty mechanic shop on the other side.

His breakfast had just arrived when Sheriff Veronica Chapman walked through the front door. Like yesterday afternoon, she was dressed in that ugly shit-brown uniform, and she stood inside the door for a beat, her hands on her hips, scanning the cafe before her eyes locked on him.

Nova made no reaction. He forked some pancakes into his mouth and chewed while the sheriff nodded and said hello to everyone sitting between them. Then she was sliding into the other side of the booth, her brown eyes narrowed.

"Sure, Sheriff, feel free to have a seat."

Veronica's jaw flexed. She opened her mouth, shut it, then glanced back to make sure nobody was within earshot before leaning in.

"How old were you when it happened?"

Nova cut a sausage link in half, chewed on it for a few seconds as he thoughtfully regarded her.

"When what happened?"

"When you hit your head so hard your brains stopped working right."

He had to bite back a grin as he scooped up some over-easy eggs.

"Not sure what you mean, Sheriff."

"Uh-huh." She leaned in even closer, folding her hands on the Formica tabletop. "Last night you were supposed to leave town. In fact, I saw you on your way."

"You did. And, I must say, that was mighty kind of you."

She ignored his playful tone.

"And then this morning I'm driving past the Millport and what do you think I spot in the parking lot?"

"Whatever it was I'm sure you're about to tell me."

She cocked her head slightly.

"Do you think this is funny?"

"Honestly, it's way too early to think anything." He gestured at his steaming mug. "The coffee hasn't kicked in yet."

"All four tires of your truck were punctured. The back window was shattered."

"Yeah, I noticed that this morning too. Weird, huh?"

"This isn't funny."

"Tell me about it. Those were brand-new tires."

"Do you want to press charges?"

"On who?"

Those brown eyes, hardening.

"You know who."

Nova looked past her at the shop across the street.

"You know, Sheriff, I was thinking about the two men who attacked the mechanic yesterday."

"What about them?"

"The mechanic seemed to be minding his own business.

Why attack him like that in broad daylight, right here along Main Street for everyone to see?"

Something in Veronica's face changed. A sense of defeat. She leaned back, sucked in a deep breath.

"What are you really doing here?"

"I'm having breakfast."

"In town, I mean."

"I told you yesterday. I'm here to fish."

"But you didn't fish this morning."

"Of course I didn't. Remember, my truck is undrivable. It took me close to twenty minutes to walk here. Not sure I could make it all the way down to the river with my gear. That's a good ten miles."

Up front, the door opened again. A woman entered with a small boy. One of the waitresses grabbed a menu and walked over to seat them.

Veronica Chapman said, "I need you to take this seriously. If you think Blake Hogan and his men will stop after last night, you're wrong."

"Again, Sheriff, I'm not sure what you mean."

Her brown eyes grew hard again. She stared at him, looked like she was going to say something else, when the woman who'd just entered the cafe sidled up next to their table.

"Excuse me, Sheriff. I'm sorry to interrupt."

Veronica smiled at the woman.

"Good morning, Mandy. Can I help you with something?"

"Actually ..." The woman tilted her head toward Nova. "I was hoping I could speak to this gentleman for a minute."

Despite the woman right next to him, Nova's attention had focused on the boy standing by the register at the front of the cafe. He looked to be five, maybe six years old, with shaggy blond hair.

Veronica Chapman, glancing over her shoulder to also note the boy, asked, "Isn't today a school day?"

Mandy's eyes lowered, and she nodded. She looked to be in her early thirties. Five foot five at the most, dark blonde hair down to her shoulders. Pretty in a rough sort of way, like she had grown up working in the sun.

"Yes, Sheriff, it is. But after what happened … I thought maybe I should keep him home for a few days."

"Of course," Veronica said. "And how is Ed doing?"

"Still unresponsive. Guess you'd say he's in a coma. We were at the hospital all last night and plan to return shortly. It's"—she paused, wiped at her eyes—"it's all just so much to deal with. And I'm real sorry having barged in like this, but again, I was hoping to speak to … I'm sorry, sir, what is your name?"

"Nova."

"Right. Nova. Well, Nova, I was hoping to speak to you for a minute, if that's all right." Her green eyes shift to the sheriff. "Alone."

It was clear Veronica Chapman didn't feel comfortable with this interaction. A victim's wife discussing something privately with a stranger who'd beat up two locals. But she wasn't going to say anything, at least not here in the cafe with all these voters around watching.

The sheriff slid out of the booth, patting Mandy gently on the shoulder as she expressed her sympathy, and then she regarded Nova one last time.

"Just think about what we discussed, okay?"

Nova didn't say anything. He didn't nod or shake his head. Instead he watched as Veronica Chapman threaded her away past the tables to the front door. Before exiting she paused to lean down to speak to the boy before giving him a gentle pat on the shoulder, just like she had with the boy's mother.

Mandy still stood beside the table, her hands clasped in front of her, fidgeting.

"Mind if I sit down?"

"Be my guest."

She slid into the booth, stared at him for a beat, then glanced back at her son.

"His name's Alex. I didn't want to bring him over here. Thought maybe it might be too much. He's already dealing with a lot."

She paused, as if remembering herself, and let loose a soft, nervous laugh.

"I'm sorry. I just realized I didn't introduce myself. I'm Mandy Schaffer. Ed Schaffer is my husband."

She paused again, maybe misunderstanding Nova's expression.

"Ed is the man you saved yesterday." She threw a thumb over her shoulder, right at the mechanic shop across the street. Then her eyes narrowed a bit, uncertain. "You *are* the guy who stepped in to save him, aren't you?"

The boy up front stood with his hands clasped in front of him like his mother did only moments earlier. Nervous. Fidgety. Looking vulnerable.

"It was no trouble," Nova said. "I just happened to be in the right place at the right time."

"Those men"—anger flared in her green eyes, her voice growing tight—"those men were animals. They could have killed him."

"I'm sorry I couldn't get there any sooner. Maybe if I had, your husband wouldn't be in the state he is right now."

Had his voice wavered when he said *your husband*? He wasn't sure. He had to be careful. This woman didn't know that Nova was her husband's son. That he was the half-brother of the little boy standing only a few yards away.

"Well," Mandy said, forcing another smile, "I just wanted to thank you. It means the world to me and Alex. In fact, I wanted to invite you to dinner tonight at our place. I'm not much of a cook, but it's the least I can do to show my gratitude."

Her tone was so earnest that it gave Nova pause. But when he started to shake his head, started to open his mouth, Mandy quickly continued.

"And I won't take no for an answer. I'm sorry, but I won't. If it wasn't for you, I'd be a widow right now. My son wouldn't have a father. Please. Just one hour. Maybe even less than that. It's the least I can do."

What was he going to say? Maybe he should have left town last night, just as Veronica Chapman had advised. If he had, his truck would still be drivable and he wouldn't be in this awkward situation, sitting across from the woman who had given birth to Nova's half-brother. A woman who had no idea that the man she thought of as her husband had once abandoned his sick wife while she was on her deathbed.

"Sure," Nova heard himself say in a hollow tone. "I'd be happy to."

Not long after that—after Mandy and her son had left the cafe, after he had paid the check and stepped out into the bright sunlight—Nova started back down the road toward the motel when somebody called his name.

"Mr. Bartkowski?"

A black GMC Sierra 1500 Denali stood gleaming in the morning sun. A man had just climbed out, sunglasses on his face.

Nova paused, conscious of the FNX-45 in his rear waistband.

"Do I know you?"

The man looked to be in his late sixties. Lean and muscular, white close-cropped hair. An ex-military man who probably still made his bed with the sheets so flat and tight you could bounce a hollow point off them.

"My name's Carson. I work for Mr. Hogan."

"Blake?"

Despite the man's neutral expression, Nova could see the disdain in the slight curl of his lip.

"No, sir. Tripp Hogan. Blake's father. He would like to meet with you."

Nova glanced again at the Sierra.

"What if I decline?"

"That's certainly your prerogative. But Mr. Hogan does express his apologies for his son's actions last night. We've transported your truck to the dealership where they're putting on new tires and replacing the broken window as we speak. At no cost to you, of course."

Interesting. The son and his goons acted like they didn't care about the law, while the old man seemed to be fixing all his son's mistakes.

Nova said, "If I come with you, full transparency: I'm carrying a piece."

The man merely smiled.

"This is Montana, Mr. Bartkowski. We wouldn't expect anything less. Now"—he opened the passenger-side door—"shall we?"

TWELVE

They drove in silence.

Down Main Street and past the Millport, Nova was surprised to find that his truck was indeed gone. Earlier that morning, he'd walked around it to inspect the damage, and there had been shards of glass littering the gravel parking lot that sparkled like diamonds in the sun.

Something told him that every one of those shards had been cleaned up as well.

Carson didn't take the same route Veronica Chapman had when she was trying to run Nova out of town. Maybe because he wanted to go past the motel and prove that Nova's truck was gone and presumably being fixed.

One backroad after another, trees and fields whipping past, and then they were on the long stretch that led to the property Nova had only glimpsed in the dark the night before.

In the sunlight, it looked even more impressive. Large swaths of open land stretched in either direction of the drive leading up to the house. Beyond the house, a hill full of trees, with a trail leading up the side.

Carson halted the Sierra in front of the house, and they both climbed out.

"If you'll follow me, sir."

Carson led him into a massive foyer and then down a long hallway. The house was still and silent. No dogs coming to greet them. No maid or butler scurrying out of view. Just the sound of two pairs of boots echoing off the hardwood until Carson stopped and rapped his knuckles on the door. A voice from inside said, "Come in," and Carson opened the door but didn't enter.

Nova stepped inside.

The room looked to be a den. A few animal heads graced the walls: buck, moose, bear. A fireplace in one corner, unlit. Bookcases lined the one wall, while two large glass display cases sat against the other wall, all showcasing what appeared to be antique firearms.

"You must be Casanova Bartkowski."

A man in his early seventies sat behind a large oak desk. For a second or two, Nova assumed the man was sitting in a chair until he wheeled himself around the desk and extended his hand to Nova.

"Pleasure to meet you."

Nova shook the man's hand and then looked at the two leather chairs in front of the desk when the man gestured for him to sit. As the man wheeled himself back behind the desk, he asked Nova if he'd like anything to drink.

"No thanks."

"Are you sure? Carson can fetch you whatever you'd like. How about some coffee?"

"I'm good."

Nodding, the man motioned for Carson to leave them. The door quietly clicked shut.

Nova said, "I'm guessing you're Tripp Hogan."

The man smiled and held his hands out wide.

"At your service."

"What am I doing here, exactly?"

"That's what I'd like to know myself. But before we get to all that, I do want to apologize for my son. I understand he ... well, caused some trouble last night."

Nova didn't say anything. He didn't nod or shake his head. He stared back at the man, waiting for him to continue.

Still with the smile: "I believe Carson told you that I'm having new tires placed on your truck, along with a replacement rear window. Free of charge, of course."

"That's kind of you."

"Well, you are a guest here in town, and you weren't treated like a guest, so it's the least I can do. My son ... he sometimes thinks he's a bit too big for his britches, if you know what I mean."

A brief silence.

"Are you married, Mr. Bartkowski?"

"No."

"Got a girlfriend?"

"Not presently."

"Have any kids?"

"Not that I know of."

Tripp Hogan chuckled softly.

"It's a great thing, being a parent. They say your whole life changes the moment your child is born, and it's true. My wife, God rest her soul, got pregnant three times before she had Blake. All miscarriages. We chalked it up to it not being in the cards. Which was disappointing for both of us, as we both badly wanted to be parents. We probably should have stopped trying, what with Dolores having turned forty-two, but then one day we got word she was pregnant and we had hope in our hearts again."

The man paused, staring at what looked to be a disassembled musket on the desk in front of him.

"She died giving birth. Can you imagine that? Going nine long months with a child growing inside you, nurturing that child by how you eat and how you take care of yourself, and then when it's time for that child to enter the world … you don't even get to see his precious face or hold him for even a minute."

Nova wasn't sure what to say to this, so he said, "My condolences."

"Thank you. I do appreciate that. But I guess the reason I'm telling you this is that Blake's momma wasn't around to raise him. It was me. Well, I shouldn't say it was *just* me. I hired a woman or two to help do the stuff women typically do, like feed him and change him and all that."

So basically everything, Nova thought but didn't say.

Tripp Hogan sucked in a breath.

"My father was a good man. He raised me right. I thought I had it in me to raise my son just as well, but I fear I may have failed. I failed him and I failed myself and I failed this town because, well, we Hogans have lived here from the very beginning. My great-great-grandfather settled here. As the story goes, on his first night in the area he dreamt he was walking through the land and all around him were bullet casings that twinkled in the harsh sunlight. It was his impression that a great battle had been waged, and that all that was left were those casings. No bodies. No blood. Not even any bullets. Just the casings."

The man cocked his head as he stared at Nova with a slight grin.

"It sounds mad, doesn't it? That story's always stuck with me. Because you listen to the media these days, they like to say we have an epidemic on our hands. Gun violence, they call it, and it's no mistake that they use that word. *Violence*. They want to demonize good men and women who simply feel it's their God-given right to bear arms. Such as you're doing today."

Nova made no reaction. Yes, the FNX-45 was snug in his

rear waistband. But he was wearing a loose jacket, making it almost impossible for someone to notice the piece. And as far as he could tell, at no point had Carson messaged ahead to let his boss know. But clearly Tripp Hogan was a man who had a particular eye, and he'd spotted the piece on Nova without missing a beat.

"Don't get me wrong, Mr. Bartkowski. I'm not saying it's an issue that you're carrying. On the contrary, I'd feel strange if you *didn't* have a weapon on you. It blows my mind that there are people in this country who choose not to own at least one handgun or rifle. As I said, it's their God-given right! Who are they to go against what God wants?"

Again, Nova said nothing. He stared back at his host, waiting for him to get to the point.

Tripp Hogan smiled again.

"I do like you, Mr. Bartkowski. You strike me as a true patriot. Someone who sees this country for what it once was and can be again. A man like you, when you see somebody in trouble, you step right up to help them. Which is what happened yesterday, from what I understand. You didn't even hesitate, did you? That's because there's something good in you. I imagine it's your patriotism. I imagine that's what called you to the service to become a SEAL in the first place."

Nova blinked. He couldn't help himself. It was only that, a simple blink, but it was enough to confirm to Tripp Hogan that he was right.

"I thought that was the case. You see, Mr. Bartkowski, I like to know who comes to my town, even for a day or two. A stranger comes to your home, you want to make sure that they're not a threat. So I reached out to some of my contacts in the government. They were able to look you up. You've got an impressive record, at least in terms of what's not classified."

Tripp Hogan fell silent again. Watching him. Waiting for him to speak.

Nova breathed calmly through his nose. Centering himself. In, out. In, out.

"What are you trying to ask me, Mr. Hogan?"

The man leaned forward in his wheelchair, placing his elbows on the desk, and knit his fingers together.

"Why are you here?"

"Because you summoned me."

"No, Mr. Bartkowski, not here in my home. Here in my *town*. Why are you here in my *town*?"

"I'm here to fish."

"Is that all?"

"Yes."

"You wouldn't be lying to me, would you?"

"I don't see why I'd have any reason to lie to you."

Tripp Hogan smiled again and nodded once more.

"Why did you leave the service?"

"Felt my time was at an end."

"During my own time in the service, I was fortunate enough to receive the Medal of Honor."

His gazed shifted past Nova, at the two glass display cases along the wall. Nova turned to see the medal hanging on the wall between the two cases.

Only three branches of the military award the Medal of Honor: Army, Navy, and Air Force. Nova clocked this one as being from the Army: the inverted five-pointed star, the cluster of laurel leaves, mixed with oak, on each of the star's five points.

The laurel leaves representing victory.

The oak representing strength.

Tripp Hogan said, "That is how I ended up in this wheelchair. It happened on my second tour in 'Nam. As soon as they told me what had happened to my spine, part of me felt a kind of despair I didn't know existed. I realized my entire world was going to change. But I sucked it up as men are supposed to, and I made the best of it, and now here I sit in this beautiful house surrounded by evidence of a hobby I enjoy. My disability doesn't make me any less of a man or patriot. If anything, it's made me stronger."

Again, Nova wasn't sure how to respond, so he didn't say anything. He was wondering where Carson had gone. He was wondering whether there was anybody else in this massive house and whether they were also carrying and if so what kind of ammunition was loaded in their weapons.

"Are you a fan of antique guns? I have quite a collection spread throughout this house, but my most valued items I keep here in my den."

Tripp Hogan wheeled himself around his desk, and Nova stood to follow him to the two display cases.

"Those two Remington revolvers on the left once belonged to Ulysses S. Grant. Do you see how the grips are carved with Grant's portrait? Absolutely stunning, aren't they?"

The old man leaned forward, squinting, and then pointed.

"And do you see the .32 caliber down there? That belonged to Adolf Hitler. It was given to the son of a bitch as a 50th birthday present by the Walthers."

The old man pointed again.

"And that Winchester up there near the top? That's one of the very first ones, the Model 1866, often called the 'Yellow Boy.' Breathtaking, isn't it?"

Tripp Hogan looked up at Nova but quickly realized his guest wasn't as impressed as he'd hoped. His grin faltered, and he cleared his throat.

"Thank you for coming to see me, Mr. Bartkowski. It was a pleasure meeting you. It's refreshing to know that true patriots are still fighting the good fight. I wish you good luck with your travels, but I ask that you not interfere with any business my son or I have going on in this town. Do I make myself clear?"

Not really. The last part sort of came out of nowhere. And

it didn't help that the man's tone had sharpened like the tip of a spike.

"Well, Mr. Bartkowski?"

Nova nodded slowly, more conscious now than ever of the pistol digging into the small of his back.

"Yes."

"Yes, what?"

"Yes, you've made yourself clear."

The smile again, like nothing at all had changed. The tone once more pleasant and welcoming.

"Excellent! Again, it was a pleasure meeting you. And again, I apologize for my son and give you my word that he will no longer be of any nuisance to you. And likewise, I'd like you to give me your word that you'll go ahead and fish until you're ready to leave and then have yourself a good and healthy rest of your life. Does that sound like a deal?"

Before, Nova had had little interest in Tripp Hogan and his son despite what the son and his men had done last night. Now…now his curiosity was piqued.

Keeping his gaze steady with Tripp Hogan's, Nova nodded.

"Deal."

THIRTEEN

Again they drove in silence.

Like before, Nova stared out the window at the passing fields and trees. He was replaying everything that happened back in the large house. A house that probably had more than six bedrooms but felt empty. The type of house that demanded to be filled with life, a family with kids and maybe even a few dogs. But Nova hadn't sensed anyone else in the home besides Tripp Hogan and Carson.

Nova said, "The two of you served together, didn't you?"

It was a risk putting it out there—part of him knew it would be better to keep his mouth shut—but he couldn't help himself.

Carson eyed him in the rearview mirror. It didn't appear as if the man was going to answer, but then after another moment he nodded.

"We did, yes. Tripp saved my life."

"And now you work for him."

"I wouldn't put it that way. I help him when I can. He's a great man, but as you saw, he has physical limitations."

"He said he was awarded the Medal of Honor."

"Yes."

"But he didn't tell me how he'd earned it. Do you know?"

Carson eyed him again.

"It's not my place to say. If Tripp wanted you to know, he would have told you."

Twenty minutes later they pulled into Hogan Auto. A mishmash of makes and models of various cars and trucks and SUVs filled almost the entire lot, shining in the late-morning sun.

His truck was sitting right near the dealership entrance. Carson parked the Sierra beside it. He left the truck idling as he said, "Your keys should already be inside."

Nova climbed out without a word. He stared at his truck for a moment—brand-new tires, new rear window, and to top it all off the thing looked washed and waxed—and then he peeked inside the driver's window to note the keys resting on the passenger seat.

He gave Carson a thumbs-up, and waited for the man to ease the pickup out of the parking space to leave.

But the man didn't move. The Sierra kept idling.

That's when Nova felt the prickle on the back of his neck and slowly turned.

The two men standing inside the dealership were being obvious. Blake Hogan and one of his lackeys. They wore slacks and dress shirts and ties, like proper salesmen. Nova and Carson appeared to be the only two people in the lot. No other customers.

Nova threw the two men a mock salute, then climbed into his truck. He backed it out and headed for the exit, noting Carson following not too far behind. They'd come to the dealership from the east and Nova figured the man would head back to the house. So Nova turned left onto the highway, heading west.

He watched the rearview mirror, waiting to see what

Carson would do. For a second or two, the Sierra didn't move, despite there being no traffic headed either way. Then finally it pulled out, headed back the way it had come.

Nova drove for another mile before looping back. He parked his truck in the same spot it had occupied only a few minutes prior.

Blake Hogan and his lackey were no longer standing at the window. The lackey was stationed behind a desk, and the man leaned forward in his seat once he realized Nova had returned.

Nova didn't go inside. Instead, he drifted into the lot to browse the vehicles. None of the cars and trucks looked brand new. He supposed this location of Hogan Auto sold cars that were pre-owned—a term he figured was more palatable to customers than *used*.

There were maybe fifty vehicles total. Nova strolled past each one, noting that there were no sticker prices, and he even peered into a few and tried some of the doors but they were all locked.

Several of the vehicles had a fine coating of dirt on them from sitting for a long time in the sun. A few were spotted with bird shit.

He was surprised nobody had come out to check on him, so he headed inside.

The lackey was still sitting behind the desk. Leaning back in his chair, his hands folded over his stomach.

Blake Hogan stood in the doorway of his office. Arms crossed, face set, his nostrils flaring the tiniest bit.

Nova said, "What would you say is the trade-in value for my truck?"

Neither man said anything.

"I mean, the brand-new tires must bring the cost up a bit more than the Kelly Blue Book value, right?"

Again, nothing.

"How about a test drive? There's an old Firebird out there I'd like to take for a spin."

He pulled out his wallet, slid out his driver's license, held it up.

"I'm guessing you'll need to make a photocopy?"

The lackey glanced over at Blake but that was the only reaction. Blake Hogan continued to stand in place, his shoulders back. Glaring at Nova.

Nova kept his gaze steady with Blake's.

"Your old man seems like a good guy. Really has a thing for antique guns, doesn't he?"

Silence.

"He said some very glowing things about you. Like how you're his favorite son."

Those nostrils, still flaring.

The lackey took the cue and stood from his chair. He stepped around the desk and gestured at the door.

"I think it's time for you to leave."

"Really? So ... no test drive?"

The lackey said nothing, now standing impatiently with his hands on his hips.

"Weird," Nova said. "I thought this was a car dealership. Don't you guys sell cars here?"

The lackey said, "This is the corporate office. We also handle the overflow from several of our other dealerships. If you'd like to get a test drive there, the closest is in Billings."

Nova glanced out the window at the vehicles in the lot.

"If that's the case, then how'd you manage to replace the tires and window on my truck so fast? I mean, this is your corporate office, right? It's not like you have mechanics working back in the garage."

Both men said nothing.

"All right, then." He tipped an invisible cowboy hat. "You boys have a nice day."

He waited to see if Blake Hogan would take the bait, but the man had become a seething statue. Nova figured he better not press his luck and pushed through the glass door.

Soon he was back in his truck and headed for the exit. He had to pause for an eighteen-wheeler as it pulled into the dealership. It was one of those multi-level multi-car carriers, with eight cars loaded onto it. None of them looking brand new.

Nova twisted in his seat to survey the lot again. As far as he could tell, every square foot of inventory space was already filled.

He whispered to himself, trying to make sense of things.

"Overflow, huh?"

He'd have to look into it later. For now, it was time to fish.

FOURTEEN

Blake Hogan stood stock-still, fuming, his jaw clenched so hard it was a wonder he didn't crack a tooth.

It had been a minute or so since the outsider had left and still Blake was standing in his office doorway, frozen, unable to trust himself to make a move. Because he worried that he might do something extreme. Like punch his fist through the wall. Or take a trash can and fling it at the plate glass that over-looked the parking lot.

"Boss?"

Marc Palmer was standing only a few feet away, watching him cautiously.

"Boss, are you okay?"

He blinked and released a breath he hadn't realized he'd been holding. Shifted his stance to regard the man.

"What?"

"New load just arrived."

He blinked again, attempted to refocus. The new load. Right. They'd been expecting it for the past hour. The driver had called ahead saying he was running behind due to a nasty accident on I-90.

Marc was still watching him, hesitant.

"You sure you're okay?"

No, he wasn't okay. His goddamned father had gone behind his back and made him look like a fool. The same truck his men vandalized last night had been brought to them so that they would fix everything they'd destroyed. On top of that, they weren't charging the asshole a penny.

But that was all right because at least they added something extra. Something special his father wouldn't have approved of and maybe that was the point when all was said and done. A big fuck you to his old man.

Marc was still watching him, so Blake grunted again that he was fine and headed back toward the garage. The rest of his men were here except Finlay, who was still in the hospital.

One of the back bay doors was open, Keith standing in the shade and directing the truck as it moved in position to unload its haul while Dominic and Gary used the time to grab a cigarette.

BJ, his casted arm in the sling, turned to Blake and said, "That asshole pick up his truck yet?"

Blake only nodded, watching Keith outside.

"Fucking prick," BJ muttered, presumably meaning the outsider, but who knows, maybe he meant Blake's father, and if that was the case Blake didn't blame him though he still couldn't have a man under his control disrespecting his old man. That was how mutinies started. To keep his men in check he needed to ensure they never disrespected Blake or his father despite the fact his father was a piece of shit.

"What did you say?"

BJ swung his face back at his boss.

"Huh?"

"Who's a fucking prick?"

"That guy. The outsider."

Blake watched BJ for a moment, studying his face. He

knew the man was telling the truth but wanted him—and the others—to feel uncomfortable just the same.

"Where are we with the schedule?"

"So far so good. This batch is a bit behind schedule, but we should make it work. All the vehicles he'll take are ready to go."

Blake gazed at the two vehicles on either side of him, the men finishing up what needed to be done so that they could get them and the other cars and trucks on the hauler.

He noted the box truck on the other side of the garage and nodded toward it.

"That's ready to go too?"

BJ nodded, clearing his throat.

"Yes, sir."

Blake said nothing and only stood there with his arm crossed, waiting. Dominic and Gary got the hint and flicked their cigarettes away to help unload the hauler now that the tractor-trailer had parked.

As he watched his men work, Blake thought about the outsider stepping into the front room and asking to take a test drive. The smile on his goddamned face.

The outsider had met with Blake's father and God only knew what his old man had told him. The only thing Blake knew for certain was that after this Friday—once there was less pressure on him—he and his men would track down the outsider even if he'd left town or, hell, the state. They'd track him across the country if need be, and they'd drag his ass out of whatever hole he called home and force him onto his knees and stick a pistol in his face and force him to watch as Blake pulled the trigger.

Good Lord, it was going to be beautiful.

FIFTEEN

Before traveling to Remington, Nova had done as much research on the town as possible. Which didn't take long as the town itself was tiny—a bedroom community, as Sheriff Veronica Chapman had put it during their first interaction, meaning its residents only lived there and commuted almost an hour to Billings for work.

Nova didn't know much about fishing, but he was a quick study. It also helped that as a kid he'd gone fishing with friends. Cheap plastic rods purchased at Walmart with a cup of worms bought at the corner store, and they'd spent more time laughing and fooling around the river than actually trying to catch anything.

This was back in middle school before the cancer in his mother's body had metastasized. Back when he had honest-to-God friends whom he hung out with after school and on the weekends. Before he dropped out and no longer saw those friends.

But Nova knew that he needed to know a good bit about fishing to make his cover work, so he watched YouTube videos and purchased the proper gear, the kind a guy like him was expected to carry, and mapped out which roads in town led to the river.

Today, he took a specific route, racing past the open fields, until he came to a deserted, gravel-packed turnoff right next to the water.

As soon as Nova climbed out and scanned the area to ensure there was nobody nearby, he began to inspect the truck.

He found the GPS tracker almost immediately. Secured under the passenger-side rear wheel well. No larger than two and a half inches wide. A super-strength magnet keeping it in place.

Nova hefted the tracker in his hand, started to grin, but then narrowed his eyes at the truck.

Way too easy.

He placed the tracker aside and dropped to the ground to peer up at the undercarriage again. He went front to back, then checked any loose sections of the tailgate, behind the bumper, the fenders, and even loosened the taillamps. He checked the truck's interior, digging through the glovebox, using a pocket flashlight to shine at the wires under the steering column and front dash. He checked under the seats and between the cushions. He popped the hood and leaned in close using the flashlight for those areas that were shadowed from the brilliant glare of the sun. Then he stood back, hands on his hips, and stared in frustration at the truck.

He closed his eyes, took a breath, attempted to center himself. What wasn't he seeing? What was he missing? He'd found one tracker already, yes, but anyone with a first-grade education would have been able to find it. There had to be something else. Tripp Hogan wouldn't have had his truck fixed out of the goodness of his heart. And if he had, then his son and his son's men certainly wouldn't have let sleeping dogs lie. They had come for him last night, and there was no doubt in Nova's mind that they would try again.

Taking another breath, he muttered, "One more time."

Undercarriage, tailgate, fenders, bumpers, engine. And it was here, peering once again at the engine block, that he realized there was something he'd missed the first time around.

"Son of a bitch."

A normal person peeks under the hood of a car and they see an engine. Only that—an engine. But as his father once told him there's so much more, and if you know what you're looking for, every engine tells a story.

Most engines tell the same story, so if you know the general outline—if you can tell the difference between a starter and an alternator, a crankshaft and a camshaft—then something wrong in the story will always stick out.

Nova had to admit, Blake and his men were good. The first tracker was a decoy. They'd expected him to find it—maybe even wanted him to. Because then he'd think it was the only one and toss it. While the entire time another tracker was positioned just underneath the battery. Vehicle-powered and inconspicuously hardwired to avoid everyday detection. But Nova had detected it.

He was still standing there, his head tilted as he stared at the second tracker, when he heard the low, quiet grumble of an oncoming engine up the road.

His hand immediately reached behind him, digging under his shirt to grasp the FNX-45. He had cover standing in front of the popped hood, but it wasn't much. He glanced over his shoulder and surveyed the river. Calm and peaceful, with nobody stationed on the other bank.

It wouldn't surprise Nova that Blake and his men had lost their patience and decided to come for him now, out here at least four miles away from the nearest home. He remembered the assault rifles the two men had carried last night and imagined each of the men would be decked out with the same. Which meant Nova didn't stand a chance with only two pistols.

His mind wheeled through different scenarios.

He considered racing to the river and diving in, swimming with the current somewhere downstream. But all that would do was get him wet and potentially mess up both pistols.

Or he could jump into his truck and try to race down the road before Blake and his men arrived. They would undoubtedly try to cut him off, but Nova was skilled enough in tactical driving to outmaneuver even the most accomplished driver.

The truck was closer now. Less than three hundred yards away. Nova could now hear the vehicle's tires skimming over the cracked pavement and remembered the fancy Range Rover from the night before. He figured it belonged to Blake Hogan and promised himself to shoot out every one of its tires if he had the chance, including the one hanging off the rear door.

Hand tight around the pistol's grip, Nova leaned to the side to view the approaching vehicle.

He didn't realize he was holding his breath until he felt the air blow out through his nostrils and his muscles relax.

A small pickup, carrying a man and a woman. The pickup's tires crunched over the gravel as it slowed and parked two spaces away from Nova's truck.

Nova gazed down the empty roadway before shutting the hood and stepping to the back of the truck to grab his gear, his hand no longer on his pistol but still hanging at his side, ready to grab it at a moment's notice.

The couple got out of the pickup. Jeans, light jackets, baseball caps. They both wore sunglasses and waved at Nova in a neighborly way before linking hands and walking down to the river.

A hike. Or stroll. Or whatever the locals called it around these parts.

The couple went north, headed upriver, which was ideal, as Nova intended to head south.

He waited five minutes to make sure they didn't double

back before grabbing one of the empty water bottles from the truck. Using his tactical knife, he tore off the top of the bottle, then dropped the small magnetic tracker inside along with a few fistfuls of gravel to give it extra weight. Next he used the roll of electrical tape from the glovebox to seal the top.

He grabbed his gear from the truck, tackle box and rod and everything else, and then headed for the river.

As he walked, he checked back over his shoulder to ensure the couple or anyone else wasn't nearby before chucking the bottle out into the dark green water.

The bottle bobbed on the glistening surface like a just-launched schooner and was quickly swept up in the current, disappearing from view as it rounded the bend.

SIXTEEN

Nova used the Google Maps app on his phone. Every half-klick he paused to survey the area to ensure nobody was following or watching him. He hated carrying the gear but didn't want to set it aside for fear that somebody might stumble across it. His fishing gear was his cover, and he needed it to be convincing.

But after three miles of working his way downriver—pushing through spots that weren't at all open—Nova eventually came to a place where he had no choice but to leave his gear behind.

He found a large viburnum bush and stowed his pack and pole under it. Then, feeling much lighter without the gear, he rechecked his phone to confirm he was headed in the right direction and started east.

It took him almost an hour before he reached what he deemed the Hogan property. There were no signs indicating as much, of course, but just a sense that Nova got. He remembered what Veronica Chapman had told him the night before, how the Hogans owned most of the land in Remington. Surely he was walking on their land now, though as far as he could see, it was all just fields and trees.

The sky was still clear, the sun extra bright. Shafts of golden rays slanted through the trees as he advanced farther onto the property. No telling if the Hogans had any sophisticated surveillance in place. He hadn't spotted anything when Carson took him to the house, but that didn't mean there wasn't some sort of setup to monitor the perimeter.

Nova moved cautiously, as though forging through enemy terrain. Which wasn't too far from the truth, based on the past twenty-four hours. Even now he saw the shock in both men's eyes as he hurried toward them. The one with the socket wrench had already swung it hard against his father's head. He remembered the smell of the grease and oil and the steadiness of his breathing as he stepped up behind the man with the socket wrench. He remembered the man swinging the socket wrench upward, meaning to catch Nova under the chin, and how Nova grabbed it and yanked it from the man's grip.

Pausing in the shade and cover of the trees, Nova took a breath. He scanned the area once again. He still wasn't sure why he was doing this. Only that something in his gut was telling him it was the right move. Especially after Blake Hogan and his men came for him last night. Especially after Tripp Hogan made a point of telling Nova to stay out of the family's business.

He remembered seeing the trail that led away from the house as Carson drove him up the drive. A wide trail that looked beaten down, like one an ATV or UTV would use. The trail had gone up the hill and disappeared into the trees. It could be anything—just a standard trail, nothing special—but without knowing for sure Nova would forever wonder, and he hated forever wondering.

There's an anger in you, isn't there?

He closed his eyes, saw his mother's gaunt face. Before she'd gotten sick she loved hiking in the woods. A simple pleasure he had never truly understood or appreciated. And on her deathbed she'd asked him to take her there. So he'd loaded her into the car and drove to the woods and wheeled her in the wheelchair a local church had donated to them, taking his time over the dirt until the stones and vines created too much of an obstacle and he had no choice but to carry her. Eventually they made it up to the top where there was a drop-off overlooking what felt like half the county.

He carefully set his mother down under a tree, so that her back was against the trunk. Sunglasses on her skeletal face, a slight smile on her colorless lips. He was sweating, trying to catch his breath, when she asked him that question.

There's an anger in you, isn't there? I can see it. It's been building for most of your life. I don't blame you—not after what all you've been through—but you can't let the anger control you. Because once the anger controls you …

"Aw, shit."

The voice came from his left, and Nova was swinging around, already reaching for the pistol secured at his back, when he caught sight of the voice's owner and paused.

The man looked harmless enough. Especially based on the fact he wasn't holding a weapon. He didn't even look like he was packing.

He had a cigarette pinched between two fingers, a ribbon of smoke curling up from the red glowing tip as he inhaled.

"Mr. Hogan sent you to come find me, didn't he?"

The man appeared to be in his forties. Early forties, most likely. Five-ten, short brown hair, brown eyes. White. He looked generic enough, though he didn't seem to fit the landscape. Probably because he was wearing Adidas sweatpants and a plain white undershirt with Nike sneakers.

"Say, I don't think I've seen you around here before."

The man was eyeing him, inhaling another puff. He noticed Nova eyeing him too, and he held up the cigarette.

"I'd prefer to keep smoking that dope you guys brought

me, but, well, can't have anything in my system, can I? Same with the coke."

The man inhaled another puff, studying Nova.

"I know I shouldn't be walking the grounds. Mr. Hogan made that very clear. But, well, I needed to stretch my legs, get some fresh air. It seems like the only time I get to walk anymore is when we hike to the shooting range."

The man took one last drag on the cigarette and tossed it to the ground and used the heel of his sneaker to make sure it was extinguished.

"It's only been a couple days I've been stuck in that cabin, but it feels like a month's gone by. Now, that isn't to say I'm not appreciative of all Mr. Hogan and his father have done for me. Especially sending the girls. The ones last night were smoking hot."

Nova said nothing. Silence seemed the most fitting reply as he tried to figure out who this man was and what the hell he was talking about.

"It's funny," the man said. "My understanding was that nobody was supposed to see me. But those girls saw me. I mean"—winking at Nova—"they saw a lot of me, if you get my drift."

Nova remained silent.

"Christ, man, you don't have to be so serious. I decided to take a walk—big fucking deal. I'm not second-guessing anything. I'm a red-blooded patriot, through and through."

Nova said, "Let's go."

The man rolled his eyes as he lit himself another cigarette, but then he nodded and started back in the direction Nova had been headed.

Nova fell in step behind him.

Insects in the tall grass around them. A hawk in the sky above their heads, riding the thermals as it searched for prey.

The man said, not looking back at Nova as they walked,

"My one regret is I can't call my mom. Typically I call her every day, and I haven't spoken to her in four days. I'm sure she's been worried sick about me. And she's gonna be even more sick once she sees … well, you know."

A glance back at Nova, the man eyeing him cautiously.

"I decided where I'm gonna do it, by the way. I ran it by Mr. Hogan, and he was impressed."

Nova said, "That's good."

Nodding, the man blew smoke out from the corner of his mouth.

"When you were a kid, did you like school? I hated it. Especially recess. Bigger kids were always bullying me on the playground. Not that I'm making any excuses—a lot of kids get bullied, and really, I wasn't bullied that much. But it definitely toughened me up. Made me realize I need to have structure in my life. And recess … it was chaos."

The ground was starting to rise. They were headed up a hill. Nova had no idea how much farther they were going and wasn't sure how he would peel off from the man before they reached the house. If the house came into view at the top of this rise, Nova would need to act fast.

"I wish I could call my mom, though. Just for a minute. I want to hear her voice one last time. To tell her that I love her and that it'll be okay. She … she wouldn't understand, though. And she's sure not gonna understand after it happens. My mom, people are gonna hate her because of me. I feel bad about it, but it has to be done. And I'm the guy to make it happen. Mr. Hogan said as much. He said I'm gonna be a hero. Can you imagine that? A hero!"

As they crested the rise, Nova held his breath. But it wasn't the house he spotted down below in the small valley.

A lone log cabin, sitting by itself in a field. Not too large—nothing luxurious—but still a nice-sized cabin.

Even from this distance Nova could make out the trampled grass of a trail snaking up the hill on the other side of the valley. No doubt the tail end of the trail that started by the house.

"There it is," the man said. "My home away from home. I'd invite you in for a beer, but something tells me that's against the rules."

"You're right," Nova said. "It is against the rules."

The man looked at Nova cautiously.

"You won't tell Mr. Hogan about this, will you?"

Nova stood silently for a beat, as if considering the question.

"Tell you what. I won't tell Mr. Hogan I saw you. You don't tell Mr. Hogan you saw me. Deal?"

The man nodded, sucking in another puff.

"I appreciate it."

"No problem. But now I should get back to patrolling the perimeter. With everything so close to happening, we can't take any chances, can we?"

The man shook his head, crunching the spent butt under his Nike.

"No, we cannot. Again, I appreciate it."

He started down the hill toward the cabin when Nova said, "Hey."

The man paused to look back at him.

"Mr. Hogan's right. You are going to be a hero."

Nova wasn't sure why he felt the need to add this, but part of him knew it was needed to keep the man on his side. Plus, he hoped that by massaging the man's ego the man would make sure to keep his promise to Nova. The last thing Nova needed was for him to mention something offhand and bring it to Tripp and Blake Hogan's attention that a stranger had been wandering the property.

The man offered up a salute before jogging down the hill.

Nova didn't wait to make sure the man entered the cabin. He turned and headed back the way they'd come, knowing he had miles to go before grabbing his gear and returning to his truck. He still didn't know what just happened, but he'd seen enough to know something was going on. Something bad.

SEVENTEEN

Nova stood in the shower, his face tilted down to allow the pulsing water to beat against the back of his head, trying to piece together and make sense of the day's events.

It was almost four o'clock and he had time to kill. After he'd returned for his gear, he'd strapped on his bootfoot waders and set up in the water, practicing the different casting techniques he'd seen on YouTube. He found it surprisingly relaxing, the silence that enveloped him. The quiet burble of the water. The air so fresh he kept breathing deeply, letting it clear out his lungs.

The other vehicle was gone when he returned to where he'd parked. Nova packed his gear in the back and then inspected the truck once again, taking his time, going over every square inch. Still the only thing he found was the tracker under the battery, which he left in place. Disposing of it would overplay his hand. He knew Blake Hogan and his men were tracking him, but they didn't know Nova knew they were tracking him. Something he could use to his advantage.

After a while he shut off the water and stepped out of the shower, grabbing the fresh towel off the counter next to his pistol. He dried off and stared at himself in the mirror. He hadn't shaved in the past two days, which was a rarity for him. He hadn't worn a beard since his time as a SEAL. He'd wanted to put that part of his life behind him, and so he'd kept himself freshly shaven ever since. Part of him missed it, though. Maybe after all of this was over—once Remington was a distant speck in his rearview—he might consider it again. Make it part of his fresh start.

He'd set the desk chair against the doorknob. It wasn't much to stop anybody from barreling into the room, but it would have at least caused enough noise to give Nova time to grab his gun from the shower. He left the chair in place as he dressed and then grabbed his phone and climbed onto the bed so that his back was against the headboard.

With a VPN initiated, he opened the web browser and googled *Hogan Auto Montana*. As Veronica Chapman had noted, there were a half-dozen locations all over the state. Billings, Missoula, Great Falls, Bozeman, Helena, Havre. Each website looked like every other car dealership's website. It appeared Hogan Auto Group carried practically every make and model of pickup and SUV. Each location's website listed the current inventory, both new and pre-owned, as well as a page that listed the staff. While Blake Hogan's face splashed every website, he was only mentioned as the president and CEO, and nothing else.

Nova recalled the Firebird in the lot earlier today. He typed it into the search box, but nothing came back.

"Overflow, my ass."

Next he googled Blake Hogan. There was a Facebook page that was public, but it was bland. Blake didn't seem to update it, and the only recent pictures were those he'd been tagged in. Some of Blake fishing. Some of Blake at a cookout. One of Blake on a hunting trip, posing in front of a dead Rocky Mountain elk.

Nova searched the friends list, trying to spot any of Blake's men.

No luck.

He googled Tripp Hogan next. Apparently, the man had a short stint in politics over two decades ago when he'd run for the US Senate. An ambitious feat for someone who hadn't even dabbled in local politics until that point. Which was probably why he'd come in fourth during the primary, and after that he hadn't bothered to try again.

Besides several news articles about the man's entrepreneurial streak when it came to local businesses, there wasn't much information. No social media sites, which wasn't at all surprising for a man Tripp Hogan's age.

Nova set the phone down and focused on the blank TV. He wasn't good with stuff like this. He knew how to use the Internet, sure, but he wasn't a whiz like his friend Scooter had been. Scooter who died only a few months ago. A young man with a stutter who'd never lived long enough to see thirty.

He wondered where Holly Lin was now. *Who* Holly Lin was now. Atticus had secured her a new identity. But she hadn't opened it by the time she and Nova parted ways after returning to the country after their bloody stint in Mexico. Nova had gone his way, Holly had gone hers, and he wasn't sure if and when he would ever see her again.

"Damn it."

Nova picked up his phone again. He'd been putting this off —even before coming to town—and now he knew he had no choice.

He googled his father's mechanic shop. He'd done so previously to verify the address but hadn't clicked on the link. He did so now and was greeted by a generic website that only included basic information, like the address and phone number and typical cost for services such as tire rotation and oil change.

Nothing on there that would give him any sense of who his

father had become in the years since he'd walked out on Nova
and his dying mother.

Next he googled his father's name. Several Edward Schaf-
fers came up, and he narrowed the search for Montana, but no
luck. Either his father kept his social media footprint restricted,
or he just didn't want to bother.

Amanda Schaffer, however, did have a Facebook account.
Nova found it without any trouble. Her profile noted that she
was married but there was no hyperlink to send someone to her
husband's account.

The most recent post on the page simply said, "Please pray
for Ed!!!"

The post had over one hundred reactions, mostly hearts and
sad-face emojis. Two dozen people had commented, assuring
Mandy that Ed was in their prayers and wishing the family well.

Nova closed his eyes, remembered sitting in the cafe and
watching the two men striding toward the mechanic shop. He
remembered the sound the socket wrench made when it struck
the side of his father's head. Then saw the spray of blood that
splattered the ground.

He pictured his father lying unconscious in a hospital bed,
surrounded by machines. A doctor conferring with Mandy out
in the hallway, solemnly shaking his head as he told her there
was nothing more they could do.

Nova opened his eyes again, went back to scanning her
Facebook page. It was mostly littered with photos—many
selfies but also selfies she'd taken with her son.

Nova's half-brother.

Christ, it was still a lot to take in. Every time he closed his
eyes he saw the kid standing at the front of the cafe, nervously
kneading his hands together.

In a good portion of the photos Mandy and Alex smiled
brightly, as though caught mid-laugh. A few showed them with

all-too-serious expressions, though the kind of expressions that they probably cracked up laughing a half second after the pictures were taken.

Only a handful featured his father.

One photo was of him and Mandy. She was clearly the one taking the photo, leaning close to him, showing her teeth. His father smiled too, but it was the kind of forced smile that didn't show any teeth. Not that he didn't look happy. Maybe just not one hundred percent comfortable. Like something about the past was still bothering him. Or maybe that was all in Nova's head.

The other photo was of the family: Nova's father and Mandy standing side by side while his father held Nova's half-brother in his arms. The boy looked maybe three years old, which meant this was taken about two years ago.

It wasn't easy to admit, but his father did look happy. Contented. Which made him wonder if maybe the happiness was forced. Knowing that whatever pictures Mandy snapped would be uploaded to social media, so he needed to make sure they looked good.

Nova wondered what photos of his father would have looked like had there been social media when he was a kid. Whether there would be the same light in the man's eyes.

He searched Mandy's friends list but didn't spot anyone that looked familiar. A few faces he'd seen around town, which was to be expected for a town this small, but not Blake Hogan or any of his men.

Releasing a breath, he tossed his phone aside and stared again at the blank TV. He wasn't sure what to do next. He wasn't sure what Blake Hogan and his men were up to. He wasn't sure why Tripp Hogan had invited him to the house only to give him a subtle threat. He wasn't sure what the stranger in the cabin was talking about. But all of it added together equaled something that didn't settle right in Nova's gut.

Maybe he should contact Atticus. Atticus had connections Nova could only dream about. Scooter may be gone, but Atticus could connect Nova with someone just as tech savvy who could look into the Hogans' business and maybe their financials and property disclosures.

But for what purpose?

That was the question. He still didn't know what any of it meant, and he wasn't going to bring something to Atticus if there was nothing there. But at least now he had an email for Atticus if and when he needed it. Before, when he was stuck in the Nevada desert, all he'd had was a phone number that turned out to be for Scout Dry Cleaning. So he'd left a voice-mail and hoped against hope that something would happen, and maybe now he needed to do the same thing too, he needed to contact Atticus—

"Stop it."

Okay, yes, he was stalling. Watching the time on his phone. He'd agreed to meet for dinner at Mandy's around six o'clock. It was now almost an hour away. He could call her and tell her that he couldn't make it. Or he could not show up. He could pack his things and drive the hell out of this town like he should have done last night.

Nova closed his eyes and once again saw the small boy standing nervously by the cash register. A small boy whose father was currently in the hospital, unresponsive. A small boy who wasn't sure whether his father would ever wake up.

"Shit."

He rose from the bed and returned to the bathroom and grabbed his razor. Might as well look presentable for when he officially met his half-brother.

EIGHTEEN

As he stepped out of the Defender, Blake Hogan checked the app on his phone to determine the outsider's location.

The blinking dot on the map told him the man was still at the motel. He'd been there when Blake left the dealership and he was still there now. Good.

He pocketed his phone as he entered the kitchen. All at once he was bombarded by the savory scent of grilled steak. His stomach rumbled but he pushed through it because the steak wasn't for him.

He breezed through the kitchen—ignoring Carson as the man stood at the stove—and went straight for his father's den. It was still his father's hour but Blake didn't care as he slammed the door open with enough force to send it smacking into the wall and bouncing back.

"What the fuck is your problem?"

His father sat at his desk, using a damp soft cloth to clean the musket's wooden stock. He barely blinked at the question, didn't even bother to look up at Blake as he stormed forward, placing his hands on his hips.

"Well?"

Tripp Hogan continued working on the stock as though his son wasn't fuming right in front of him.

Blake, his teeth clenched: "Don't make me snap those fucking pieces in half."

That elicited a smile from his old man. It was slight—just the twitch of one corner of his mouth—but it was still something.

"I'd like to see you try that," his father said. Then paused to lift his eyes to meet Blake's. "How's your leg feeling, by the way?"

Blake knew he was in a precarious position. His father was disabled and forever stuck to that goddamned wheelchair. Without any pistols involved, Blake knew he could beat the shit out of him … as long as Carson wasn't around. But Carson was in the house, presumably still in the kitchen. The man may have abandoned the steak, however, seeing as how amped up Blake had entered the house. He could be standing in the hallway, waiting for the right moment to strike.

"You embarrassed me," Blake said, doing everything he could to keep his emotions in check. "You embarrassed *us*."

Tripp casually stripped off his gloves and tilted his chin up.

"What are you going on about now?"

"The outsider!"

"Yes, what about him?"

"The new tires. The new window."

"And? You and your men shouldn't have caused the damage in the first place."

"That's not the point, and you know it."

"He's a SEAL."

The flatness of his father's tone, the declarative nature, caused Blake to pause.

"What did you say?"

"A SEAL. A frogman. The man you refer to as an outsider was in the Navy. He served, unlike someone else I know."

Blake felt his eye starting to twitch. He did everything he could to stop it, but no luck—it kept twitching, and the more Blake tried to will it to stop the more it felt like it was going.

His father always knew the things to say to get under his skin. The right words, the right tone. Blake having never served was one of those things. There had been a time when it was all but decreed that Blake would enlist just like his old man. But the truth was Blake was scared to go into the military. After all, this was back during the height of the Iraq war, so there was a good chance Blake would have seen combat. And while he was proficient with a weapon, he wasn't brave. He knew that, despite how much he played it up otherwise. But he was smart —much smarter than his old man, by a mile—and managed to build a whole new empire because he saw an opening and grabbed it while the grabbing was good.

Blake said, because he didn't know what else to say, "Who gives a shit if the guy was a SEAL?"

"He's a patriot. He fought for our country. I guarantee you he's one of us."

"He beat up Finlay and BJ!"

"He saw a situation going south and stepped in to help who he deemed was the victim. And I can't say I fault him for it. Whatever weird obsession you and your guys have with this man needs to stop. He's a guest in this town and will remain that way until he leaves. Speaking of guests, I believe Carson should have the steak done about now. Why don't you go deliver it?"

He checked the app on his phone again as he drove up the hill. One hand on the steering wheel, the other holding his phone and thumbing at the screen.

The outsider was still at the motel.

The two tracking devices had been Blake's idea. One that wasn't easy to find but was still in a place that was sure to be found assuming the outsider looked. And then a second, smaller device hidden in a place the outsider was almost certain not to look.

If the outsider didn't bother to look for any tracking devices —or anything that they may have put on the truck—then maybe their fears were unwarranted. In that case the outsider was just a guy who saw somebody getting roughed up and decided to intervene. Nothing to worry about.

But if the outsider found the first device and tossed it, then it was clear the outsider was more than he appeared.

And, well, based on the fact that one of the devices looked to be right now moving down the Yellowstone, it was clear the outsider had found that first device and chucked it into the water. Which meant he'd been smart enough to check the truck in the first place. Though maybe that wasn't so surprising, now knowing the man was a SEAL. The military trained its boys well, which was why the US had the greatest soldiers in the world. It would make sense the outsider would look to see if Blake and his boys had left anything behind on his truck.

He parked the UTV by the cabin and grabbed the large cooler off the seat beside him.

Darrell was alone—a new batch of girls was scheduled to arrive later tonight—but still Blake knocked on the door and waited for the man to answer.

"Mr. Hogan!"

"Brought you dinner."

Blake entered the cabin and did his best not to make a face at the smell. Darrell had been drinking and doing drugs and having sex with countless women for the past several days. Carson had come out to clean up every day, but still there was an underlying stench—a miasma of sex and drugs—that they'd need to do something about once this was all over.

"Steak, right?"

Darrell knew it was steak—he'd requested it—but Blake merely nodded with a smile as he set the cooler down on the table.

"Anything else I can get for you?"

The man shook his head, smiling, though something in his eyes gave Blake pause. Part of him chalked it up to nerves as they were now less than forty-eight hours away—Blake imagined he'd have some doubts himself—while another part wondered if it was something else.

"Everything okay?"

Darrell nodded, saying, "Oh yeah, everything's good. I'm just hungry, is all."

And he smiled again, a bit too widely this time, which made Blake look at him curiously.

"Are you sure?"

The man maintained the smile for another beat before it faded, and he closed his eyes and sucked in a breath.

"I can't lie to you, Mr. Hogan. It just doesn't feel right, not after everything you and your pops have done for me."

Blake felt the hairs on the back of his neck stand on end.

"Lie to me about what?"

"I went for a walk," the man said sheepishly, now having a hard time meeting Blake's gaze. "I know the rules are to always stay in the cabin, but I just … I needed to get some fresh air. And, well, I wandered a bit farther than I probably should have."

Darrell saw something enter Blake's face and quickly shook his head.

"Nobody saw me, Mr. Hogan. I didn't leave the property or anything like that. I mean, one of your men saw me, and he walked me back here, but that was it."

Blake wasn't sure what to say at first. They had people who worked the property, but everyone was off this week while

Darrell was here—the groundskeepers and the maids. It was of the utmost importance that nobody saw the man or even knew he existed. No reason anyone else would have been on the property except Blake's guys or Carson.

"Do you know which one of my men it was?"

Darrell seemed to have to think about it a bit too long before shaking his head.

"No, sorry, I don't."

"That's okay," Blake said, feeling his nails digging into his palms. "What did he look like?"

For once in Tripp Hogan's life the arrogance had disappeared from his eyes. He stared back at his son in silence, contemplating what he'd just been told.

"Well?" Blake said. "What do you think of your precious frogman now?"

Carson was in the room too, standing back in the corner like always. Blake couldn't help but sneer at the man.

"How about you?"

Carson didn't respond.

Tripp cleared his throat.

"Are we sure it's him?"

"Darrell described him to a T."

"And he was on our property."

"That's right."

"And he interacted with Darrell."

"Yes."

Tripp Hogan was quiet for another moment, absorbing this. Finally he sighed.

"Well, that's certainly unfortunate. Even if the man had a valid reason for being on our property, having seen our guest—having *interacted* with him—complicates things."

If you want to call it that, Blake thought.

Tripp Hogan asked his son, "What do you propose?"

"He needs to be eliminated."

"I agree. I suppose now we need to come up with a plan to—"

Blake cut his father off.

"No need." He held up his phone, his expression solemn despite the large grin he was holding back. "I've already taken care of it."

NINETEEN

"Would you like more garlic bread?"

Mandy Schaffer held the basket out to him. The oven-warmed garlic bread was the frozen kind that came from a box, and while Nova had already taken one to be polite, he took another and set it on the edge of his plate.

She gave him a warm smile and then turned to Alex, sitting between them. The boy was preoccupied with a game on his mother's phone; from where Nova sat, all he could see were bright frantic seizure-inducing colors.

"Alex, keep eating."

The boy used his left hand to fork some lasagna into his mouth, his right hand tapping the screen as the tiniest sound emitted from the phone's speaker. Initially Mandy had told him to mute the phone, but Alex had put up a fuss, practically begging to hear his game, so they'd compromised on the lowest volume setting.

Nova was still having a hard time accepting that this boy was related to him. He remembered his own childhood and how strict his parents had been. Well, more his father than his mother, especially when his old man was having a bad day.

If Nova slouched, he got a smack. If Nova talked out of line, he got a smack. If Nova burbled his milk out of boredom, he got a smack.

His mother often tried calming his father, reminding him that Nova was only a boy. His father often countered with how Nova should know better, even though he was about Alex's age. *I don't want to raise no ingrate*, Nova's father had once said, though years later he'd decided enough was enough and ran for the hills.

Mandy said, "How's the lasagna? I hope I left it in long enough. I have to admit it's not homemade."

She smiled at him as if he was in on the joke, because the large Stouffer's box was sitting on the counter across the kitchen.

"It's great," Nova said. "Thank you."

Another lapse of silence, except for the barest hint of noise coming from Mandy's phone. He'd been here now for about twenty minutes. Had sat out in the driveway for close to five debating whether he should bother walking up to the door. Mandy had greeted him like a lifelong friend, even going so far as to give him a hug. She had dressed up a bit since this morning: a nice blouse, earrings, makeup. Alex was also wearing nicer clothes than he had earlier at the cafe. A light-blue polo shirt that looked brand-new.

"So," Mandy said when the silence stretched too long for her liking. "What was it you said you did for work again?"

He hadn't said anything about his work, but he understood her unease.

"I'm between jobs right now."

"Oh," she said and gave him a quick wink. "I know what that's code for."

Alex glanced up from the phone.

"What's what code for?"

"Never you mind. Keep eating, mister." Then back to Nova: "So what did you do?"

"I worked for the IRS."

Might as well stay consistent.

"Jeez," Mandy said. "That doesn't sound fun."

"It wasn't."

"What did you do there? Like, did you audit people and stuff?"

"A little bit of this, a little bit of that. Not really worth talking about, to be honest. What do you do?"

"I've got the most important job in the world. I'm a mother and a wife."

She smiled down at her son, then looked wistful for a beat.

"I never had a chance to go to college. I'd wanted to—had even been planning to go—but it didn't work out. So I did some odd jobs here and there, and then … I met Ed."

Nova felt his stomach tighten at the sound of his father's name. He figured they'd get here eventually, but it had come way too fast.

"How is he doing?"

A cautious glance toward her son.

"He's doing better, I think. The doctors sound positive."

Her tone, however, betrayed that she didn't know at all. Clearly she wanted to put on a brave face for the boy.

"We were down at the hospital earlier today. Then I swung by the school to pick up some homework, but do you know what they told me? All the work's online! Duh. I guess I knew that already, but I've just been so frazzled."

"That's understandable."

"School just started the other week. Part of me didn't want to keep Alex home, but another part …"

She glanced back at her son, whose gaze was laser-focused on the phone, his eyes wide and bright.

"You're real worried about Daddy, aren't you?"

Alex blinked. He looked up at his mom, nodded solemnly. Nova wasn't sure why this surprised him. He'd assumed the boy was too enthralled by the game to be aware of his surroundings. It hit him a second later that maybe the gaming was a coping mechanism. Made it easier for him to lose himself in the digital world than to concentrate on whether his father would still be breathing tomorrow.

Nova asked Mandy, "How did you meet?"

"Ed? Oh, I'd known him for a while before we started dating. He was always so sweet. So polite. A true *gentleman*, you know? People like to give us a hard time because of our age difference, but age is just a number. I hated dating men my age because they were all so immature. Not Ed. He's gentle and kind and smart."

Nova marveled about this man she was talking about. Gentle and kind and smart. Those weren't traits Nova had ever associated with his father. *Distant* was one that stood out most. *Grouchy*, another. Though maybe age had changed the man. Maybe guilt and regret had done it too.

"Are you from Remington?"

Mandy nodded, her smile bright and proud.

"Born and raised."

"The same with Ed?"

"No, he only moved here maybe fifteen years ago. Took a while for everyone to warm up to him, but they've come around."

"How'd he end up here? No offense, but there isn't much going on in Remington."

"Oh, don't I know it! It's a good town with friendly, hardworking people, and … I don't know, I guess Ed just saw something here that made him want to stay."

"Where's he from?" Nova asked and immediately wondered if he'd pushed things too far. He wanted the questions to be conversational, not edging toward interrogatory.

But he didn't sense anything in Mandy's eyes, no seed of doubt.

"To tell you the truth, I'm not sure. I know he's from out east. But Ed … he doesn't like to talk much about his life before coming to Remington. I used to try to push him but realized my time was better spent worrying about the future and not the past, you know?"

A brief silence, other than the quiet noise coming from the phone, and then Mandy asked, "So you're in town to fish, is that right?"

Nova tried remembering if he'd mentioned this already. He didn't think so, but Remington was a small town and word surely got around fast. Besides, why else would he come to town?

"That's right."

"How are you enjoying it so far?"

"So far, so good."

"Catch any big fish?"

This came from Alex, who'd paused his game. The question threw Nova. He was surprised the boy had said anything at all.

"Yeah, I got some big fish."

A grin grew on the boy's face.

"How big?"

Mandy, chuckling: "You're gonna have to excuse Alex. He loves fishing."

"Is that right?"

Alex nodded eagerly.

"Then again," Mandy said, "he's never actually been fishing. Ed has talked about taking him a few times—he'd even bought some fishing rods, which have been collecting dust in the garage—but Alex likes the fish he sees on YouTube. The ones out in the ocean. The *big* fish. Not the fish you find in the Yellowstone."

She regarded Nova again, a thoughtful look on her face.

"Have you always liked fishing?"

"Yes."

An easy lie.

"How did you get into it?"

"My father."

Another easy lie.

"That's sweet," Mandy said. She stared back down at the table, then grabbed the basket again. "Would you like more garlic bread?"

He hadn't even touched his second one.

"No, thank you."

"Alex, keep eating."

"I'm full."

"Have one more bite, at least."

Eyes back on the phone, Alex grabbed his fork and dug out another clump of lasagna. This one didn't reach his mouth, instead dripping onto his shirt.

"Alex!"

Mandy was on her feet in an instant, grabbing the fork and what little food remained and placing it back on the plate.

"Your new shirt!"

"I'm sorry, Mama."

Mandy sighed with irritation, a hand on her hip.

"Come on, let's get you upstairs and find you a new shirt."

Alex looked abashed as he rose to his feet. He started to take the phone with him.

"Leave it," Mandy said.

"But my game—"

"Your game will be fine."

Alex grumbled as he set the phone on the table and led his mother toward the stairs.

When they returned a few minutes later, Alex beelined straight for the phone. His face fell.

"Hey! The game restarted!"

"Maybe you should have thought about that before you got your new shirt dirty."

Mandy noted that Nova had already started clearing the table. He stood at the sink, rinsing the dishes.

"You don't have to do that."

"I don't mind."

"But you're our guest!"

He shut off the water and wandered over to the wall of pictures. He'd noticed them earlier but had only seen them from a distance. They were all family photos: Mandy and Alex and his father. Like the ones he'd seen on Facebook, his father looked happy.

Alex asked his mom, "Can I go play this in the living room?"

"Yes, fine, go ahead."

Alex bounded out of the room, leaving the two of them alone.

Nova watched Mandy Schaffer's faint reflection in one of the glass panes. She looked to be gathering herself.

"Mr. Bartkowski?"

He turned to face her.

"You can call me Nova."

"Nova, yes. Thank you again for coming tonight."

"Thank you for inviting me."

"It was kind of you to come. I know it's been awkward. But it's just ... I don't think Alex is taking it all too well. He was real close with his dad, and now ..."

She shook her head slowly, the ghost of tears in her eyes.

"He's always liked video games, but I worry he's become too obsessed with them. I'm not so sure it's healthy. And his father ... well, the fact is I lied to you earlier. I couldn't tell the truth in front of Alex."

She wiped at her eyes, lowered her voice to a whisper.

"Ed is still unconscious. The doctors aren't sure when he'll wake up, or *if* he'll wake up. They said it could be days, or weeks, or months, or …"

Mandy shook her head again, sucked in a deep breath.

"I feel like Alex needs a good distraction. Something to take his mind off everything that's going on. So that's why I was wondering …"

Nova said nothing, waiting for her to continue.

"Well," she said, now having trouble meeting his eyes, "you've been fishing down at the river and everything, and Alex, he really likes fish and all."

"Fish he sees on YouTube, you mean."

Another wistful smile.

"Yes, that's true. But still, I was wondering if you'd be willing to take him along. Take *us* along. Just for an hour or two. I hate to ask this after everything you've already done for our family, but I think it would be good for him to … you know, focus on something other than that darned game."

Her green eyes shifted all around the kitchen, as though not wanting to meet his own, until finally they did.

"What do you say, Nova? Is that something you can do? Please?"

TWENTY

The Thirsty Moose Tavern was a rundown place that had probably never seen better days, at least not in this century. But it was dark and loud and had cold beer, so that was where Nova found himself at nine o'clock that evening. Sitting at a booth in the rear corner, drinking a sweating bottle of Budweiser and thinking about his life choices.

At just after nine thirty, George Murphy entered the bar.

The scrawny mechanic paused in the doorway, squinting so that his eyes would adjust. He scanned the room, his face swiveling from one end to the other. He almost missed Nova in the shadows until he took a second look and craned his neck even more.

Nova watched the man grab a soda from the bar before threading his way through the tables to his booth.

"Mind if I sit?"

Nova didn't want to deal with people right now. He wanted to review the dinner he'd just had and the choice he'd made and what it all meant. But he recognized this man from his father's mechanic shop and figured he might have some information to give him, even if he didn't realize he was giving it.

"Sure."

George lowered himself down onto the booth across from Nova, suddenly looking nervous. He gazed around the bar as he sucked on a straw.

"Ginger ale," he said, indicating the drink as though Nova had asked. "Soda's all I drink these days. Well, except water. Haven't had a drop of alcohol in almost five years. If you knew me five years ago, you'd realize just what a big deal that is."

He offered up an awkward grin, maybe expecting Nova to say something to this, to congratulate him, but when Nova remained silent the grin faded.

"I'm George, by the way. George Murphy. You maybe remember me from yesterday at the shop."

Still Nova said nothing, waiting for the man to get to the point.

"I never got a chance to thank you for what you did. It was real kind of you. Real *brave*. I saw those guys coming, and I … I froze. Part of me always imagined how I'd react in a situation like that—whether I'd be brave—but it's different when something like that actually happens. There's no time to think. You just … well, I guess you react."

Silent, Nova took a slow sip of his beer.

George shifted uncomfortably, sipping again from his soda.

"Did Ed's wife track you down? She'd asked me about you. I saw her at the hospital. I went to visit Ed, but they wouldn't let me in. Said only family is allowed. It's funny, because I think of Ed as family, what with how long we've known each other, but of course I'm not blood or nothing like that."

Okay, so the guy was just going to keep rambling.

"What can I do for you, Mr. Murphy?"

"George. Please call me George."

"All right, George. What can I help you with?"

"Nothing. I don't mean to be any bother. Like I said, I

never got a chance to talk to you and, well, I wanted to talk to you."

"About what?"

"Well, about what happened. Maybe I'm not saying things right."

Nova remembered this man from yesterday. How he stood off to the side, frozen like a tree in winter, eyes wide and mouth hanging open to catch flies. Nova had seen it before, that shock at witnessing sudden violence, and he didn't fault the man. Either you were wired to step in when the shit got rough, or you weren't.

"It's okay, George. I saw somebody in trouble and wanted to help. That's all."

"Yeah, I know, and that's great. But the thing is … those guys could've killed Ed. I mean, they put him in the hospital! He's in a coma! For all we know, he might never wake up."

That wasn't something Nova wanted to contemplate. Because it made him wonder what would have happened had he acted quicker. He'd been watching the garage since he'd taken his seat in the far booth of the cafe. He'd seen the two men pull up, noticed the tightness in their shoulders as they stepped out of the truck. Knew exactly the men's intention before the first one even picked up the socket wrench.

George Murphy took another sip of his soda, glancing over his shoulder to make sure nobody was close enough to listen in despite the loud country music. He lowered his voice.

"Blake Hogan and his guys are a menace to this town."

Nova said, "You don't say."

"I've lived here about five years. Came here because … well, it don't matter why I came here, but I've lived here and have put up with the Hogans' bullshit for too long."

"What bullshit?"

"See, that's the thing. I don't know for sure. Nobody knows from what I can tell. But they run this town like they're mobsters. Everybody has to kiss the ring whenever the old man comes through. You ask me, Blake's jealous of him, wants to take over, but I don't think he has the balls."

"What beef do the Hogans have with your boss?"

"I don't think it is the Hogans, to be honest with you. I mean, I don't want to talk out of turn or anything, but one guy in particular—the one whose leg you broke—he used to go with Ed's wife. But then he went to prison for a couple years. Got out recently and started coming back and harassing Ed. Saying he's too old to satisfy a young woman like Mandy. Shit like that."

"How long ago did he go away?"

George gave Nova a knowing look.

"Long enough that the math works. Mandy practically threw herself at Ed right after he went away. I told him he should get a paternity test, just to be sure, but he kept waving me off. Got real angry about it too. Fact is, I sorta worried that I might piss him off so much he might let me go, so I stopped pushing and kept my mouth shut."

The door up front opened again. This time Veronica Chapman entered. Like George Murphy, she paused in the doorway to scan the bar but spotted Nova immediately.

Others in the bar noticed her too. A few threw her some nods while a few others purposely ignored her. She didn't seem to notice or care as she bypassed the bar and headed straight for where Nova was sitting.

George Murphy dug out a pen from his pocket and scribbled on a napkin and slid it across the table.

"If you're free to talk later, that's my number. I hate what happened to Ed and want to help any way I can to expose the Hogans for what they are."

Veronica Chapman was halfway to the table. Nova took his eyes off her long enough to look at the man sitting across from him. He frowned, not sure what to say because taking down the Hogans hadn't been on his mind, but George Murphy quickly slid out of the booth, taking his soda with him.

"Sheriff," he said as he stepped past Veronica Chapman, who halted by the table with a quizzical expression.

Nova said, "Howdy."

She slid into the booth across from him and gazed around the bar before leaning in like the mechanic had done a few minutes ago.

"Should I save myself the time and not bother asking what you're doing here?"

"I'm enjoying the cigarette smoke and loud music, obviously."

"I understand Tripp Hogan had your truck fixed."

"That he did."

"You think he'll fix your truck a second time?"

"Maybe if I ask nicely."

She stared at him for a beat, those beautiful brown eyes especially striking in the dark.

"I'm tired of trying to do you favors."

"Um ... thanks?"

"Will you do me a favor?"

"What's that?"

She reached under the table, and her long fingers touched his leg.

"Come home with me."

TWENTY-ONE

Veronica Chapman lived in a small two-story located near the edge of town.

The moon was large and bright and riding a sea of clouds as Nova followed her home in his truck. He parked behind her in the driveway and stepped out and gazed about the area, noting the handful of other houses along the road, orange light leaking around drawn curtains. He heard the steady crunch of Veronica Chapman's boots against the driveway and turned to find her approaching him, a seductive smile on her face.

She leaned in and kissed him hard, then broke the kiss and took his hand and pulled him along with her up the walkway to the front porch and inside. As soon as the door clicked shut Nova pulled her close to kiss her again, but she stepped back.

"Do you want a beer?"

"Sure."

She left him in the living room as she went into the kitchen. Nova took off his jacket as he heard the fridge open and close, and he looked around the living room to note that there wasn't much to it except the usual couch and recliner and TV sitting on a stand with a grandfather clock standing in the corner. Only one photo on the wall, Veronica with an older couple who he assumed were her parents.

Returning to the living room, Veronica handed him a Coors Light and clinked her bottle against his.

Nova took a long swallow. He set the bottle aside and leaned in to kiss her again when Veronica placed her hand against his chest.

"I need to be honest with you about something."

The tone of her voice caused whatever passion that had been sparked inside of him to flicker out.

"I have no intention of sleeping with you."

Nova said nothing.

"The truth is, I used you. As a prop, I guess you could say. You're a single, handsome guy visiting town, and I'm a single woman who hasn't been seen in public with another man in over a year."

Nova saw it now.

"I get it."

She tilted her head, staring at him with a thoughtful expression.

"Do you?"

"Yes."

"I do feel bad misleading you. But I also thought it was a good opportunity to get us alone so that we can talk."

She gestured for him to sit on the couch as she lowered herself onto the recliner. The thing looked about three decades old, its brown leather worn in places.

"This used to be my father's chair. He bought it a few years before he passed away. Said he needed a good chair to sit in after a long day at work. It's funny to think about, but he loved this chair. He'd sit in it with a beer and watch the TV to unwind. I always thought it was odd—not to mention cliché—until I became sheriff and began seeing the world through his eyes."

She took a sip of the beer, gestured with the bottle around the room.

"As you probably guessed, I grew up in this house. Had always told myself I would leave one day, but … I don't know. Most of us aren't destined to leave their hometowns, I guess. I never had any desire to work in law enforcement either. But, well, like father, like daughter."

Nova stared down at his beer, not sure what to say. Then he took another swallow and cleared his throat.

"Do you like it?"

"What, being sheriff? I don't *hate* it. I'm good at my job, and the public seems to like me overall. Though maybe that's because a lot of them still remember my father."

"Why did you kiss me outside?"

"There's an old lady who lives across the road. She's a night owl. As soon as she heard me pull into the driveway, I guarantee you she hobbled over to the window to peek outside."

"And you think that'll be enough."

Veronica grinned.

"Trust me, that woman leaks as easily as a sieve. I wouldn't be surprised if half the town knows by now that I've got a man over here. *An outsider*, no less."

Nova tipped an imaginary hat.

"I live to serve."

The grin faded, and she studied him carefully.

"You're not mad?"

"No."

"Are you sure?"

"Yes."

She was quiet for another moment, debating whether she should continue with whatever she wanted to tell him. In the corner, the grandfather clock quietly counted the seconds.

"I told you that story about Petra Kovačević last night. Do

you remember? That's when I knew. Even at such a young age —just a girl—I knew I wasn't right."

She snorted a laugh, shaking her head.

"*Wasn't right*. God, that's the kind of thing my mother would say. She was very religious, you know. Both her and my father. I had to hide it from them their whole lives. I dated boys because that's what a nice girl like me was supposed to do. I even got engaged, though I kept putting off the wedding until…well, until my father passed away. Then I broke things off. Told my fiancé I wasn't sure we should be together anymore. He understood, what with my father having passed, though part of me always wondered if he suspected."

"I'm sorry."

"For what?"

"For having to live like this. Pretending to be someone you're not."

"That's kind of you, but I've made my choices. There's a woman I chat with on one of the apps. She lives all the way out in Butte. I go out there every once in a while to see her. She's stuck in a relationship with a man. Wants to break things off but knows it'll hurt her career. She knows how important it is to keep quiet. As much as the people in this county might like me, it's still a very conservative county, and I guarantee you if word got out I'd lose the next election in a landslide."

She paused again, still with that thoughtful expression as she gazed off toward the sole picture on the wall, before blinking and focusing on Nova.

"I assume you left your piece in your truck."

Nova wasn't surprised that she spotted his pistol as they'd left the bar. He'd kept it snug in his rear waistband, but even with his jacket it wasn't like the thing was invisible. And Veronica Chapman had probably been taught at an early age how to spot someone concealing a weapon.

She said, "It's not a big deal that you're carrying a gun.

Especially around here. State law allows anyone to conceal carry a weapon without a concealed weapon permit, so long as they're eligible to possess a firearm under state or federal law. I'm just surprised someone who recently worked for the IRS feels the need to carry a weapon on him at all."

"Why are you surprised? It's my constitutional right."

She snorted a laugh.

Nova asked, "What's so funny?"

"Nothing. It's just you remind me of the stuff a lot of people around here say. Take some of our ranchers and farmers, for instance. Walking around with a nine-millimeter doesn't appease them. They want to carry ARs wherever they go. Stockpile them like they're preparing for the zombie apocalypse."

"You don't think the Founding Fathers intended us to have automatic weapons that fire thirty rounds in five seconds?"

She stared at him for another moment and then chuckled when she noted his grin. Then soon the laugh faded, and she studied him closely again.

"You served, didn't you?"

"Yes."

"I thought so." A beat of silence. "What about your parents?"

"What about them?"

"Are they still alive?"

"No."

"And they actually named you Casanova."

"Apparently."

"Did they ever say why?"

"Nope."

"Didn't you ask?"

"Of course. Neither of my parents ever wanted to talk about it, my dad especially. I was told that what happened had happened and there was no changing it."

This wasn't necessarily the truth, but Nova didn't want to

get into it with her. He didn't want to tell her that as soon as he'd turned eighteen—two years after his father had walked out on them—he'd legally changed his last name to his mother's maiden name. He'd considered changing his first name too—Christ, who named their kid Casanova?—but decided to keep it because it was what his mom had named him.

The story he'd been told was that his mom was loopy on pain medication after giving birth and his dad had stepped out for a while, to get a smoke or drink or who the fuck knew, and his mom, for some reason thinking of the name, had put it down on the birth certificate.

Why, Mom? he'd asked her once while she was on her deathbed, after yet another long day of taking care of her, just the two of them in the house and nobody else in the world. *Why that name?*

And she'd smiled at him with her thin lips, her eyes unsteady, and said, *Because it's perfect, just like you.*

In the corner, the grandfather clock continued to count the seconds. On the recliner, Veronica Chapman shifted as she stared down at her beer.

"I really do think you should leave town."

Nova made no reply as he took another swallow of his beer.

"Blake Hogan isn't the type of guy you want to mess with."

Nova considered what to tell her. Whether to tell her about the two tracking devices he'd found on his truck or the stranger he'd met on the Hogans' property or his dinner tonight with Mandy Schaffer and her son who may or may not be Nova's half-brother.

"How long have you known him?"

"Blake? I've known him my entire life. Even dated him briefly in high school. Mostly because our fathers were so close."

"Did your father serve too?"

"He did. Vietnam, just like Tripp. Though"—and here she grinned—"he didn't return a quote-unquote *war hero*."

"How so?"

She held his gaze, debating whether to tell him. A sly smile played on her lips, and maybe it was the beer or maybe it was the fact she felt bad bringing him home under false pretenses, but she sucked in a heavy breath.

"You said you met him, right? Tripp, I mean."

Nova nodded.

"He tell you how he ended up in the wheelchair?"

"He said it happened during the war."

"That's true, it did. But it didn't happen during a firefight or anything."

"What do you mean?"

"He fell out of a helicopter. They weren't even going into combat. It was like his second week there. That's what paralyzed him from the waist down."

"He said he was awarded the Medal of Honor."

Veronica burst out laughing, then held up her hand to hide her laugh as if she was embarrassed.

"It's true, he was, but that was some bullshit, the way my father told it to me. Tripp comes from money, as I'm sure you realize. Generational wealth. His father knew someone in the military who was able to pull the right strings, and then, voilà, suddenly Tripp Hogan is a war hero."

"Did that come out during his Senate campaign?"

"No, but that was also a long time ago, and politics wasn't as dirty as it is now. I mean, politics has always been dirty, but it's more of a blood sport these days. My guess is if he'd become the nominee, his opponent would have dug around and found out what happened. My father even told me Tripp still has nightmares about it. But that was a long time ago, so maybe he's gotten over it."

"What about Blake?"

"What about him?"

"You said you dated. That you've known him your entire life. What's his deal?"

She took a long swallow of her beer, thinking about it. Finally shrugged.

"I don't know. Blake's just Blake. He's always lived in his father's shadow, and he hates it. Back in high school he once told me he'd rather get shot in the head than not being able to use his legs like his father. Living the rest of his life in a wheelchair is what scared him most, he said. Lovely, huh?"

He smiled at her sardonic tone and decided to keep pushing.

"And what does Blake do?"

"What do you mean? He runs Hogan Auto Group."

Nova waited, expecting her to say more, but she finished her beer and asked him if he wanted another. He nodded, and she went back into the kitchen and returned with two fresh bottles.

He said, "So that's all he does, just oversees the car dealerships?"

"Yeah. Why do you ask?"

Nova shrugged, taking another sip of his beer. He knew now he couldn't tell Veronica any of his suspicions. Because the truth was, he still didn't know anything for sure. Other than what George Murphy had told him, and he wasn't about to share that.

Veronica said, "You're welcome to stay as long as you'd like. In fact, if you want to stay the night, I can bring down some blankets and pillows for the couch."

"I appreciate it, but I think I'll head out soon. Or, well, maybe give it another hour or so to make sure it looks good for the old lady across the road."

Veronica Chapman smiled, leaning forward to gently tap her bottle against his.

"Cheers."

Two hours later, with the clock almost ready to hit midnight, Nova headed back to the Millport Motel. Steering with his knee, he glanced at the folded-up napkin by the dashboard light as he dialed the number.

George Murphy answered after three rings, his voice hesitant and sleepy.

"Hello?"

"It's Nova Bartkowski, George. I think I could use your help after all."

TWENTY-TWO

Weasel-faced Wayne was working late again.

Nova waited until ten minutes after one o'clock before calling the motel. He muted his phone and held it to his ear as he opened his door and peeked outside. The gravel parking lot was empty except for the few vehicles that had been there when he returned from Veronica Chapman's house. He leaned out to watch Wayne standing up from the chair behind the counter to answer the phone, placing his back to the parking lot.

"Millport Motel."

Wayne's nasal voice came through the phone's earpiece as Nova locked the door and hurried down the walkway to the other end of the motel, keeping an eye on the office.

"Hello?"

The tone now irritated. Any second Wayne would disconnect by probably slamming the phone in exasperation.

Nova ducked around the corner, out of sight, and severed the connection before Wayne had the chance.

Like last night, he skirted the back of the motel and disappeared into the trees. He tracked his progress using his phone's

GPS and broke through the tree line twenty seconds before a pair of distant headlights appeared.

Nova waited in the trees until the pickup slowed and halted. The headlights winked out, but the engine kept running. For a truck that looked to be fifteen years old, the engine sounded healthy. Nova wouldn't expect anything less from a mechanic.

Hurrying out from the tree cover, he circled the truck and slipped into the passenger seat.

George Murphy gazed at him cautiously, his Adam's apple bobbing as he swallowed.

"We really gonna do this?"

"Not if you don't feel comfortable about it."

"No, I ... I feel comfortable. I mean, not *comfortable*, but I think I'm good. I *know* I'm good. Just ... anxious."

Nova studied the man's face in the dark cabin, wondering if he'd made a mistake by calling him. But the truth was he had no other options. Not with a tracking device on his truck and a weasel-faced clerk keeping an eye out for him.

"George?"

"Yeah?"

"Let's go."

They drove in silence, the pickup's high beams spotlighting the blacktop.

Nova tracked their location on his phone. When they were a mile away, he tilted the screen toward George so he could see where Nova wanted to go. George stared a beat too long and shrugged.

"I think that might work."

"You think? George, you've lived here for years. Don't you know the area?"

"I live here, yeah, but I don't know this town that well. I mostly stay to myself. I don't go joyriding on backroads."

George took the turn and soon they were on a long stretch of road that looked like any other. Nova watched the blue dot on his phone moving steadily and then pointed toward a line of ponderosa pines standing in a field.

"How about there?"

George twisted the wheel. The bright moon swept a silver glow over the open field. George killed the headlights and drove slowly over the uneven terrain, not wanting to use the brakes. The last thing they needed was for someone to spot tail-lights flaring up in the middle of nowhere. George eased the truck between two trees so that they wouldn't be easily seen from the road.

Nova pulled the sound suppressor from his jacket pocket and started screwing it onto the threaded barrel of his pistol.

George's eyes grew wide.

"You're not gonna kill anybody, are you?"

"Not planning on it."

"Then why the gun? Why the silencer?"

"I told you—the only way this is going to work is if we kill the power. We won't have much time. We need to be in and out. Normally I'd say five minutes, but seeing as we're in the middle of nowhere, I don't want to be in there for more than ten."

"I'm still not sure what you expect to find."

"I don't either. That's why we're looking. You sure you're still up for this?"

George's Adam's apple bobbed again as he swallowed. His voice, a nervous whisper.

"Yes."

They approached Hogan Auto from the rear. Nova had noted the security cameras when he stopped by earlier in the day. Those had made sense, what with them being out front and overlooking the inventory, though he assumed the back would have security cameras too. But it was doubtful those cameras were aimed at the field.

Once they drew close enough—staying low to the ground in an awkward crouch—Nova spotted the cameras. Two of them, positioned on each corner of the building. Aimed at the back lot and not the field.

The other thing Nova had noted on his visit earlier was the power setup. The electrical wires had come through from the highway, which was to be expected. Those wires met up with a transformer box. Nova hadn't spied the box but figured it would either be on the back of the building or on the side.

The box was on the left side.

Nova motioned for George to stay back before he advanced farther, the FNX-45 at his side. The night was silent except for the insects and the distant rumble of big rigs on the interstate. He was conscious of his heart beating in his ears, of his steady breathing. Slow in, slow out. Slow in, slow out.

Bright lights illuminated the inventory. He noted a few of the new vehicles dropped off by the car-hauler earlier in the day.

Nova wished he had a rifle for this next part. The closer the distance between the muzzle and backend, the less accurate a shot. That's why snipers didn't use pistols.

He noted the position of the security cameras and made sure to stay far enough out of view before crouching to one knee. Using his other knee to balance his elbow, he aimed with the pistol at the transformer box. Tilted his head down just a bit to aim.

Slow breath in, slow breath out.

Three squeezes of the trigger, three kicks from the pistol as each .45 ACP round fired a 230-grain bullet that traveled at just over eight hundred feet per second. All three bullets met their mark, tearing into the transformer box and creating a spray of sparks.

At least one of the rounds did the trick. The bright lights overlooking the inventory flickered and then went out. The whole area was enveloped in darkness.

Nova rose to his feet, turned back to George.

"Remember—ten minutes, in and out."

It took a minute for him to pick the lock on the back door. Then they were in, both of them wearing latex gloves, both with flashlights, the beams crisscrossing through the dark.

The place smelled like a garage. It was probably second nature to George but it made Nova sick, reminding him of the days he'd been in his father's garage as a boy. His father with his greasy hands showing him the ins and outs of cars because he would be damned if his son would grow up to become a waste of space like so many other people in the world. The whir of a pneumatic wrench as someone tightened the lug nuts on a tire. The groan of a hydraulic lift as it raised a car into the air. The melodic crash of a wrench as it fell into a service pit.

The garage housed only two cars, along with a large box truck. For whatever reason, the box truck looked out of place. It was parked off to the side, as if it was being held for some reason and not to be worked on. Nova found himself gravitating toward it when he realized George was standing in the middle of the garage, motionless.

"What are you doing?"

"I ... I'm not sure. What do you want me to do?"

"Check those cars."

"And ... and what am I looking for again?"

"You're a mechanic, George. You work on vehicles every day. Look for something that's out of place."

George nodded and started toward one of the cars. An older Chrysler with faded paint. As he did, Nova turned back to the box truck.

Again, he wasn't sure why he was drawn to it, but he unlatched the roll-top door and pushed it up just enough to shine his flashlight inside.

A car was squeezed in there. A decade-old Honda Accord. Its silver paint faded. It had been backed in so that its front faced out, no license plate on the front bumper.

Why was the car in this box truck and not out like the others?

George's voice cut through the oil-soaked dark.

"Holy shit."

Nova turned away from the truck. His flashlight beam found George standing by the Chrysler. He'd popped the hood and now stepped back, slowly shaking his head. In the bright light of his own flashlight, Nova noted that the man's face had become ashen.

"You're never gonna believe what's in here."

TWENTY-THREE

Blake Hogan was spent.

That's what usually happened when you went a half-dozen rounds with a girl who was just one week over eighteen.

It also didn't hurt that he'd popped a Viagra a few hours earlier. Not that he ever had any trouble getting it up, but tonight he especially didn't want the good times to end prematurely.

Four girls had been brought in, each a smidge above eighteen. That had been important to Darrell, and Blake respected the man for it. A while back, they'd hosted another guest who had a penchant for young girls. Like, *very* young. It had twisted Blake's stomach to coordinate that, especially knowing what would happen after the girls' night spent with the guy. But the guy was invaluable to the cause, just like Darrell, so Blake had gritted his teeth and made it happen.

He didn't know the name of tonight's girl. He didn't care. She'd come in with the three because Darrell had asked for three, but Blake had ordered four. And as soon as they'd arrived he'd appraised them and picked the one he liked the most. Petite and blonde with a crooked smile. She seemed confused at first and a bit worried, what with the others going in another direction, but once she realized they were headed into the big house a spark of delight entered her voided eyes.

He'd offered a variety of drugs, and in the end she'd gone with the coke. Based on Blake's experience, that was typically the preferred party favor. She'd snorted it like a pro, just as Blake snorted his Adderall. He'd tried different drugs in the past and found that he much preferred Adderall to the rest. Plus in some ways it was a big fuck you to his old man.

Growing up, Blake had always had trouble focusing, especially in school. His teachers suspected attention deficit hyperactivity disorder and recommended his father take him to a psychiatrist. But his father was old school—he didn't buy into the notion of mental health. If you were struggling with something, like your emotions or just plain focusing, then clearly that meant there was something wrong with you that only hard work could change.

It wasn't until Blake was twenty years old that he'd gone to see a psychiatrist on his own. He'd done it secretly, knowing what kind of shit his father would give him if he ever found out. The psychiatrist confirmed what the teachers had suspected—he had ADHD. Untreated for most of his life at that point. The doctor had prescribed Adderall, which he'd started taking that day, and immediately felt the benefits, the blurry corners of the world finally coming into focus.

His bedroom was on the second floor, what had once been his parents' room and his grandparents' room before them. That part he often forced himself to forget. The quickest way of losing his mojo was to be reminded that he was fucking a girl in the same place his old man had fucked his mother and his grandfather had fucked his grandmother.

Nowadays his father slept on the first floor, as did Carson. Blake had the second floor to himself. Most of the rooms were empty and he sometimes wondered what the house would feel like once his father was dead and buried. When Blake wouldn't be nervous to bring a girl home for fear of how his father would demean him in front of her and make him look like less of a man.

That's why he only saw women in the city, often from the apps, though nothing ever got past the physical. But Blake did want to start a family someday. He wanted a kid or two who he'd treat like they were supposed to be treated and not the way his bastard father treated him—cold and distant and ashamed.

A quiet buzzing interrupted his thoughts.

Blake blinked, realizing where he was and who he was with. Lying naked in his massive bed, the girl lying beside him on her belly, drugstore-blonde hair and perky breasts and tight in all the right places.

She was asleep or acting like she was asleep, maybe hoping that they wouldn't go another round, what with the fact the Viagra gave Blake the stamina to keep powering away like a jackhammer. The girl was sore, no doubt about it—that much was evident by the spots of blood already soaking the sheets—though that wouldn't matter to her by tomorrow.

Pushing himself up onto an elbow, Blake stared at his phone on the bedside table. It lay screen down as it buzzed so he couldn't see who was calling, but he knew that whatever this call was it wasn't good. Because his men knew about the girls coming in tonight—they knew about how he'd likely take one of them for his own. On nights like these, Blake wasn't to be interrupted for any reason.

Unless it was an absolute emergency.

He picked the phone up and saw it was Marc Palmer calling. Marc whose voice was hesitant and quiet and full of concern.

"Umm, boss? I just got notified that the dealership's lost all power."

TWENTY-FOUR

Nova stared under the hood of the Chrysler, his body entirely still.

An engine block was what you'd expect to see 99.9% of the time once you popped the hood of a car.

Not a cluster of military-grade automatic weapons.

They were lined up orderly, every other carbine going barrel to stalk. There looked to be at least twenty rifles in total.

George Murphy's hushed voice cut through the dark.

"Same with this one too."

Nova tore his gaze away from the rifles to swing his flashlight over at George, who stood by the other car with its hood up.

"Check the rest of the car."

"Like the trunk?"

"It's doubtful they'd stock the trunk too. Too much chance of having it inspected during transport."

Nova pulled out his phone and snapped photos of the guns, then stepped over to the other car and took pictures of those guns too. Like the Chrysler, the engine block and other parts had been torn out to make room to fit the assault rifles.

George said, "I think I found something here."

He was standing by the driver's side, the door open, the dome light on. He waited until Nova had joined him before shining his flashlight beam on the edge of the door.

"See this gap here? That's not normal. And then—"

He ducked down and pointed. Nova lowered himself too. The two combined flashlight beams were more than enough to show that weapons had been fitted into the paneling as well.

"These don't look the same as the others," George said.

Nova shook his head.

"That's because they're not."

"What are they?"

"Uzis."

George looked at him cautiously.

"What the hell is going on here?"

Nova didn't answer. He took a few more photos of the weapons in the paneling before standing back up. He checked his watch and the time he'd set. They'd already been in the garage for just over eight minutes.

"We should get going."

"But shouldn't we, I don't know, call the police?"

Nova shook his head again, staring at the rifles stacked in the front of the car.

"There's someone I know to call. But we should leave now. Put everything back the way it was."

As George closed the hoods to both cars, Nova circled each car and took photos of the license plates. Then he started for the door they'd entered before beelining for the box truck.

He took a photo of the truck's plate, then pushed open the roll-top door again and snapped a photo of the Honda.

Nova stuffed the phone into his pocket, turned to George standing by the door.

"Let's move."

They made it back to the pickup without trouble, moving swiftly through the field and the trees. The moon was still bright enough that they didn't need their flashlights. George had already disabled the interior lights so the overhead dome light didn't blink on when they slipped inside.

George went to jam the key in the ignition to get them the hell out of there.

Nova stayed the mechanic's arm with his hand.

"Don't."

George's eyes were as wide as teacup saucers.

"Are you nuts? We need to *leave*."

Nova placed a finger to his lips, slowly shook his head.

"Not yet."

"But what are we waiting on?"

That's when George seemed to remember the backroad ahead of them also led to the Hogans' place.

"Okay, I see."

They sat in silence for several minutes, watching the dark back road. The dewed field shimmered in the moonlight. Finally George broke the silence, his voice a whisper.

"What were those rifles?"

"M4A1s."

"They use those in the military, right?"

"Special Forces. They're not supposed to be available to the general public."

"Jesus Christ. I *knew* Blake Hogan and his guys were up to no good. I knew it!"

Nova said nothing. He was thinking about the photos he'd taken. He wanted to get back to his room so he could review them more closely.

Blake Hogan and his people were trafficking automatic rifles, most likely all over the country. That was obvious. But why? People could easily purchase semiautomatic rifles online or at gun shops or even at gun shows. Those hosted more than enough gunfire for the regular Joe Schmo.

Unless …

No, he wasn't sure he wanted to jump to that conclusion. Not yet. Even with the evidence he already had. He could email Atticus Caine these photos and explain where he'd found them, but it wasn't clear yet what Atticus could do with that information other than contacting somebody at the ATF or even the FBI. Nova needed to determine what Blake Hogan was up to first.

"Overflow," Nova murmured.

George said, "Huh?"

"That's what one of Blake's guys told me when I was at the dealership earlier today. That the vehicles there are their overflow from the other dealerships. I looked one of them up on the website, but it wasn't listed. Maybe a fluke, but my guess is none of them are listed anywhere."

"Why's that?"

"Because none of those vehicles are meant to be sold as actual vehicles."

"So they're, what, smuggling weapons?"

"That's my guess. You see those trailers with the half-dozen or so vehicles on the highway every day, headed to what you figure is another dealership or car show. They can transport these hollowed-out vehicles all across the country without anyone knowing."

"But … why?"

The million-dollar question.

After another beat of silence, George said, "Once Blake and his boys learn about the transformer and realize somebody shot at it, they're gonna suspect you, won't they?"

"Seems most likely."

"Aren't you afraid?"

Nova kept his gaze steady on the empty back road.

"I'm never afraid."

George Murphy snorted.

"Man, you're nuts. I'm terrified. Now more than ever I could use a drink, but ..."

His voice faltered, and he shook his head, issued a heavy sigh.

"I'm an alcoholic. Just like my old man, and my old man before him. Runs in the family, I guess. Usually I drank until I blacked out. And when I was out, I ... did stuff I'm not so proud of. That's how I lost custody of my daughter. I never hurt her or nothing, but one time I did beat the shit out of her mother, and for what? No reason at all. Not that you ever have a reason to hit a woman, I know, but ..."

His voice trailed off. He stared out the windshield, and in the faint moonlight Nova could see tears in the man's eyes.

"That's why I left the state. Didn't want to be anywhere near them. Not that I don't miss my daughter like crazy. But knowing that I'll never have contact with her ever again? I know it's probably for the best, and I haven't had a drop of alcohol since. I've thought about calling up my ex and explaining how I've changed, but I don't think it'll matter. She'll never let me see my daughter again, and I couldn't deal with it anymore, so I left. Kept moving about until I came to this town and met Ed and he gave me a job. Ed never asked me about my past, but I think he might suspect. He's been a good boss. Real supportive."

Nova didn't say anything. He wanted to make sure his focus was on the automatic rifles being trafficked across the country rather than be reminded the whole reason he'd come to this town in the first place was to confront the man who had walked out on him and his dying mother.

George's tone spiked with anticipation.

"You think this is them?"

Headlights appeared from the north. Seconds later the Defender zoomed past, a silver streak in the moonlight.

As soon as it was gone, Nova said, "Wait another minute."

The minute seemed to last forever, but no additional vehicles came through, and then George turned the key in the ignition and with the headlights off crawled the truck back to the road.

———

They passed the Millport and the motel looked just like it had when Nova had left two hours ago, the parking lot semi-deserted and the light on in the manager's office with Wayne sitting behind the counter.

George muttered, "That's weird. That place is typically never open later than eight o'clock."

Of course it wasn't. More than likely Blake Hogan had paid the clerk to stay late to keep an eye on Nova.

As George halted the truck along the side of the road, Nova said, "Do me a favor, George."

"What's that?"

"Go back to your apartment, pack your things, and get the hell out of this town."

George seemed to think about this a second too long, biting his lower lip.

"It's not safe to be here no more, is it?"

"No, it's not. I appreciate your help tonight, but I don't want anyone else getting hurt. Got it?"

Still biting his lip, George nodded solemnly.

"Got it."

TWENTY-FIVE

Blake Hogan stared down at his phone, at the dot on the screen indicating the location of the outsider's truck. He'd checked it right before leaving the house after he'd gotten the call, and he'd checked it again fifteen minutes later when he arrived at the dealership, and now he checked it a third time.

That damned dot hadn't moved one bit.

Marc said, "I won't know until the power's back on and I can do a more thorough search, but there doesn't appear to be anything missing."

They were standing in the garage, both gripping flashlights. Blake had gotten distracted from his portion of the search because he wanted to check on the outsider again.

Keith filled the doorway up front, flashlight in hand.

"Boss, the police are here."

Blake pocketed the phone and headed out to the front. He unlocked the glass doors and stepped into the cool night air to meet Jamie Bennett and another deputy.

Jamie asked, "Anything stolen?"

"Doesn't appear to be."

"Any idea what caused the power to go out?"

Blake gestured for the two deputies to follow him. He led them around the side of the building to the transformer box. Or what was left of it.

The other deputy said, "Ouch."

Jamie Bennett shined his flashlight at the ravaged box.

"Any chance it somehow blew on its own?"

Blake shook his head.

"If you look there, on what's left of the door?"

He waited for Jamie Bennett to comply, then waited another moment for the man to glance back at him, a frown on his face.

"Is that a bullet hole?"

Blake said, "Looks like one, doesn't it?"

The deputy turned back to the transformer box to take a closer look. Then he stepped away, shaking his head, his flashlight beam dipping low and illuminating the ground at their feet.

"Who do you think would do something like that?"

Blake somehow managed to keep his emotions in check as he answered.

"I've got one suspect in mind."

Wayne had had three cups of coffee and was working on his fourth when Blake Hogan's Defender and a deputy's SUV pulled into the parking lot.

Truth be told, Wayne's eyelids had been growing heavy despite all the caffeine in his system, and for a minute or two he started to feel like he might drift off, but thank the good Lord in heaven he managed to stay awake. He couldn't even imagine the wrath that would fall on his head if Blake Hogan found him dozing off when he'd been instructed to stay awake all night to keep an eye on the outsider.

Wayne hurried out from behind the counter and met Blake Hogan and Deputy Bennett in the parking lot.

"Evening, Mr. Hogan. I didn't expect to see you here tonight."

Blake's jaw was tense as he poked a finger at the row of motel rooms.

"Has he left his room?"

Wayne knew exactly who Blake meant but still felt strange talking about it in front of the deputy. To give himself time he cleared his throat, frowned, seemed to think about it for a moment.

"Sir?"

Blake Hogan noted the clerk's worried expression and said, "Don't worry about Deputy Bennett. Just answer the question. Has the outsider left his room?"

"Well, sir, his truck's been here all night—"

"I *know* his truck's been here all night. But has *he*?"

Wayne wasn't sure what to say. The confidence in the man's tone at knowing the outsider's truck was here all night had thrown him for a loop.

"Of course, sir. He hasn't left his room at all."

But as soon as the words tumbled out of his mouth like Jack and Jill going down the hill, Wayne felt every muscle in his back tighten. Because suddenly he thought about the phone calls. Two phone calls to be exact. One earlier in the night and then another maybe a half hour ago. Both times nobody had been on the other end ... or, well, if somebody had been there, they hadn't said a word.

Wayne suddenly had the terrible notion the outsider had called the motel both times. That he'd used the calls to distract Wayne so he could slip out and then slip back into his room.

The night all at once felt suffocating, the infinite darkness from the star-studded sky pushing down on him. The quiet buzz from the neon sign above them sounded like a swarm of bees in his head.

"Wayne."

Blake Hogan's stern, commanding voice fought past the buzzing swarm.

He blinked. Focused on the two men standing in front of him.

"Yes?"

Blake gestured at the room again.

"Go on."

"Sir?"

"Check on your guest."

Wayne glanced nervously toward the deputy again.

"Are you sure—"

"Goddamn it, Wayne, don't make me tell you again. Check on your guest *now*."

Nova heard them out there in the parking lot. At least three people, including the clerk.

He lay on the top of the bed. His boots and shirt off. He still wore his socks and jeans and undershirt. With his hand under the pillow, gripping his FNX-45.

Nova listened to two distinct pairs of footsteps approach the room, then a soft tap at the door.

A beat of silence, then a stronger tap.

"Mr. Bartknowsee?"

Wayne's voice, sounding hesitant. Totally butchering his last name.

Nova waited ten seconds—what he figured would be enough time to rouse himself from sleep—before standing up from the bed. He went to the door in a groggy manner, forcing himself to yawn as he slipped the pistol into the back waistband of his jeans. He forced another yawn so that he was mid-yawn when he opened the door.

"Yes?"

The deputy from the other day stood on the walkway with Wayne, Blake Hogan lingering behind them in the parking lot with his arms crossed.

Wayne looked nervous.

The deputy looked somewhat inconvenienced.

"Sorry to bother you, sir, but I was hoping you could tell me where you were earlier tonight."

Another yawn, this one genuine.

"What's this about?"

"Please answer the question, sir."

"Well, I guess it depends on what time. I've been in my room since I got back here after midnight."

"And where were you before that, sir?"

"That's … a private matter."

This answer didn't seem to sit well with the deputy. His shoulders went back slightly as he hitched his belt and cleared his throat.

"I need to know where you were, sir."

Nova frowned at the two men on the walkway, then out at Blake Hogan.

"Is there some kind of problem?"

"Where were you earlier tonight?"

Nova gave it a moment, as if considering. He didn't want to draw Veronica Chapman into this, but she did say she needed the cover.

"If you must know, I spent some time over at your boss's place before coming back here."

Clearly the young deputy hadn't been expecting this answer. His mouth started to open but it was obvious he wasn't sure how to respond.

Nova said, "If you don't believe me, call her. I'm sure she'd love to be awakened in the middle of the night for whatever the hell this is."

The deputy shook his head.

"That's all right, sir. Thank you for your time. Sorry to wake you."

Nova made sure to not even glance at Blake Hogan as he shut the door and latched it. His hand went to the pistol in his waistband, squeezing the grip as he listened to the hushed voices outside. Blake Hogan saying that Nova was lying and the deputy saying there was nothing they could do about it and Wayne assuring Blake Hogan that Nova hadn't left his room all night.

Eventually, the men dispersed. He heard two sets of engines start up and then the sound of tires aggressively spinning out of the parking lot onto the road. Wayne's footsteps on the gravel growing fainter as he returned to the office.

He waited another minute, listening to the silence, before returning to bed.

Slipping the FNX-45 under his pillow again, Nova lay down and stared up at the dark ceiling.

He thought about automatic weapons hidden in cars and the stranger in the cabin on the Hogans' property. He thought about Mandy Schaffer and her son who may or may not be his half-brother. He thought about Veronica Chapman and the tightrope she saw herself walking every day.

Part of him was exhausted. Another part, wired. But he knew he needed to rest.

Tomorrow was going to be a busy day.

TWENTY-SIX

The sky was cloudless and bright, the temperature edging just over seventy degrees, when Nova pulled into the driveway at nine o'clock that Thursday morning.

Mandy Schaffer must have been watching for him. Before he could even put his truck in park, the front door opened and she hurried down the steps, her dark blonde hair bouncing in the breeze.

He met her on the walkway and asked if something had happened to her husband.

"No changes," she said. "I spoke to one of Ed's doctors this morning. They said he's still unresponsive. But my work— they just told me I have to come in. Only for an hour or two, but still. I didn't have your number; otherwise, I would have called."

She glanced over her shoulder at Alex standing behind the storm door, peering out. She sucked in a breath and spoke in a quiet tone.

"He was really looking forward to it too. So was I. He needs a good distraction that isn't on a screen."

Something changed in her face as she paused, staring up at him.

"You … you wouldn't be open to taking him anyway, would you?"

Nova started to open his mouth, but she kept going, cutting him off.

"I know, I know. A crazy question. It's just … I heard him crying in his room last night. He really misses his dad. And I hate that he can't go fishing because of my stupid job."

Nova wasn't sure Mandy had ever told him what it was she did for work. Last night when he'd asked all she said was that she was a mother and a wife.

He said, "I don't feel comfortable taking him, just the two of us."

Mandy's face dipped as she sniffed back what were presumably tears.

"I get it. I do. But, I mean, it wouldn't be for the entire time. Like I said, I only have to go into work for an hour or two. I could meet you there!"

Her tone had ticked up with hope, her green eyes now searching his for any slight trace of compassion.

He let the silence stretch for a moment before he said, "Only an hour or two."

Nodding her head adamantly, her eyes bright: "Yes, absolutely, only an hour or two. I'll meet you there and take him home when you're done."

Nova glanced back up at the boy standing behind the storm door.

"Okay."

A small gasp escaped Mandy's throat.

"Really? Are you serious?"

"An hour or two. No more than that."

"Yes, of course. I promise. Do you know where you'll be?"

"We'll park down at the end of Patterson Road."

"Great! I'll go get his fishing rod from the garage. Oh, and can you call my phone? That way I'll have your number."

She'd given him her number at the diner yesterday and she read off the number again, and Nova dialed it so it went through.

Beaming, Mandy turned and motioned for Alex to come outside.

"Baby, I have great news! You're going fishing!"

Patterson Road was twenty minutes from the house. For the first ten minutes or so, they drove in silence. The wind streaming in from the open windows. The bright sun gleaming off the truck's hood. Because of his age, Alex sat in the back. His seat belt snug, his head tilted back as he stared out at the passing scenery.

Nova kept checking on him in the rearview mirror. Wanting to say something. Not sure what to say. Until, after another minute or so, something finally came to him.

"What's your favorite fish?"

Alex tilted his face to look back at Nova watching him. He seemed to have to think about the question for a long time before a grin spread across his face.

"Shark."

"What kind of shark?"

"Hammerhead shark."

"Why the hammerhead shark?"

"Haven't you ever seen one? They're so cool looking!"

The boy's face now animated with excitement. He obviously had a passion for fish—or at least this one fish.

Then the smile faded, and the boy looked sad.

"But they're gonna become extinct."

"Really?"

A somber nod.

"I saw it on YouTube. There are only like two hundred still alive in the entire ocean. It will probably be too late by the time I get old enough to swim with them."

Great, Nova thought. His job was to lift the kid's spirits and already the kid was depressed.

Not sure why, he asked, "Does your dad like hammerhead sharks?"

A small grin.

"He says they look cool. But his favorite is the great white. He told me about that one movie, the one about the shark, but he won't let me watch it until I'm older. But I watched some scenes on YouTube. *Everything's* on YouTube."

Nova tried remembering if his father had ever mentioned *Jaws* to him when he was a kid. Or any movie, for that matter. It was a rare treat when the family went to the movie theater, but it had usually been his mom who planned those trips with his father complaining most of the time about the cost.

Patterson Road was coming up in the next mile. Nova kept an eye out, his finger unconsciously ready to hit the turn signal. But as soon as he spotted the road, he kept his foot on the gas pedal, and the road sign zipped past them.

He drove for another five miles and then turned off onto Herron Road. It was deserted here, trees stretching everywhere except ahead. An opening soon appeared and the river was right in front of them, its swiftly moving current sparkling in the morning sunlight.

No other vehicles present.

Nova parked the truck, shut off the engine, glanced back at the boy.

"We're here."

"Mister, what time is it?"

Checking his watch, Nova twisted his arm around so the boy could see the time.

Ten fourteen a.m.

It was the third time the boy had asked the time since they'd set up along the riverbank, casting their lines into the water.

"Getting anxious for your mom to show up?"

The boy only nodded, staring at the red-and-white bobber floating on the water's surface.

Part of Nova wished the boy wasn't here. That he could put on his bootfoot waders like yesterday and continue working on his casting techniques. Just him and the fish and nobody else.

Because the truth was he enjoyed himself out here. The silence was part of it, yes, but also the clear blue of the sky and the cool breeze rustling the tops of the trees and the birdsong echoing all around him.

He'd never been one to want to commune with nature, but this was a start.

There was so much he wanted to ask the boy. Not just about his father, either, but what it was like growing up in the middle of nowhere. Did he have any friends? What types of things did he do for fun besides playing games on his mom's phone and watching YouTube videos?

Of course, he wanted to ask about his father too. About what he was like when he was home with the boy and the boy's mother. Whether he told any jokes or stories. Whether he made them laugh. Or whether he spent all his time in front of the TV drinking beer after beer, crumbling up one can of PBR after another, refusing to make eye contact.

They'd been here now for just over an hour and hadn't caught one fish. Though the boy had gotten a nibble, the end of his rod dipping low. The same bright smile that had appeared on his face when he talked about hammerhead sharks had shone again, but disappeared as soon as it became clear the fish had managed to get away.

Nova had told him not to get upset, that it was all about patience, and coached him to throw out his line again.

After another ten minutes, the boy asked again what time it was and Nova showed him his watch.

The boy said, "I have to use the bathroom."

"One or two?"

The boy thought about it for a moment.

"One."

Nova gestured back at the trees behind them.

"Will you be okay on your own?"

The boy nodded, his face set as he reeled in his line and set his rod down beside the tackle box between them and started off into the trees.

Nova watched him go, then turned his attention back to the river. The sun was still bright, sequinning the water. He closed his eyes and listened to the boy's fading footsteps. To the wind in the trees. To the steady sound of his heart beating in his head.

A minute or so passed, and then he heard footsteps approaching.

"You all good?"

Keeping his rod pointed toward the water, he turned around—and froze.

It wasn't the boy standing only a few yards away. It was the man he'd beat up the other day. The one whose arm he'd broken and which was still in a sling.

In the man's good hand was a Beretta APX.

"Die, you piece of shit."

And the man raised the pistol and shot Nova in the chest.

TWENTY-SEVEN

The nine-millimeter round struck Nova with enough force to knock him off his feet.

He landed on his back, hard, tipping the tackle box over in the process.

The shot had hit him center mass and he couldn't breathe —all oxygen had disappeared—and his right hand clutched for the contents spilled out from the tackle box as he listened to the shooter's boots crunching over the earth.

"Finlay wanted to be here for this, but his fucking crutches made it impossible. He and I debated on how I should do it— whether I should just shoot you in the head and call it a day. But me, well, I decided to make it painful. So that way you ..."

The man paused, standing over him now, squinting.

"Are you wearing a vest?"

Nova's fingers squeezed around the grip of the FNX-45, which he'd stashed in the bottom of the tackle box. With effort he lifted it up and aimed it at the man, all within the space of a second. The man, caught off guard, never had a chance to raise the Beretta again before Nova shot him in the face.

As the man's body fell over, Nova struggled to sit up. He

still couldn't breathe right—it felt like a boulder was sitting on his chest—but he managed to get up onto an elbow and swing the pistol back and forth, searching for others.

He didn't see anyone in the trees, but he heard voices—hushed, whispering back and forth—and a twig snap somewhere in the foliage.

The fibers of the ballistic vest he wore under his shirt were designed to absorb and disperse the impact and force of bullets. That, in addition to the lightweight armor panels, was enough to stop a bullet from a certain distance.

But that didn't mean an impact didn't hurt like fuck.

Movement caught his attention, another man's head peeking around a tree.

Nova squeezed off two rounds, watching pieces of bark splinter off the tree as the head disappeared for cover. By then he was on his feet, grimacing in pain. But still, he was on his feet, mobile.

In the distance, Alex cried out for help.

Nova started moving swiftly along the riverbank. He and the boy had walked a good half mile from the truck before settling on their spot, and Nova imagined the men who'd come to kill him had parked in the same area.

At one point he heard Alex cry out again, sounding closer, and he quickly veered into the trees. Pressed himself up against the trunk of a ponderosa pine and listened for any movement. Nothing coming from behind, but he did hear something farther ahead, the rapid bustle of departing footsteps.

He stayed close to the trees for cover, looking every which way as he moved, before he spotted a man in camouflage carrying Alex over one shoulder like a fireman.

They were maybe fifty yards away.

Nova hurried forward, ignoring the potential threat behind him and solely focusing on the danger ahead.

His chest still felt tight but he could breathe again, and he ran as fast as possible, trying not to trip over anything in his path.

A tree a few feet ahead spat up bark as a half second later a shot sounded out behind him.

Nova reflexively ducked. He didn't bother glancing over his shoulder, though, instead keeping his focus on the man in camouflage running off with Alex. But the gunshot was enough to catch the man's attention. As he ran, the man glanced back to see where the shot had come from, and in doing so tripped and fell forward, spilling Alex onto the ground like a discarded bag of groceries.

Alex cried out again, this time much louder and sharper, but Nova kept his eyes on the man. The man who was now turning around, reaching for the pistol he had holstered to his belt. Nova didn't give the man a chance to clear leather before he fired two rounds—one in the chest and another in the man's throat.

By the time he reached them, the man was gurgling blood and Alex was writhing in pain. Nova saw why immediately—a thick sliver of bone protruded from the boy's arm.

Nova twisted around to check the trees behind him. Hazy sunlight filtered through the overhanging branches. No movement. The man he'd shot was still gurgling on the ground, one hand to his neck, his other hand trying in vain to grab for his weapon.

Nova bent down, wrested the gun from the holster, and stuck it in his waistband. He considered putting the man out of his misery, but Alex's cries drew his attention and he knelt down beside the boy.

"Ow, ow, ow, ow, ow!"

The boy's face was beet-red and streaming with tears. He screamed when Nova picked him up.

"It's okay, Alex, everything's okay. Just hold your arm in place. Yes, just like that—that's perfect."

The clearing was coming up, less than one hundred yards away. Nova slowed before they reached the bright sunlight. He peered out to see if anyone was waiting for them by the truck, then glanced back over his shoulder.

Still no movement.

Alex was still crying, murmuring now, "I'm sorry, I'm sorry, I'm sorry."

Nova shushed the boy as he darted out from the trees. They were in the open now, easy targets. He hoped that carrying the boy made it less likely that Blake's men would fire on them.

He started for his truck but then paused.

Coming down the road was a car.

Nova moved to take cover behind his truck. He only realized seconds later that the approaching car belonged to Mandy Schaffer.

The car screeching to a halt, Mandy jumped out, frantic.

"He is bleeding? What happened?"

She stopped suddenly then, her eyes on the gun in Nova's hand.

Nova said, "His arm is broken."

"How—"

"There's no time to explain. Take him and head straight to the hospital. You'll both be safe there."

She stared at him, eyes wide, face ashen. It looked like she wanted to say something but couldn't find the words, so Nova didn't give her the chance.

"Go!"

She took her son from Nova, hurried him to the car, and buckled him into the back. She paused, staring at him for another moment, before climbing inside and kicking up grass in her wake as she sped away.

Nova watched them go, then opened his door and reached under the front seat for the two extra magazines he had squirreled away that morning.

Slipping the mags into his back pocket, he slammed the door shut and gazed at the tree line.

Except for the wind pushing through and the burble of the river, the area was still and quiet.

Pistol in hand, he started back into the woods.

TWENTY-EIGHT

Nova moved quietly through the trees, FNX-45 held at the ready, backtracking to the spot where he'd shot the man who had attempted to abduct Alex. He assumed if there were others they would want to check on their fallen comrade, and he was in luck—as he rounded the corner he spotted a man with a beard standing over the body, a pistol held at his side.

He crouched behind a tree and leaned out far enough to watch the man, debating on what his next move would be. His focus so trained on the man—with blood thumping quietly in his ears, his breathing shallow—that for a half second he didn't sense the movement to his side before it was too late.

Nova swung his gaze over to the left. To another man standing only a few yards away, a SIG P226 in hand. In that split second, he realized that the man with the beard was the bait, to draw his attention, to get him to drop his guard so that this other man could steady his aim.

The split second felt like a minute, both of them frozen in time. Then the suppressed snap of a gunshot broke the silence. Nova didn't realize until another half second passed that he hadn't been shot and that the man with the SIG was now falling to the ground, half his face torn away.

Nova spun back toward the man with the beard. The man who had turned away from the body on the ground and who was now lowering his own fired pistol as he approached, slow and steady.

The shooter's gaze stayed locked on Nova's until he reached the man he'd just shot. He glanced down at the body, and sighed.

"I didn't want to do that, but I had no choice."

The man's voice was a whisper, so Nova answered in the same tone.

"Then why'd you do it?"

"Because he was going to kill you."

"And that concerned you how?"

The man studied Nova for a beat.

"I'm FBI, undercover."

Part of Nova wanted to laugh out loud.

"How long?"

"Coming up on three years now. I got close to one of Blake Hogan's men in prison, and they brought me on once I was released."

"What does the FBI care about the Hogans trafficking weapons? I thought that fell under the ATF's purview."

The man grinned, not looking at all surprised.

"Figured that was you at the dealership. Blake did too, only he can't prove it."

"That why you guys came to kill me today?"

"I'm not entirely sure why we came to kill you today. But those were the orders. Blake plays his cards very close to the chest. I've been working with him and his crew for two years and they still hardly tell me shit. Same with a lot of the other guys."

"Still doesn't explain why the FBI cares about trafficking

weapons."

"Trafficking weapons is only part of what the Hogans are into. But that's not why I've spent three years of my life on this."

"Then what's the FBI's interest?"

"Domestic terrorism."

Nova arched an eyebrow.

"How are the Hogans associated with domestic terrorism?"

The man glanced around the area, looking even more guarded than before. He took a half step toward Nova.

"We don't have time to get into it. But something big's going down very soon."

Nova said, "The guy staying on the Hogan's property."

A flicker of surprise flashed through the man's eyes.

"How'd you know about him?"

"Let's just say we ran into each other."

"That means you were trespassing on Hogan's land. Good thing you weren't caught."

"Who is that guy?"

"No idea. They keep him well secluded. Only Blake and Carson deal with him, as far as I can tell. I think the idea is that none of us are supposed to see his face."

"Why?"

"Again, no clue. Look, we've already talked longer than we should. Marc took off for the truck. Piece of shit was scared, I think. If I don't show up soon, he'll probably take off without me."

Nova lifted his chin at the body lying on the ground between them.

"How are you going to explain that?"

"Simple. You did that. But me ... I can't walk away from this unscathed."

Nova realized what the man meant, and asked, "Where do you want it?"

"Shoulder or leg. Someplace clean. I don't want to bleed out."

His grip tight on the FNX-45, Nova nodded.

"Say when."

"Wait. I need you to deliver a message. Two agents have been holed up in town for the past year. It's been nearly impossible to make contact with them. I need you to go to them and tell them exactly what I told you."

"Where are they?"

"Red house at the end of Mottley Lane. You can't miss it."

"Their names?"

"Special Agents Dennis Heller and Janelle Barton."

"And yours?"

"Special Agent Dean Roberts. But I've been undercover as Keith Thompson."

"Thank you for saving my life, Agent Roberts."

The man nodded, already gritting his teeth.

"Just make it quick."

Nova lifted his pistol and fired three rounds in the air, then aimed and squeezed off one round straight into the man's left shoulder.

Dean Roberts clenched his face against the pain but didn't make a sound. He only nodded again at Nova, and started back through the woods.

Nova watched him go, paying attention to his peripheral vision for any other movement.

When the man had disappeared, Nova turned and hurried back to where he'd parked.

A marked deputy's SUV sat idling behind Nova's truck. A deputy was peering inside when he heard Nova emerge from the trees.

The deputy grabbed his service weapon and aimed it at him.

"Freeze!"

TWENTY-NINE

By the time Veronica Chapman arrived, two hours had passed and the scene was crawling with deputies and highway patrol. At least a half-dozen vehicles in total, cruisers and SUVs, their roof racks flashing.

Nova sat in the back of a marked SUV, handcuffed, thinking about everything that had happened so far this morning and what it all meant. Also wondering what would happen if Blake Hogan showed up and simply put a gun to Nova's head—would any of these cops stop him?

Veronica conferred with the deputy who was first on scene, glancing toward Nova every couple of seconds, before patting the deputy on the shoulder and striding over to the SUV.

She opened the door and said, her tone flat, "Get out."

It was awkward climbing out, what with his hands secured behind his back, but then he was standing and slowly stretching the muscles in his neck.

"Thanks."

Her expression was dark, her brown eyes hidden by the Ray-Bans

"Don't thank me yet."

She shut the door and motioned for him to follow her a few paces away from the others. Nova noted many were eyeballing him but that wasn't surprising, seeing as how he had emerged from the woods carrying a pistol in his hand with another in his waistband and three dead men lying in his wake.

Turning back to him as she squared her shoulders, Veronica Chapman said, "Tell me what happened."

Nova couldn't help but grin, and her expression darkened even more.

"What's so funny?"

"Nothing. Just feels like déjà vu."

The sheriff clearly didn't see the humor in it.

"Tell me what happened."

"How about you let me out of these cuffs first?"

"Tell me what happened, and we'll see."

Nova sucked in a breath and told her about coming out here to fish with Alex Schaffer and how after Alex had gone off to pee behind a tree one of Blake Hogan's men approached him with a gun and shot him in the chest.

She stopped him there.

"How do you know it was one of Blake's men?"

"It was the guy whose arm I broke the other day."

"Christ," she muttered, staring at the other cops on the scene. Then crossing her arms, shifting on her feet: "So he shot you in the chest. You don't look dead."

"That's very astute of you, Sheriff."

She ignored his tone.

"Why are you wearing a Kevlar vest?"

"I like the style."

Not the glimmer of a smile. Her expression, hard as steel.

"This isn't funny. Three men are dead. Men who, from what I understand, all worked for Blake Hogan. I told you about how the Hogans run this town. I don't care whether you were once a SEAL or if you were indeed acting in self-defense,

I'm already having a hard time seeing how you manage to walk away from this without doing any jail time."

"I felt threatened for my life, so I asserted my Second Amendment right. Isn't that what I'm supposed to say?"

Again, no reaction.

"So he shot you."

"Yes, he shot me."

"And then what happened?"

He told her about grasping his pistol, about managing to squeeze off a round before the other man could fire a second shot. About hearing Alex Schaffer screaming for help and chasing after him.

"How is he, anyway?"

"Who, the boy? Mandy got him to the hospital just fine. The doctors are taking care of him. Stay on topic. What happened to that man?"

"After he dropped Alex he reached for a weapon, so I shot him."

"So that's two. What about the third?"

"I carried Alex out here right as his mom arrived. As soon as they were gone, I went back into the woods."

"Why?"

"I paid a lot of money for my fishing gear. I wasn't going to leave it behind."

Veronica Chapman didn't look amused. She glanced back at the others before taking a half step closer to Nova.

"I don't want you to go down for any of these assholes' deaths, you got it? So I need you to make sure your story stays consistent."

"It's not a story, Sheriff. It's the truth."

"You went back into the woods."

"Yes."

"And then?"

"Two more men came at me. I managed to shoot the one in the head, but I only nicked the other."

"What do you mean, nicked?"

"I think I got him in the shoulder. He ran off, so I decided to come back here and call for the police. By the time I got out of the trees, your deputy was already here."

"That's because Mandy called 911 as soon as she drove off with Alex." She tilted her head, and his reflection in her sunglasses shifted. "Is that all? Nothing else you want to tell me?"

Nova stared at the sheriff's face in the low light. Clouds had appeared in the sky within the past hour, blocking out the sun.

He glanced over at the others, then dropped his voice.

"What are you talking about?"

She stared at him as her jaw went tight. When she spoke, she barely moved her lips.

"I just hope you didn't kill him."

Nova eyed the others nearby, determined they weren't in earshot.

"Who?"

Reaching into her pocket, she glanced back over her shoulder at the others. The sun broke through the clouds, momentarily making the handcuff key in her hand glint as she stepped behind him.

"It's come to my attention there's an undercover FBI agent working in Blake Hogan's crew. If you killed him …"

She released one cuff, then the other, and stepped back.

Nova turned to face her, rubbing at his wrists where the cuffs had bit into his skin.

"What makes you think there's an undercover agent?"

"I'm the chief law enforcement officer in this county. I get a heads-up about certain things, especially when they're delicate."

Clouds slid in front of the sun again, masking Veronica's face in shadow.

"I didn't kill him."

"How can you be so sure?"

"Because I know who he is."

Another half step forward, so close they were almost touching. Even with the breeze and the river right next to them he could smell her shampoo and sweat and anxiety.

"How?"

"He spoke to me."

Veronica opened her mouth, but it was clear she didn't know what to say. She stared at him for another moment and then nodded.

"Okay, that's good."

"I don't want this guy caught in any crossfire."

"I don't either."

"He told me something big is going down soon. Your people should probably arrest Blake Hogan and his father."

"On what charge?"

"Conspiracy, for one."

She glanced again at the others, her throat moving as she swallowed.

"You said it yourself," Nova whispered, "they aren't good people. Maybe now's the time to take them off the board."

"But this agent—"

Nova cut her off.

"Is on his own. That's why he felt the need to expose himself to me. So that I could reach out to the right people to get help."

Nova waited a beat, staring at his reflection.

"I'll tell you who the agent is."

Her throat moving again, she whispered, "You know his name?"

"No, but I know what he looks like."

Veronica shifted her body so her back was to the others as she slipped her phone from her pocket.

"Luckily I keep photos of Blake's crew in a folder, just in case."

She held the phone out so Nova could see the screen and started swiping through. A few were mugshots, but others had been taken off social media.

Nova told her to stop on the fifth photo.

"Him?" she said.

"Yes. What's his name?"

She stared down at the photo, her jaw once again tight.

"Marc Palmer."

THIRTY

The main area of the barn was wide open, just empty space all over, which was more than enough room for them to have laid down the tarp.

On the tarp was a single metal folding chair, and secured to the chair—his ankles bound to the legs with his wrists tied behind him—sat Marc Palmer.

If it wasn't for the strip of duct tape over his mouth, the man probably would have shouted his head off, but as it was his face was red and his eyes were wide as he stared in vain at the men standing in front of him.

Blake Hogan said, "Stop squirming—you're just going to wear yourself out."

Marc stared up at Blake beseechingly, hoping for an ally.

"I'm disappointed, Marc. I've known you most of my life. I considered you a true patriot. My father did too."

In his wheelchair, Tripp Hogan made no reaction, his gaze steady on Marc.

Blake said, "The FBI sure likes to play the long game, don't they?"

Marc's eyes went wide again, and he bucked in the chair violently, almost tipping it over.

"Enough! I've already dealt with too much bullshit today. Three of my guys are dead—BJ, Gary, and Dominic, all of them damned fine men—and what did you do but run off like a scared chickenshit."

Blake motioned at Keith, who stood off to the side, his bullet wound patched up the best they could for right now.

"At least Keith didn't run away like a little bitch. But that's because he's a *true* patriot. He knows what's at stake. But you… you're a fucking traitor."

Still Marc bucked violently in the chair, screaming despite the tape over his mouth.

Blake motioned again at Keith.

"I shouldn't be surprised, because he rescued your ass while you were in the joint. Isn't that what you told me? Three niggers were going to beat you to death, but then Keith stepped in and fought them off for you. God, I can't believe I didn't see it sooner, how weak you are. And then to learn that you're a goddamned traitor?"

Blake shook his head and drew his SIG. He held it at his side, his fingers white around the grip, as Marc's wide eyes zeroed in on the black matte finish.

"Dad?"

Tripp Hogan grunted, "Yes?"

"What did they do to traitors back during the Civil War?'

"They executed them."

"How'd they execute them?"

"They lined them up and let a firing squad send them to their maker."

Blake nodded slowly, his heavy gaze not once leaving Marc.

"Firing squad sounds just like what this son of a bitch deserves. But, well, I don't want to waste the ammunition. Keith?"

Keith blinked, at first not realizing that Blake was holding out the SIG to him.

"Boss?"

"Take it. Put the bastard out of his misery."

Keith took the proffered pistol. He stepped forward onto the tarp, Marc still trying to shout behind the strip of duct tape.

Press-checking the pistol to confirm that there was a live round in the chamber, Keith aimed the SIG so that the barrel was only two inches away from the side of Marc's head.

But he didn't squeeze the trigger. Not for a second or two, and then he glanced up at Blake and Tripp and Carson.

"Shouldn't we at least—"

A single round, expertly placed, created a hole in the center of Keith's forehead.

His head snapped back, and the rest of his body went with it, crumbling onto the tarp.

Carson lowered his Glock and placed it back in his holster without a word. Blake had to hand it to the older man: he was a great shot, even after all these years.

Marc had stopped bucking in the chair. He no longer attempted to shout behind the duct tape. Instead he waited for Blake to step forward and peel the tape off his mouth and use a knife to cut off his bindings.

"Christ, he could have killed me!"

Blake said, "He wasn't going to kill you. We would never have let it get to that point."

"He held the barrel to my head!"

"He was an FBI agent. He wasn't going to kill you."

As soon as his bindings fell away Marc bolted up from the chair, pacing around the tarp to stretch his legs.

Tripp Hogan called, "You can come out now."

Veronica Chapman emerged from the shadows, where she'd been standing in the dark the entire time, watching.

Blake said, "So what do you think, Sheriff?"

She stared down at the body on the tarp. Blake figured she was doing her best not to show emotion, but he could tell it unnerved her. Good.

She asked, "Why bother?"

"What's that?"

"With the whole dog and pony show. If you were going to kill him right here right now anyway."

Blake shrugged and grinned down at his father.

"We wanted to see how far he'd let us take things."

A moment of silence stretched where the gunshot still echoed in their ears.

Tripp Hogan said to Veronica, "You know what this means, don't you?"

She nodded silently, still staring down at the body.

"Mr. Bartkowski identified the wrong man on purpose. Which means you failed to do your job."

Her face snapped up, her expression tense.

"My job?"

"To get him to trust you. So that we can determine his true reason for being here."

"I told you his true reason. He came to fish. But then, well, shit happened."

Blake laughed out loud.

"You're damn right shit happened. And it's just going to get worse. Why didn't you place him under arrest back at the river?"

"Highway patrol was there. And some of my people are straight. They would have expected him to be taken to jail if I had placed him under arrest. But I guess it doesn't really matter anymore. How are you going to get to him now that you've lost half of your men?"

Blake's brow squished, and he shrugged.

"We've got more men coming. They'll be here shortly."

"I don't want any more bloodshed in this town. It's going to be hard enough to explain what happened with the dead bodies we already have."

"That's not our problem, Sheriff. If you had done your job in the first place and got the prick to leave town, those men would still be alive."

Veronica was silent for a moment, biting her lip.

"Do you know where he is now?"

Blake pulled his iPhone from his pocket, opened the GPS tracking app.

"The bug we placed on his truck has him already on the interstate forty miles outside of town. But I don't buy that's him. He likely found the tracker and tossed it on a passing truck."

"Great," Veronica said. "So we've lost him."

Blake grinned, and shook his head.

"Not quite. I have a pretty good idea I know exactly where he's headed."

THIRTY-ONE

Nova couldn't wait any longer.

For more than an hour he'd been sitting in his truck, the engine off, the FNX-45 resting on his lap.

Veronica Chapman and her deputies hadn't taken his weapons before they let him go. That was one red flag. He was having trouble believing the entire police force was crooked, but believing Veronica was bent wasn't a stretch at all.

He had to give her a name, so he gave her Marc Palmer's. Blake had already lost several men and Nova wasn't sure how many were left, but he imagined they were dropping off fast. He wasn't sure how much time he'd granted the FBI agent, but he hoped it would be enough.

As soon as the sheriff allowed him to leave with the promise that he would stay in town in case they had any further questions, he drove for a few miles before pulling off, popping the hood, and extracting the tracking device.

Next he stopped at the gas station. Waited until a trucker had stepped away from his rig before ducking behind the trailer and affixing the tracker to its undercarriage.

Then, back in his truck, he finally emailed Atticus. He kept it short and concise, still not sure how to explain what was going on because he still wasn't entirely sure himself.

Potential trouble in Remington, MT. Still investigating. Can you confirm three FBI special agents? Dean Roberts. Dennis Heller. Janelle Barton. Send photos if possible.

As soon as he'd pressed SEND, he was hoping for a quick response, but now nearly an hour had passed and Nova realized he couldn't wait any longer.

He headed for Mottley Lane, which was located right off Main Street and a mile away from the heart of town.

A few houses dotted Mottley, and there at the end, as promised, sat the red house. Two stories tall and looking almost abandoned except for a pickup in the driveway.

Something about the truck was familiar but Nova couldn't place it.

He'd debated on how he should move forward and ultimately decided to be upfront. So he parked his truck behind the pickup and purposefully strode up the walkway to the porch.

Before he could advance up the three steps, the front door opened and a man peered out at him. He kept the pistol at his side, hidden from anyone passing by on the road but visible to Nova. A warning.

"Help you with something?"

Nova momentarily wasn't sure what to say. At once he realized where he'd seen this man before, and the pickup. It had parked near his truck yesterday near the river. The man had been with a woman, and they'd given him a friendly wave as they started on their walk, hand in hand.

He'd paused on the steps, his hand itching to grab for the FNX-45 he had stashed in his waistband.

"Your undercover man sent me."

The corners of the man's eyes creased.

"I don't know what you're talking about."

"Dennis Heller. Special Agent Dennis Heller?"

The man was just under six feet tall, close-cropped black hair and green eyes. He stared at Nova for another moment before leaning out to survey the empty road and then stepped back, motioning with the pistol for him to enter.

As Nova stepped into the foyer, he found the woman— Special Agent Janelle Barton—standing in the living room doorway, leveling her own pistol at him.

Dennis Heller asked him, "You carrying?"

Keeping his hands held out at his sides, Nova nodded.

Heller traced Nova's gaze at Barton, and grinned.

"Forgive my partner's caution. She's been a bit jumpy the past couple of days. Ever since ... well, ever since you came to town."

The agent hadn't asked Nova to hand over his weapon. At least not yet.

Nova said, "Three of Blake Hogan's men were killed only a few hours ago."

Heller nodded, his face solemn. He shot a glance at his partner before clearing his throat.

"Yeah, we heard."

"How'd you hear?"

"We've been in this town for a while now. Word spreads fast. But it also helps that we keep an ear on the police line. God, when we heard, we were worried Dean had gone down too."

"He saved my life. Told me to come find you."

"Why's that?"

"He said that whatever's going down is happening very soon."

Dennis Heller stared at Nova for a long moment, considering these words, before he realized that his partner hadn't lowered her pistol.

"Christ, Janelle, ease up."

Barton stood about five-five, her strawberry-blonde hair pulled back in a ponytail. Keeping both the pistol and her blue eyes steady on Nova, she said, "We don't know who this guy is."

Heller sighed and rolled his eyes.

"Dean sent him. Dean saved his life!"

"Says the stranger."

"Janelle."

Barton lowered the pistol, only a bit.

"Who do you work for, anyway?"

Heller said, "Yeah, you're not with us, are you? Christ, all this time undercover messes with your head. Fries something in your brain, I swear. So what is it—ATF, Homeland Security?"

Nova said, "Something like that."

Heller shot another glance at his partner.

"See? I told you so. Now put that thing away before you shoot someone."

Barton didn't put her pistol away as she kept her eyes locked on Nova.

"Show us some identification."

"I'm undercover too. I don't carry my credentials with me. What are you both doing here, anyway?"

Dennis Heller made a dismissive sound as he rolled his eyes again.

"Surveillance, obviously."

"But why? The automatic rifles?"

"Those, yeah, but also something else. Hey, you hungry? We were about to have lunch. Nothing fancy, I'm afraid. Just cold cuts."

Nova shook his head. Dennis Heller shrugged and motioned again for Janelle to put her pistol away before heading deeper into the house. Nova shared another staring contest with the woman before she turned away and followed her partner.

Nothing in the kitchen seemed out of place. The counters bare except for a roll of paper towels by the sink. The fridge looked like it had been bought back in the 1950s.

Nova said, "Where's your setup?"

Heller started pulling out meat and cheese and mayo and mustard from the fridge.

"Down in the basement. We can't afford to have anything out in the open on the first floor. We've tried keeping to ourselves, but this is a small town, and the locals talk. As far as they're concerned, I work in Bozeman, while Janelle works from home doing web design. We've needed to integrate ourselves, which means having people over occasionally. You want a soda or some water or something?"

"Water's fine."

Heller tossed him a bottle before handing his partner a can of Diet Coke. Then he closed the fridge door with his hip and placed everything on the kitchen table.

"Take a seat."

He turned to the cabinets, pulled out a loaf of bread and some bags of potato chips and Doritos.

"Worst part about staying undercover for so long—besides not seeing your family—is you don't get to eat as healthy as you'd like."

Now it was Barton who made a dismissive sound as she rolled his eyes.

"I try to make healthy meals as much as possible. *You're* the one who continues to eat this junk."

"What"—Dennis Heller's expression was wounded—"frozen pizza seven nights in a row is unhealthy all of a sudden?"

Nova had yet to uncap his water bottle. He was still assessing the situation, listening to the house for any noises.

"So what else is there?"

Heller blinked at him as he started making a sandwich.

"You mean condiments?"

"Besides the automatic weapons."

"Ah, yeah. Well, there's a white national angle to this too."

Hence the concerns about domestic terrorism.

"How so?"

"It's our belief Blake Hogan is using message boards to incite these so-called patriots all over the country. We believe that's who he's sending these weapons to. But you must already know that, otherwise they wouldn't have sent you here in the first place. Honestly, if these agencies communicated every once in a while, it would save a lot of time and headache, not to mention paperwork. So spill, my friend—what's your angle on this?"

Nova still hadn't opened the bottle. He twisted it back and forth on the tabletop, watching both Dennis Heller as he dug into his sandwich and Janelle Barton as she took a sip of her soda.

His phone vibrated in his pocket, one quick buzz signaling an email.

"Excuse me. I think this might be my superior."

He drew his phone from his pocket and saw that Atticus had finally gotten back to him.

What concerns do you have? Do you need backup?
Confirmed identities of all three agents—they are active
and undercover. See attached photos.

Atticus had attached three headshots for each agent, no doubt taken from their files.

The first Nova recognized as Dean Roberts, who had saved his life only a few hours ago. His hair was shorter and his eyes didn't look as stressed, but it was definitely him.

The other two—Special Agents Dennis Heller and Janelle Barton—he didn't recognize at all.

THIRTY-TWO

Nova stared at the photographs on his phone. First Dennis Heller, then Janelle Barton, then Heller again.

A man in his mid-forties. Short brown hair, blue eyes.

A woman in her early forties. Long red hair, brown eyes.

The Heller sitting across from him had close-cropped black hair and green eyes, while the Barton sitting beside him had strawberry-blonde hair and blue eyes. And she looked to be about thirty years old.

Nova didn't think anything had changed about his posture or expression, but the imposter Dennis Heller sighed as he carefully set his sandwich down.

"That didn't take long, did it?"

There was a heavy silence as Nova stared across the table at the man while also watching the woman in his peripheral vision.

The woman twisted in her seat, reaching for her pistol, so she was the one Nova targeted. He whipped the water bottle at her face, then pushed back his chair as he flipped the table over with one hand while simultaneously reaching for his gun with the other.

The man was on his feet a second later, Glock in hand. He aimed for Nova but Nova fired off four rounds as he scrambled backward into the living room, taking cover around the corner.

In the sudden aftermath, his ears ringing, Nova heard the man speak quietly to the woman.

"You hit?"

"Yeah, but I think I'm good."

His back against the wall, Nova surveyed the living room. Like Veronica Chapman's, it was sparse. Photos dotted the walls, a middle-aged couple smiling for the camera. They were of the real Heller and Barton, not these two imposters. Which was why Nova hadn't been invited into the living room. And which also made him think that these two hadn't taken over the agents' lives until very recently.

A large mirror hung over the fireplace. It gave Nova an excellent view of the kitchen, but it also gave the two imposters an excellent view of him.

He watched the man motion for the woman to head around the other way, and then the man saw Nova watching him and grinned—and immediately fired at the wall where Nova stood.

Nova ducked as a storm of plaster flew everywhere. He dove to the side, shooting as he fell, and watched the man's body jerk as at least two rounds tore into it.

As soon as he hit the ground Nova twisted to aim toward the other entrance into the living room, expecting the woman to appear.

Nothing. No movement. Just silence.

Nova climbed to his feet, splitting his focus between the two entrances and keeping his pistol aimed in the middle so that he could swing it in either direction.

He realized the man in the kitchen wasn't dead. He heard the man gurgling blood and watched as the man groped for the

Glock on the kitchen floor that had fallen only inches away from his splayed fingers.

Rechecking both entrances, Nova pivoted and put a bead on the man's head and squeezed the trigger.

A single shot, that's all it took, and the man was no longer gurgling.

Nova continued to cover both entrances, waiting for the woman to make some noise. Still only silence. He backed up toward the wall, sidestepping the couch to get a better angle. Then he started moving toward the left, taking slow, steady steps.

A foot came into view. The woman's foot. Another couple of steps and the foot grew into a leg and then her entire body.

She was sitting on the floor, her back against the wall. Gun in her right hand, her head slumped forward. She didn't appear to be breathing.

Nova said, "Bullshit."

With a ferocious screech the woman jerked up, bringing her gun with her, but Nova already had his pistol aimed and placed a bullet right in the side of her head.

Playing possum. Christ, he didn't think he'd ever seen that before.

The two imposters were down, but that didn't mean there weren't others. He cautiously moved through the first floor, checking that both the man and the woman were dead. He found the basement door and debated checking there first or checking the second floor.

He decided on the second floor and did a quick sweep. Nothing but two bedrooms and a bathroom and none of it looked out of place.

In the basement he found the two bodies. They were squeezed into a large chest freezer, wrapped tightly in a clear tarp. Or rather *pieces* of them were wrapped in the tarp—to fit both bodies, their arms and legs had been severed from their torsos.

Taking up the rest of the basement were two long tables with several computers and files. The command center for the op.

But what was the op, exactly?

He found some file folders with photographs in them. Surveillance shots of Hogan Auto as well as Blake Hogan and his men. Some of the photos had time stamps and dates that went back more than a year.

Keeping his gun in one hand, Nova pulled out his phone. He decided to forego spending the extra time to send an email and called the number he had saved in his contacts—the number Atticus Caine had given him to call in case of emergency and which he'd used previously during his time in Parrot Spur, Nevada.

"Thank you for calling Scout Dry Cleaners. Our normal business hours are Monday through Friday, seven a.m to seven p.m., and on Saturday eight a.m. to three p.m. We are closed Sundays."

As soon as he heard the beep, Nova said, "Backup is needed. ASAP. I've got at least two FBI agents dead. My guess is they've been dead for a few days now. Something big is going down and I'm still not sure what it is, but they've been trafficking military-grade weapons out of Hogan Auto. I'll try to stay low until I hear back from you."

Back upstairs, he did another sweep of the first floor to be safe before stuffing the FNX-45 in his waistband as he stepped outside.

The sun was shining again, so bright he had to squint as he scanned the houses farther along the road. If any of them were occupied, there was little doubt someone had heard the gunshots. A worried neighbor would have called the police by now, and the last thing he needed was to deal with Veronica Chapman and her bent police force.

Tires squealed farther down the road, accompanied by an engine that roared like a pissed-off dinosaur.

A jacked-up Dodge Ram with massive wheels was headed to this location, fast. In fact, it was so fast Nova barely had a chance to make it to his truck before the Ram screeched to a halt in front of the house and the two passenger-side doors popped open, depositing a pair of men with M4A1s.

Nova turned and fled behind the house as the men opened fire.

THIRTY-THREE

Sprinting through one backyard after another, pistol now in hand. Dodging trees and ducking limbs. Glancing over his shoulder every couple of seconds to gauge the distance between him and the men with the assault rifles.

Nova had a good one hundred yards on them, but that didn't stop both men from momentarily pausing to fire off three-round bursts. A few of the shots were wide, but one caused the tree Nova was bounding past to spit up bark.

When he recognized where he was, he veered off past another house and came out onto Main Street.

The sun was out in full force now, spotlighting the deserted stretch of roadway. Nova looked both ways, thinking about the handful of businesses nearby, and then jogged up the sidewalk toward the Yellow Bird Cafe, concealing his pistol in his waistband.

The parking lot was moderately full, which for a Thursday afternoon meant maybe a dozen customers.

That should do.

He glanced down the street and watched the two men appear from the front yard of the house he'd run past, the

American and Gadsden flags hanging limp from their perches on the front porch.

The men spotted him, said something to one another, and then lowered their rifles as one of the men pulled out his phone to make a call.

Drawing his own phone as he stepped into the cafe, Nova saw that Atticus hadn't yet responded.

"Good afternoon. Please sit wherever you'd like."

The waitress behind the counter smiled at him as she filled someone's mug with coffee. She had told him the same thing yesterday when he'd come in for lunch and would probably tell him the same thing tomorrow if he lived to see it.

Nova beelined for the same table he'd sat at the past three days, sliding into the booth so that his back was to the wall.

The waitress ambled over to him, pad and pen already in hand.

"Know what you want, or do you need a minute to look at the menu?"

Nova watched the jacked-up truck slide into view. It motored slowly past the cafe and then pulled into the parking lot so that its grille faced the building.

"I'll just have coffee for now, thanks."

The waitress nodded and turned away to check on another table, but Nova barely paid any attention, his focus shifting to the two men with assault rifles striding past the front windows.

The men went straight for the truck. The driver climbed out, also with an assault rifle, and joined the other two men as they stood in front of the truck. Two of them lit cigarettes. Another pulled out a can of Skoal from his pocket as he checked something on his phone.

Nova realized others in the cafe were looking out the windows now. A low, curious murmur filled the air.

The waitress brought a mug and carafe of coffee, and as she poured, she frowned out the window.

"I wonder what they want."

Nova asked, "Do you recognize them?"

She bent her head a bit to get a better view. Stared a moment and then shook her head.

"Don't believe so. At least they're not from here, I can tell you that."

Curious.

As the waitress turned away, Nova checked his phone again. Still nothing from Atticus. He thought about calling the FBI. The closest field office was in Salt Lake City. They oversaw ten satellite offices in three states, a half-dozen of which were in Montana. He could call any one of them, but what would he say?

Ah, yeah, hi, so two of your undercover agents? I found them wrapped in a tarp in the basement of this house that's been all shot up. And your other undercover agent is in grave danger if he isn't already dead.

Nova took a sip of his coffee as he watched the three men out in the parking lot. Large men with beards, wraparound shades, drab-colored baseball caps. Most likely local militia members, called in by Blake Hogan as his own crew had started to dwindle. And Nova had no doubt that these were just the first to arrive.

Scanning the cafe to make sure nobody was watching, he pulled his pistol from his waistband and set it on the booth next to his leg.

He rechecked his phone.

Still nothing from Atticus.

A few others in the cafe were still glancing out at the men, but everybody else seemed to have forgotten them. Outsiders carrying automatic rifles wasn't a major concern, apparently.

Nova kept watching the men, sipping his coffee, until a deputy's SUV pulled into the parking lot.

He recognized the deputy from earlier today. The deputy

went over to speak to the men, but he did so casually, not even resting his hand on the butt of his service pistol.

As the deputy spoke to the men, another vehicle slid into view from the other direction down Main Street.

Veronica Chapman's unmarked Ford F-150.

She pulled into the parking lot, ignored the deputy and the three men, and entered through the front door.

The waitress called out, "Afternoon, Sheriff!"

Veronica nodded in acknowledgment and headed straight for Nova, propping her Ray-Bans on the top of her head. Like yesterday, she slid into the other side of the booth without asking.

Nova took a sip of his coffee.

"Fancy seeing you here."

She stared at him, her face blank. Then her lips pressed together in a tight line, and she shook her head with a sigh.

"Why didn't you listen to me the first time I told you to leave?"

"I've been asking myself that same question."

"It didn't have to be like this, Nova. It really didn't."

"And what exactly is *this*, Sheriff?"

"You know very well."

"Do I?"

She paused as a thought entered her head, and then glanced around the cafe at the others.

"Did you think coming here would save you?"

"It was a thought."

"All it gave you was a little reprieve. That's all."

"How do you know?"

Still watching him, she called out, her voice loud and commanding.

"I need everyone to vacate this building immediately. Even you, Joyce. Now!"

A moment of stunned silence. Then the sound of chairs

scraping against the linoleum floor, the low squeak of the vinyl upholstery as people slid out of their booths.

Everyone filed out the front door, including the waitress and the cook who appeared from the back.

It took less than a minute, and then the cafe was empty except for the two of them. In the corner, the TV turned to cable news played silently.

"Impressive," Nova said. "What other tricks can you do?"

"This isn't a laughing matter."

"You're telling me." A pause, then: "What happened to him?"

"Who?"

"You know who."

She hesitated, and that was all Nova needed to confirm what he didn't want to accept.

"You do realize what will happen once the FBI learns you're involved in the death of three of their agents."

"I didn't kill any of them."

"Is that what you'll tell yourself to fall asleep tonight?"

"I never wanted to end up like this."

"Like what?"

"Like my father. Under the thumb of Tripp Hogan and his son. But ... in the end, I didn't have any other choice."

"So what's the plan, Sheriff? You're going to march me out the door and have those men execute me in the middle of Main Street?"

She glanced out the window at the men standing by the Ram. The three militiamen and the deputy. They stood in a circle, chatting like they were waiting for a ball game to start.

"How did you know?" she asked.

"How did I know what?"

"That you couldn't trust me."

"You mean besides the fact this county is, what, several

hundred square miles, and you as the sheriff have spent the past
two days in town babysitting me?"

"Yes."

"Well, for starters, I never told you I was a SEAL. Which
means you must have gotten that from Blake or his old man,
who I imagine have some powerful friends in the government."

"What else?"

"Even if you are the chief law enforcement officer in this
county, the FBI wouldn't give you a heads-up about an undercover agent."

She stared out at the men in the parking lot for a moment,
and nodded.

"I wasn't thinking straight. I thought I'd been doing a good
job, and suddenly realized I'd messed up."

"Regarding what?"

"Once it became clear you weren't going to leave town, my
orders were to build trust with you. To try to determine what
agency you work for. Obviously, I failed."

Veronica looked at him again, intensity flashing in her
brown eyes.

She said, "Are you aiming your gun at me under the table
right now?"

"What if I am?"

"If you do anything stupid, those men will race in here and
kill you."

"Something tells me they're going to kill me anyway, so
why not rid the world of one more corrupt cop before it
happens?"

Her phone buzzed. Veronica held it to her ear, listened for a
moment, and then placed the phone down and slid it across
the table to Nova.

"It's for you."

THIRTY-FOUR

Even in the musty dark, the whiskey's amber glow was mesmerizing.

George Murphy couldn't take his eyes off it. Not as he sat hunched at the bar, on a leather stool that somehow felt way too familiar. Not as he twisted the shot glass, a quarter inch at a time, building up the nerve to take the drink.

"You okay?"

He didn't realize the question was directed his way until he sensed the bartender standing in front of him, a towel draped over his shoulder. He almost looked like the old bartender on *Cheers*, the one before Woody Harrelson joined the show. George remembered watching it with his old man, George sitting on the floor while his dad sat on his recliner, a cigarette in one hand, a beer in the other.

Young George had savored those moments, because when his father was smoking and drinking and watching TV he wasn't raging at George and his mother and using his fists to work out his anger.

George said, "Huh?"

The bartender nodded at the shot glass in front of him.

"You've been playing with that for a half hour now."

"I have?"

He honestly hadn't been paying any attention to the time. All he knew was that he'd sat in his truck for close to an hour before breathing in a heavy sigh and climbing out. Then pausing at the front door, feeling the thump of the loud country music inside, as though crossing the threshold would be like entering Mordor.

The bartender leaned forward and squinted as he studied George.

"I shouldn't be worried about you, should I?"

"What do you mean?"

"You ain't planning on doing something stupid."

George couldn't look at the man as he shook his head, his gaze once more focusing on the amber liquid.

"It's just been a stressful couple of days."

"Oh, shit. That's right. You work for Ed. Hey, how's he doing?"

"Still unresponsive, last I heard."

"Well, damn. I'm sorry to hear that. I've never seen you in here before, but I've seen you at the shop. I hope Ed wakes up real soon."

George merely nodded and watched as the bartender sauntered down the bar to get somebody else a drink. Not even one o'clock in the afternoon and there were maybe a half-dozen people here. Regulars, George figured, and in the men's faces he saw a ghost of his own, of what was waiting for him if he went ahead and took that drink.

Because he knew he couldn't just have one. That had never been the case. One drink led to another which led to another which led to another until it got to the point George woke up in some strange place he'd never been before, his mouth sour and his head pounding.

He never knew how many drinks it took before he got to

the blackout stage, but he could hold his liquor well, right up there with the best of them.

Just like his old man.

Like father, like son.

Father ... shit, thinking of himself as a father was the only thing holding him back right now.

But what was the point? He hadn't seen his daughter in years. He doubted she would recognize him if he ever did happen to cross paths with her. A distant memory, that's all he was, and so nothing was keeping him from enjoying this drink.

Every time he closed his eyes, he saw those rifles where the engines should have been. George wasn't sure why they bothered him so much. He was used to seeing guns all over the place, but something about this was different. Something that caused him to lose sleep last night.

Maybe because he'd seen on the news yesterday morning that there'd been another school shooting—the woman on the TV said it was the twentieth this year. Only four people had been shot, no fatalities yet, so while that was something to be grateful for, George knew just like everybody else in the country that this shooting wasn't going to be the last.

And then there was his daughter to consider. Beautiful, sweet, precious Nina. She would be in, what, the seventh grade now? He couldn't even imagine receiving the call that she'd been gunned down by another classmate or some psycho who'd decided to breach the doors of her school.

That man from last night, Nova, had told him to pack up and leave town, and for about an hour or two George had honestly considered it.

But then the more he thought about it, the more he wondered just what the point would be. If he was in danger, that danger was sure to follow him wherever he went. And if he ended up in another town ... he didn't want to start all over again. Even though he didn't know many people here in

Remington, he had begun to think of it as home. And it also didn't feel right leaving while Ed—the only man who'd ever seemed to give a damn about him—lay on what very well may be his deathbed.

So he broke his word to Nova. He didn't pack his things. He didn't hightail it out of town. And because the world was so messed up and there was absolutely nothing he could do about it, he found himself out in the parking lot an hour ago, staring at the bar that he'd passed by thousands of times without even a second glance.

"Hot damn!"

The voice broke through the country music with enough force to make George jump.

The guy George recognized who worked at the motel slapped his hand on the bar and waved at the bartender.

"Get me a round, Jerry! It's time to celebrate."

The bartender grabbed a bottle and poured a shot.

"What're we celebrating, Wayne?"

"Word just got out. That outsider who's been causin' all that trouble? He's 'bout to get his ass handed to him."

"How so?"

"He's holed up in the Yellow Bird. They've cleared the place out. The sheriff's in there with him now, and there's some guys from out of town who are standin' guard to make sure he don't ever leave, if you get my drift."

Wayne threw back the shot, slammed the glass down with a whoop.

"Jesus, that's strong. Hey, did you know Mr. Hogan had me watchin' him? Paid me a hundred dollars a night to keep an eye on the bastard."

George said, "They're going to kill him?"

Wayne glanced over at him, irritated at first by the interruption. Then, an unnatural light in his eyes, he grinned.

"No, they're gonna arrest him, put him in jail, and let him

stand in front of a judge. Gimme a break. Course they're gonna kill him!"

The glee in Wayne's voice at the thought of a man dying sent a shot of ice through George's veins.

"Hey, where you goin'?"

George wasn't even aware that he'd stepped off his stool and was heading straight for the door until Wayne's voice cut through the fog in his head.

"Can I have your shot if you're not gonna drink it?"

Without answering, George pushed the bar door open and stepped into the light.

THIRTY-FIVE

Watching Veronica Chapman, Nova picked up her phone and placed it to his ear.

"I must have missed them when you and I met last night."

A brief pause on the line, and then Blake Hogan said, "What's that?"

"Your massive balls. After all, it takes giant cojones to kill three FBI agents and expect to get away with it."

Blake Hogan chuckled.

"Casanova, Casanova, Casanova. You have no idea what's going on. I can kill anyone I want and get away with it. Besides, once everything is all said and done, it will be *you* they believe killed those agents."

Nova was silent, staring out the window at the deputy and the three militiamen. They saw that he was on the phone and started forward, heading for the entrance. The driver lingered, keeping his rifle still strapped over his shoulder, wraparound shades zeroed in on Nova behind the plate glass.

"Casanova, are you there?"

"I'm here."

"And did you hear what I said?"

"Not really. It all just sounded like bullshit to me."

"We set up cameras in the house, you know. So I watched the entire thing. I think it's hilarious my girl tried to play possum with you."

Another chuckle, then a sigh.

"I was hoping they would have gotten it out of you before everything ... well, went sideways."

"You were hoping they would have gotten what out of me?"

"The truth. Of who you are. Of who you work for."

"I don't work for anyone."

"I find that very hard to believe."

"You want the truth, that's the truth."

"I don't think so. Ending up in this town right when you did ... I don't buy it."

"I don't care if you don't buy it."

"We know you were a SEAL. That you did some off-the-books work for the government. What that work is, I can only imagine, but a good portion of your file is redacted so it must have been a doozy."

Silent again, Nova watched as the deputy and the two men entered the cafe.

Blake Hogan said, "The official story will be that you went rogue. You're white, so they'll blame it on mental health. Maybe explain it on some belated PTSD from your time in the Navy. Whatever the case, you snapped and went on a killing spree. Who knows, maybe you didn't even know those three were agents. Or maybe you did—maybe you were targeting them specifically because ... well, we'll get that sorted out soon enough."

"All this just to keep trafficking weapons?"

"Is that all you think we're doing? Well, maybe you aren't so well informed after all. Trafficking those weapons is part of what we do, yes. We're patriots, you see. The only thing more

precious to us besides life and liberty is the Second Amendment. It's our God-given right."

"Sure it is."

Blake Hogan paused, and then laughed.

"Do I come off too strong? It's a persona, you know. Those
men there with you now are true believers. They actually
believe this shit. Whatever BS you feed them, they slurp it up."

"I'm sure they'd love to hear that."

"Go ahead and tell them. Do you think they'll believe
anything you say? As far as they're concerned, you're public
enemy number one."

"So then what's this all about?"

"What is pretty much everything about? Money. Power.
Legacy. You see, when my dad ran for the Senate, he realized
something about his constituency. And not just here in the
state, but all over the country. He realized that most people are
already wired to think a certain way. And he realized he would
have more power manipulating them to his own benefit than
trying to get anything done in Congress."

"How so?"

"Well, I'll tell you, things changed once the Internet came
around. Made it much easier to influence and indoctrinate
others. You ever heard of 4chan? We run a similar message
board dedicated to weapons. Weapons of all kinds. And we
play footsie with the skinheads and the militias and the like.
Basically, anybody who gets a hard-on reading the Turner
Diaries. There's one board in particular that attracts the real
crazies. We call it Bullet Country. It's named after the legend of
my great-great-grandfather—"

Nova cut him off.

"I've already heard the story. What do you do on the
board?"

"Oh, nothing much. Just stir the pot when the pot needs
stirring. That's where we attract the true believers. The ones

who are convinced any day now the government is going to show up on their doorstep with tanks. For whatever reason, they think they'd stand a chance against the entire United States military."

"Is that why you're selling them the automatic weapons?"

"Of course! These idiots think they're getting one up on the government by hoarding those guns. They'll pay whatever crazy markup we price them at."

"So you're not actually planning some kind of revolution."

Blake snorted and said, "We're just making money. If those true believer nutsos want to think they're building themselves some kind of army, then more power to them."

"Why are you telling me this?"

"Because you'll soon be dead, and it's not like you'll be able to tell anyone else. And the truth is it's difficult some days to keep a secret this big."

He was trying to impress him, Nova realized. Despite everything that Nova had done, this man was trying to make Nova respect him.

"Tell me, Blake, who's your guest staying in the cabin?"

Silence.

Nova grinned as he watched a pickup truck ease past the cafe. For a second or two, he almost didn't recognize it or the driver, but then those seconds passed and the pickup had slid out of view.

"Blake, you still there?"

"Nobody is staying in our cabin."

"Uh-huh."

"You really don't know what's going on, do you? Maybe you are telling the truth and you were just passing through. Interesting. Either way, it doesn't matter at this point. What's done is done."

Nova stared past Veronica Chapman at the deputy and the two militiamen. Each of the men stood motionless, sunglasses on their faces, gripping their rifles with the barrels pointed toward the faded linoleum. They each wore camo-colored tactical vests with quick release buckles and pouches already stuffed with magazines and flashbang grenades.

"Tell you what, Blake, I'm going to give you one last chance."

Another chuckle.

"One last chance?"

"Call off your men. Stop whatever it is you have planned."

"Or else what?"

"Or else I'll kill you."

This time Blake Hogan coughed out a full-throated laugh.

"You'll kill me? Why, Casanova, that's quite a scary threat. But no, I think I'll let my men take care of you as planned."

"Of course you will. Because you don't have the balls to do it yourself."

Silence.

"Tell me, Blake, did your daddy cut them off when you were a kid? Is that why you're such a bitch?"

More silence. It lasted five seconds. Ten.

Until he heard Blake Hogan's voice again, low and razor-sharp.

"Goodbye, asshole."

And the line went dead.

THIRTY-SIX

George parked his pickup behind the laundromat so that it was out of view of anyone driving down Main Street. He didn't shut the truck off right away and just sat there, staring ahead at nothing, trying to breathe normally.

He'd spotted Nova in the cafe. Along with at least three other men, all of whom were carrying weapons.

Wayne was right—they were going to kill him, no question about it.

The only question, really, was what did George think he could do about any of it?

He was no hero. He wasn't brave. Didn't he even tell Nova that he was a coward? Yes, he had, so why'd he leave the dark safety of the bar and park his truck here?

"Screw it."

He killed the engine and quickly climbed out. Then, before he could psych himself out of it, he hurried toward the garage, skirting the rear of the three buildings in between.

Stepping up to the back door, he already had his key in hand and was inside a second later, quietly pulling the door shut behind him.

The garage was silent, as expected. The only sound was George's heart thumping in his ears and a voice in his head reminding him that he was no hero.

"Shut up."

His whisper sounded like a cry in the silence.

He wasn't sure what the plan was or if he even had the slightest hint of one. All he knew was that the guy who'd saved Ed Schaffer's life was in danger. And if George could help him, then … well, maybe his own life wouldn't feel like such a waste.

Peeking out the window in the large bay door, he saw Nova and the others were still in the cafe.

Would the men kill him there or take him someplace else to kill him?

He gazed around the shop, trying to find something that might work. A weapon that he could use against men with assault rifles like the ones hidden under the hoods of those cars last night.

Besides a bunch of ratchets and socket wrenches and other tools, nothing looked promising, and that voice whispering in his head suddenly sounded vindicated.

See? that voice said. There's nothing you can do. You're no hero. You've never been, and you never will be.

Maybe.

Maybe not.

Because George now found himself staring at the truck parked in the middle of the garage.

Ed's 2010 Toyota Tacoma.

The other day, after the ambulance had taken Ed away and the police were done with their questions, George called Mandy to ask what she wanted to do with Ed's truck and Mandy had said to leave it there for now. So he'd parked the truck in the garage, backing it in so that once Ed woke up and returned from the hospital he could drive it right out with no trouble.

Now he realized the truck was more or less aimed straight at the cafe.

It took him only a minute to find the items he needed.

Several rubber bungee cords, which he'd use to keep the steering wheel in place.

And a dead car battery, which he'd use to keep the gas pedal applied.

The trick would be putting it in gear without George being inside.

For a minute or two, he realized this wasn't going to work.

Then an idea hit him, and he found himself smiling. His voice, an eager whisper.

"Ed, please forgive me. But I hope you've got good insurance."

THIRTY-SEVEN

Nova slid the phone back across the table.

"Blake told me to tell you it's all a big misunderstanding and to let me go."

Veronica Chapman took her phone back, tapped her fingernail thoughtfully on the tabletop, and issued a heavy sigh.

"All right, it's time to go."

Nova was watching the deputy and the two men with the assault rifles again. It was hard to look away. Especially when you realized one if not more of these men would be shooting him in the head in the next couple of minutes.

He still had his FNX-45, but no way he could clear it before one of the men, already holding their weapons at the ready, placed a bullet in his face.

He could wait for Veronica Chapman to slide out of the booth first and step up behind her and use her as a shield.

But no, she wouldn't be so stupid, as proven a second later when she called out.

"David, come escort Mr. Bartkowski outside."

The deputy started forward, hand on the butt of his service pistol, his other hand reaching for a pair of handcuffs … while outside, directly across the street, the large garage door was starting to rise.

One of the men with the rifles whispered something to the other, who nodded and looked like he was going to turn around to head outside.

Nova shouted, "Hey, you two assholes!"

Both men paused. Turned to look back at him. Their faces, stone.

"Yeah, I'm talking to you two lame-dick losers."

The garage door had risen the entire way up. Nova could see a Toyota pickup parked in the bay. And George Murphy standing beside the truck, reaching in the open window.

Nova said, "Want to hear a joke?"

The two men made no reply.

The deputy started to glance back at them, and Nova raised his voice even louder.

"What about you, deputy no-dick?"

The deputy focused again on Nova, his eyes narrowed. His jaw, clenched.

Nova didn't have any joke in mind, but he needed to stall because he realized what George Murphy was doing and felt conflicted—on the one hand, George shouldn't be anywhere near what was about to happen, while on the other hand, this might give Nova the slimmest of chances.

"What do you call three assholes who just walked into a cafe?"

Across the street, the Toyota bucked and shot forward, the sun glinting off its front windshield as it raced right for the Yellow Bird.

All three men were watching him, as was Veronica Chapman, a slight frown on her face.

Nova said, "Roadkill."

The Toyota's tires jumped the curb with ease. The front end bounced up and the grille came smashing through the front door, a tornado of glass spraying everywhere.

One of the militiamen was struck with such force that he flew through the air, while the other man was clipped and sent reeling to the floor.

The truck didn't slow, though, and kept coming, straight for the deputy. The man was standing far enough from the door that he managed to dive out of the way in time, and then the truck slammed into the rear wall and stalled out.

Veronica started to slide out of the booth, reaching for her gun. Nova made a split-second decision and abandoned the FNX-45, jumping out of the booth right as she did. The sheriff standing tall, bringing up her weapon—which Nova latched onto as he twisted her around and aimed at the deputy climbing to his feet, and with his finger over the sheriff's, squeezed the trigger three times.

Two of the rounds hit the deputy—one in the chest, the other in the throat—and as he fell back to the ground, Nova jerked Veronica's arm so that her pistol was now aimed at the militiaman who'd gotten clipped by the truck.

The man was back on his feet now too, having regained control of his weapon, bringing up the barrel of his M4A1 as Nova again squeezed his finger over Veronica Chapman's, firing another three rounds.

One of the rounds hit the man in the shoulder, spinning him around as he applied pressure to the rifle's trigger, a spray of bullets tearing into the cafe's ceiling.

By that point Veronica must have realized wresting the pistol from Nova's grip was useless. So instead she clamped her teeth on his arm and bit.

Instinctively he fell back, reaching for the FNX-45 on the booth as he tripped and stumbled onto his ass.

Nova aimed up at Veronica Chapman as she aimed down at him.

"Don't make me shoot you," he said.

The man who'd gotten shot in the shoulder was back on his feet. He rushed forward, kicking aside a broken chair, and shouted at Veronica, "Get out of the way!"

She glanced back at him, then did a double take.

"Watch out!"

Before the man could turn, George Murphy had appeared behind him, having followed in the wake of the pickup's destruction. He raised the socket wrench in his hand and brought it down on the back of the man's head, a solid strike that resulted in the man dropping to the floor like a rag doll.

When Veronica turned back to Nova, he was already on his feet, less than a yard away, his pistol aimed right at her head.

"Set it on the table."

Glare full of acid, it didn't look like she was going to comply until after a beat she carefully placed her Glock on the table.

Nova shifted his aim as the driver of the Ram—who'd decided to come running into the fray instead of burning rubber down Main Street—charged around the corner to enter the cafe through the open space the Toyota had created. As the man stepped inside, raising his assault rifle, Nova's bullet entered the front of his face and exited through the back, spraying the wall with blood.

Shifting his aim back at the sheriff, Nova said, "Now pull out your keys, slowly."

Her glare drilling into him, she pulled out her keys and placed them on the table next to her gun.

Nova grabbed the keys as well his iPhone, then motioned with the FNX-45 for her to move toward the front of the cafe.

"Let's move."

George made sure to give Veronica Chapman a wide berth as she stepped over one of the dead militiamen. George still gripped the socket wrench dripping with blood in his hand. His eyes found Nova's, and Nova saw the fear and panic there.

Nova motioned for the mechanic to follow, and then bent to grab one of the militiamen's rifle and gear.

They headed for Veronica's truck. The sun momentarily displayed the empty street with its bright glare before ducking behind another cloud.

Nova had her lean up against the side and keeping his pistol trained on her quickly patted her down. The only thing he took away was her pair of handcuffs. He opened the passenger-side door and motioned for her to get in.

She hesitated.

"Where are we going?"

Nova didn't answer, only stared back at her, the FNX-45 trained on her chest.

As soon as she'd climbed up into the Ford, Nova pocketed his pistol and leaned in and grabbed her left arm. Snapping one of the cuffs around it, he threaded the rest of the handcuffs through the grab bar on the A-pillar before snapping the other cuff onto her other wrist.

"What are you *doing*?"

Nova slammed the door shut without a word, then headed around the back of the truck where he found George Murphy standing with the socket wrench still in his hand, looking dazed.

"Hey."

Nova gently grabbed the mechanic's shoulder to get his attention.

"You okay?"

The man blinked, swallowed.

"I … I can't believe that just happened."

"Thank you, by the way."

"Did I … did I kill that man?"

"Probably."

"Oh my God."

Nova's iPhone buzzed in his pocket. He pulled it out, saw that Atticus had emailed him.

Backup on its way. Should be there in less than an hour.

Slipping the phone back into his pocket, he glanced up at George and noted the man's pale face.

"Are you sure you're okay?"

George stared at him for a moment, and then shook his head.

"I saw you were in trouble, and I did what I did. After I sent the truck in, I grabbed this"—he hesitantly hefted the socket wrench, as if it were alien technology—"and came running."

Nova knew the man was still trying to process what just happened, and he gently patted him on the shoulder.

"I'm glad you did. And I wouldn't fault you at all if you want to get the hell out of here. But I could use your help with one more thing."

When they got into the truck, Veronica Chapman sat awkwardly in the shotgun seat. She looked first at George Murphy as he slid behind the steering wheel, then back at Nova.

"Where are you taking me?"

"To see your boss."

THIRTY-EIGHT

Blake Hogan sat in silence for a long time, his phone in hand, thinking about his conversation with Casanova Bartkowski.

He didn't like not knowing who the man worked for. Sure, the outsider claimed he didn't work for anyone, but that had to be bullshit, right?

No matter. He'd be brought here very soon. They already had a new tarp laid out in the barn, the same metal folding chair on top that Marc had been secured to earlier in the day.

Truth be told, Blake didn't relish torturing people. He didn't like watching it done, and he certainly didn't like doing it himself.

But it wasn't like the outsider had given him much choice. Half his men were dead, and he wasn't sure how far to trust these patriots he'd called for help. The first team had arrived in no time, and they would bring the outsider here. Others were on their way and should arrive shortly.

He hit the mouse to wake up all his screens. There were a half-dozen in total, all logged into various message boards. As he did every time he was online, he used a secure web browser and a VPN to mask his location.

He browsed the different boards, grinning as he read posts mentioning "deep state" and "civil war" and "Soros-backed communists." Typically he would chime in from one of his countless accounts, trying to stir the pot, but the truth was he didn't need to stir the pot much anymore. Every day that went by these posters became even more obsessed, more agitated, more enraged. Each a stick of dynamite just waiting to be set off.

A knock sounded at his office door.

Closing out his monitors, he called, "Come in."

Marc opened the door and stepped inside.

"It's done."

"They're on the road?"

"Yes."

Blake stood, stretching his back and neck to the point he heard a soft pop.

"Hungry?"

"I could eat."

The help would be back on Monday, but in the meantime they could scrounge something up. He motioned for Marc to follow him and headed down the hallway toward the kitchen. The midafternoon sun slanted through the windows, dust motes floating in the bars of golden light.

Halfway to the kitchen, Carson stepped around the corner, halting them.

"Your father would like to see you."

Blake made to step past the man, saying, "It can wait," but Carson's hand against his chest stopped him.

"He wants to see you now."

His jaw tightening, Blake told Marc to go on ahead and that he'd catch up. Then he turned back and headed straight for his father's den. There wasn't any place else his old man was during the day. He found his father staring at his large computer monitor, the screen's soft glow shining off his glasses.

Tripp Hogan clicked something with his mouse, then turned his attention to his son.

"Our guest?"

"Is already on his way."

"Who's driving?"

"Finlay."

"Finlay," his father echoed, tone flat. "The man with a broken leg."

"He can still drive."

"That distance?"

"Look, the options were slim. With everything going on, I felt it was better to keep Marc close by. Especially with the outsider coming here soon."

Tripp glanced again at his screen, then shook his head.

"I don't agree with this plan."

"I know you don't."

"I will admit, I made a mistake. The man is more dangerous than I believed him to be. He should be eliminated as soon as possible."

"I agree. But first, I think we might be able to get information out of him."

"Suppose he is working for someone—what's to say he hasn't already contacted them?"

"Dad, this is the only way we'll know for sure."

Glancing again at the monitor, Tripp Hogan said, "Everything's already in place on our end."

"How many shares?"

"The max."

Blake grinned. For months now they'd been buying up thousands of shares every couple of weeks so as not to tip off the FTC once the stock prices surged. They were already rich but were soon going to be even richer.

Then he noticed something in his father's face, and his grin faded.

"What is it?"

"I thought I taught you better."

"What are you talking about?"

"You shouldn't have told the outsider anything. Not even a hint."

"How did you—"

But Blake stopped himself, immediately seeing it.

"You were spying on me? Listening in on my phone call?"

His father stared back at him without any emotion.

"Spare me your outrage. This is my house. I can do whatever the hell I please."

"How often are you spying on me?" His throat suddenly went dry. "What about my bedroom?"

His father said nothing.

Warmth entered Blake's face. His fingers flexed into fists.

A broad smile spread across Tripp Hogan's face.

"You want to hit me? Go ahead, Son. See what happens."

He sensed Carson lingering in the doorway, a rabid dog obedient to do whatever its master commanded.

Silent, he turned away and strode toward the door. Carson's large frame filled the doorway as he watched Blake, and then he slowly moved aside to let Blake pass.

As Blake stepped out into the hallway, he was half-conscious of Carson turning away, so that his back was to Blake.

Carson thought he knew everything there was to know about Blake—what he would do, how he would react.

That assumption was his downfall.

Because Blake immediately spun around, drawing his pistol from his holster, and fired a round into the back of Carson's head.

The man hit the ground with a hollow thud. A wisp of smoke haunted the air from the barrel of Blake's pistol. He stepped back into the room as Tripp reached for the gun in his desk drawer.

"I wouldn't do that if I were you."

Tripp Hogan's face rippled with rage.

"You've made a grave error in judgment, Son."

Blake merely smiled as he advanced closer, keeping his pistol aimed at his father's face.

"Not so tough anymore without your attack dog, are you?"

"Carson was family."

"Spare me. I'm sick and tired of you thinking that you're the one running the show. *I'm* the one who's running it."

His father shook his head, his expression sorrowful.

"I failed you, Son."

Footsteps stormed up the hallway, and Marc appeared, SIG in hand. He paused when he noted Carson's body on the floor and Blake walking behind the desk, aiming his gun at the back of his father's head.

"Everything okay?"

Blake said, "Everything's peachy."

He grabbed the pistol from the drawer, stuffed it in his waistband, then motioned for his father to move out from behind the desk.

That's when an alert came up on the computer monitor.

A security alert, signaling that a vehicle had just pulled into the driveway.

On the monitor, a box in the lower left-hand corner popped open, showing a familiar F-150 headed up the drive.

Keeping his pistol aimed at his father, Blake Hogan grinned at Marc.

"Looks like our new guest has arrived."

THIRTY-NINE

The whole ride Veronica Chapman had stayed silent, fuming as she sat leaning forward with her hands secured to the grab bar, but when they headed up the long drive toward the house, she finally shifted in her seat to glance back at Nova.

"You don't have to do this."

Nova rechecked the load on the M4A1 as well as the sheriff's Glock. He trusted the FNX-45 because it was his and he'd loaded it, but it was never wise to trust a weapon you haven't taken apart and put back together again.

"Do what?"

"Whatever it is you're planning to do."

Nova smiled at her.

"Who says I'm planning to do anything? I'd just like to have a little chat with Blake about the guy he's been hosting."

A genuine frown crossed Veronica's face.

"What guy he's been hosting?"

Interesting. Nova had assumed the sheriff was privy to everything going on in Hogan World. If she didn't know about the guy in the cabin, that presented an extra wrinkle that Nova hadn't anticipated.

Just who the hell was this guy?

George Murphy had also stayed silent the entire drive, sitting rigid, both hands on the wheel. Now as the pickup began to decelerate, he cleared his throat.

"What … what do you want me to do now?"

The hesitant tone gave Nova pause. He worried the man might not manage to keep going until the cavalry arrived. Whenever that would be.

"See Blake's Range Rover? Park right behind it."

The truth was, Nova still didn't have a solid plan in mind. But they couldn't wait at the cafe or someplace else in town. Other militiamen might show up before the FBI, and Nova wasn't sure he could hold them off alone. And besides, he remembered Dean Roberts's words about how whatever was going to happen was going to happen very soon, and he didn't want to wait because what if whatever that was happened within the hour?

Veronica Chapman sneered, "What do you think you're going to do—ring the doorbell?"

As the Ford came to a halt, Nova strapped the rifle over his shoulder and grabbed the door handle.

"Guess we'll see in about fifteen seconds."

Then he paused, meeting George's eyes in the rearview mirror. He held up the sheriff's Glock.

"Can you handle this if I leave it with you?"

George's eyes were wide in the mirror. He nodded, swallowing.

Nova hesitated again, then passed the gun up to George.

"If you need to use it, just hold it tight and squeeze the trigger." He took a breath. "I'll be back as soon as I can."

He hadn't taken even ten steps past the truck when the side door leading into the kitchen—the same door he'd entered yesterday—opened.

Blake Hogan stepped out. By the expression on his face,

plus the easiness in which he carried himself, it was clear he hadn't expected to find Nova headed toward him, an assault rifle strapped over his shoulder with a pistol in his hand.

Following Blake a step behind was another man. Nova recognized him as the lackey from Hogan Auto yesterday. Marc Palmer.

The man already had his gun in hand and brought it up, but Nova was faster, firing off two rounds into his chest.

Blake froze, but only for a second. Even from forty feet away, Nova saw the conflict flash through his eyes: grab for his pistol or dive back inside the house.

The coward he was, Blake dove back inside.

Nova sprinted forward. He checked that the other man was dead, then, crouching, moved closer to the house. Clouds dipped in front of the sun again, shadowing the earth. Silence except for the familiar ringing in his ears.

"Blake! Can you hear me? I just want to talk!"

A beat of silence, and then three rounds tore through the side of the house from inside the kitchen.

Blake's voice, hoarse and full of energy: "Fuck you!"

From his back pocket, Nova fished out the flashbang grenade he'd lifted from the dead militiaman back at the cafe.

"Are you sure you don't want to talk this out?"

Four more rounds tore through the side of the house, the window shattering and sending a shower of shards down on top of him.

Nova pulled the pin and tossed the grenade through the broken window.

Two and a half seconds—that's all the time the grenade allowed—before a raucous *BOOM* exploded from inside with enough force to cause the loose shards of glass on the windowsill to shake.

Nova tore around the corner, sweeping his pistol left and

right. Blake Hogan was crouched behind a long table, gun in hand, pressing on his ear with the heel of his other hand.

"Put it down!"

Blake, his face twisted in pain, glanced up at him only briefly before he started to raise his gun.

Before Nova could fire, the cabinet beside his head burst apart. Ducking, he swung back and saw Tripp Hogan in the doorway now, one of the antique rifles in his hands. The recoil had caused the wheelchair to roll back. The old man worked the bolt, ejecting the spent cartridge and pushing a new cartridge into the chamber, but his finger barely touched the trigger before Nova's bullet punched through the front of his face.

"Dad!"

Blake Hogan started toward his father, instantly realized he was dead, then wheeled around and fired wildly in Nova's direction until, all at once, his pistol's slide kicked back.

Empty.

Nova advanced through the kitchen, keeping the FNX-45 trained on Blake as he watched in his peripheral vision for anyone else popping out of a doorway.

"You killed him," Blake said quietly, staring down at his father. Then, gun having dropped from his hand, his fingers squeezed into fists, he turned, his face bunched up in rage: "You killed him!"

Now only ten feet separated them. Nova kept his aim on Blake's face, though he didn't intend on killing the man. Not until he got the information he needed.

"Where's Carson?"

"Fuck you!"

"Who's the guy staying in the cabin?"

"Fuck you!"

"You want to end up like your father? Because if you don't

tell me what I want to know, I'll put a bullet in both of your knees. You'll never walk again."

Blake squared his shoulders, his hands still balling in and out of fists. His lips moving silently until, after a second, they made sound.

"Fuck … you."

Nova's grip tightened on the pistol. They didn't have time to screw around.

But before he could say or do anything, the steady beat of rapid gunfire—what was clearly from an assault rifle—sounded from outside.

FORTY

"You're in a lot of trouble, George. You realize that, don't you?"

George Murphy ignored the dead body lying on the ground only yards away from them and kept his eyes glued on the door where Nova had disappeared only seconds ago. He held the gun Nova had given him—the sheriff's gun—so tight his hand was shaking.

"You can still make things right. I can help you."

As soon as Nova had disappeared into the house, Sheriff Chapman started talking. Trying to get into this head. Trying to mess with him.

He said quietly, as though to himself, "Stop it."

"Nova isn't your friend. He's a criminal. This whole thing— it's one big misunderstanding."

"I said, stop it!"

He saw a flicker of surprise cross the sheriff's face. Her eyes quickly darted down at the gun in his hand.

"Do you even know how to use that? I don't want you hurting yourself, George."

George realized there was some gunfire coming from inside the house. It had almost gotten lost behind the blood pounding in his ears. Nova and Blake Hogan and whoever else was in there were shooting at each other.

For a brief second, George thought about racing in there too, the sheriff's gun at his side. Stepping in at the last moment to save Nova's life, just like back at the cafe.

But no, that wasn't going to happen. He wasn't brave, no matter what he might tell himself.

"You don't want to go to prison. Do you, George?"

He looked at her again, saw the smugness on her face, and found himself grinning.

"*I'm* not going to prison. *You* are."

She stared at him for a beat, tilted her head slightly.

"Are you sure about that?"

George didn't answer. He was listening to the gunfire again.

Sheriff Chapman said, "Well, well, well. What do we have here?"

He didn't know what she meant at first—did she see something about the house he'd missed?—but then he realized she had shifted in her seat with her neck twisted back to look out the rear of the truck.

That's when he glanced up at the rearview mirror.

That's when he saw the two trucks—one SUV, one pickup —speeding up the long drive.

"Who … who is that?"

"My guess, George? More militiamen. Those back at the cafe were only the first to arrive."

George felt his blood go cold.

"Let me go, George. I'll talk to them. I'll make sure they understand the situation. I'll work it out so that they don't kill you."

"You … you're lying."

She tilted her head slightly again, her eyes large and full of empathy.

"Do you want to bet your life on it?"

He eyed the rearview mirror again. The two trucks were now halfway up the drive.

Licking his dry lips, he asked, "How would I let you go?"

The sheriff lifted her chin.

"I keep a spare key under the floor mat."

George figured she was lying, but when he eyed the rearview mirror again—the trucks almost here—he leaned down and felt around under the mat until his fingers touched the cool metal.

A second later he'd handed her the key, and five seconds later she'd unclasped the one cuff and then slid her other arm free.

"Now give me my gun."

George pressed his back against the door, aiming the gun at her. He shook his head.

Her jaw clenching, she glared back at him one last time before opening her door.

"Stay low and out of sight until I've handled this."

Then she stepped out of the truck, keeping the door open, and started moving toward the two approaching vehicles, raising her hands high to get their attention.

The SUV was ahead of the pickup—not even one hundred feet away—and it slid to a halt at once. The passenger-side door swung open, and a man stepped out with an assault rifle in hand.

Sheriff Chapman, maybe realizing her uniform put her at a disadvantage, raised her voice to almost a scream.

"Wait! I'm on your side! I'm working with—"

The rest of her words were drowned out by the sudden roar of the man's rifle. A score of bullets tore into the sheriff's body, causing it to jitter and shake like a marionette.

She was on the ground, dead, a second later, and George found his hands shaking even harder than before, knowing that the sheriff's gun was in no way enough to protect him against the firepower these men possessed.

His mind raced. He realized the key was still in the ignition at the same moment he glanced up back and saw the man who'd killed Sheriff Chapman notice him in the truck and swing up the barrel.

George had the Ford started and in reverse in less than a second. He ducked low as the man opened fire and the rear window shattered and bullets thumped into the truck, and then it was the man's body that thumped into the truck before a second later the tailgate crashed right into the front of the SUV. George reached up to put the truck in drive before slamming on the gas and lurching forward, still staying low so he didn't see where he was going, until suddenly the airbag popped as the truck slammed into a wall.

Dazed, George grabbed the gun off the floor and crawled across the seat toward the passenger door that Sheriff Chapman had left open. He didn't realize he'd crashed into Blake Hogan's Defender until he dropped to the ground. He heard shouting and he heard shooting, and it didn't hit him right away that he was hearing several different guns shooting and realized that Nova was back outside, using Blake's truck for cover as he returned fire on the militiamen.

George's ears were ringing from the airbag. He felt blood on his face and realized it was coming from his nose. The gun was still in his hand but it felt like a stone and he looked around, still not sure what was going on, when he heard someone shouting at him.

"Get behind something!"

Nova. Nova was shouting at him. Nova was scrambling forward to grab his shoulder and yank him to his feet and push him toward the house.

"Run!"

George's body moved on autopilot, hurrying along the side

of the massive house, while Nova disappeared around the corner and even more gunfire rang out.

How many men were in those two vehicles? How many guns? How many bullets?

George didn't know where to go, where to hide, so he kept moving. Staying low. Staying close to the house for cover.

He heard more thumping and for a second wondered if that was his heart again but then realized it was a helicopter flying over the house.

He shuffled forward, tasting blood in his mouth, seeing snapshots of Sheriff Chapman's body being ravaged by bullets, when suddenly a man appeared in front of him.

The man had rounded the corner, looking for cover just like George. He carried the same assault rifle the other men had at the cafe. For a moment, he looked anxious, like he didn't know where to hide, and then his eyes fixed on George and the barrel of the rifle started to swing up, and George wanted to raise the gun too—he wanted to aim it at the man and squeeze the trigger like they do in all the movies—but his hand wouldn't move and instead of watching the man kill him he squeezed his eyes shut and braced for the bullet's impact.

A single shot, one that was somehow louder than all the rest.

George flinched.

He stood partly crouched, his eyes closed, waiting for the pain.

After two seconds, he opened his eyes.

The man with the rifle was on the ground. Half of his head blown apart.

And stepping around the corner, a pistol in hand, was Nova.

Nova scanned the area for any other militiamen. Then he started forward, holstering his gun, and gently grabbed George by the arm to help him stand.

"Come on, let's go."

"What … what about the others?"

"The others are all dead. Or under arrest."

The words—George heard them, but they didn't make any sense.

"Under … arrest?"

"Yes, George. Backup finally arrived. The FBI is here."

FORTY-ONE

But it wasn't only the FBI.

The Air Force had arrived too, flying straight from Malmstrom Air Force Base near Great Falls in a Sikorsky HH-60G Pave Hawk. The helo's max speed was 184 mph, so it traveled the 170 miles in less than an hour, beating SWAT by mere minutes.

Now the helicopter sat perched on the massive field in front of the house, the late-afternoon sun cutting a long shadow. Several black SUVs had also arrived within the past two hours, parked every which way.

Due to the potential threat of more militiamen showing up, several agents patrolled the perimeter while checkpoints were set up on all roads leading into town.

Two ambulances had shown up. EMTs looked over George Murphy and helped set his broken nose while another pair of EMTs looked over Nova as he recounted the events of the past several days to FBI agents while a man from the Air Force stood nearby.

Nova kept a few details to himself as he wasn't sure how to proceed with them just yet, and he made sure to keep that in mind when he recounted his story yet again for another pair of agents.

Then another car arrived, a black sedan. Two agents climbed out—a middle-aged man with short brown hair and an Asian woman in her thirties. Both wore suits and sunglasses, and the man introduced himself as Special Agent James McGuire and the woman as Special Agent Angela Bowen.

Agent Bowen barely glanced at Nova before stepping away to meet with another agent.

James McGuire looked stressed beyond belief, which was to be expected when Nova learned he was the one who'd sent Dean Roberts and the other two agents in on this operation.

"Christ," he said, rubbing his jaw, "they've all got families."

Then McGuire's eyes narrowed a bit at Nova.

"Why did you come to this town again?"

"To fish."

"You killed, what, at least a half-dozen men? The answer *to fish* isn't going to cut it."

That's when the man from the Air Force cleared his throat.

"Unfortunately, his answer will need to suffice."

Agent McGuire said, "Who the hell are you again?"

"Chief Master Sergeant Ben Howard."

In his early fifties, muscular jaw and piercing blue eyes, the man wore the Army combat uniform that the Air Force had adopted in 2018. The four other men who'd flown in on the Pave Hawk and who were helping to patrol the perimeter wore the same.

Agent McGuire stared at Howard for a moment, then shook his head as he surveyed the bodies lying around the property. One of those bodies was Veronica Chapman, who George Murphy stated was killed by the militiamen.

Finally the agent turned to Nova.

"You must have friends in some pretty high places."

Howard said, "He does. How else do you think your agency and ours mobilized so fast?"

McGuire placed a hand on his forehead and massaged his temple with his fingers.

"They were still checking in, just like before. Those assholes who killed my agents, I mean. That's how we had no idea anything had happened."

Nova said, "It's not over."

McGuire's eyes narrowed again as he frowned.

"What do you mean?"

"A man was staying in the cabin out in the valley. I told your agents when they first arrived. They went to check the cabin but said it was empty."

McGuire said, "We don't know who this man is?"

"No idea. Blake Hogan refuses even to acknowledge he exists."

"Blake Hogan," the agent said, nearly spitting the words. "Where is that piece of shit?"

Howard motioned toward the house.

"He's inside with a few of your agents. From what I understand, he keeps asking for a lawyer. Plus"—the chief master sergeant's eyes slid to Nova—"he has a nasty bruise on the side of his head."

Nova shrugged.

"Those militia assholes showed up and I didn't have an extra pair of handcuffs, so I knocked him out with the butt of my rifle."

Agent Bowen returned to the group.

"We have people at the dealership now. They're going over everything."

"Any rifles?" McGuire asked.

"Quite a few."

"What else?"

"We also have people searching the grounds. But there's a

lot of ground to cover, so it's unclear how much longer it will take."

Nova said, "Where'd they get the rifles, anyway?"

Agents McGuire and Bowen shared a glance but said nothing.

"Well?"

McGuire cleared his throat, clearly not happy about having to explain himself to a man he'd only met ten minutes ago.

"We're still not entirely sure. That's why we've been keeping this op going for so long. To determine not just who is getting these weapons, but where they're coming from."

Howard said, "There can't be that many choices. It's either the manufacturer or an armory."

"Or both," Nova said. "Blake Hogan made it sound like they've got a lot of 'patriots' stationed in every agency. In fact, Special Agent McGuire, how well do you trust your people?"

McGuire's glare burned almost as hot as the sun above them.

"I still don't understand why you're still here. You want a pat on the back for doing such a swell job?"

"What I want, Agent McGuire, is to figure out what's going on and stop it before it happens."

"Before what happens?"

"Agent Roberts told me that something big was going to happen very soon. And based on how adamant Blake Hogan has been at denying the man in the cabin even exists, I'm guessing it has something to do with his mystery guest."

McGuire turned to Agent Bowen.

"Has the cabin been swept?"

"It has. They've found some prints, but it could take a while before we get back any matches, assuming we get anything at all."

Another agent hurried over to them, radio in hand. Agent Bowen stepped away to speak to the agent, and as she did Nova glanced over at where George Murphy was sitting near the barn. The man had a white bandage on his nose. Even now, almost two hours later, he looked dazed, staring out at the helicopter in the field but not really seeing it.

Agent Bowen thanked the agent and rejoined the group.

McGuire read the worry on her face and asked, "What's wrong?"

She said, "Our people found something we need to see."

FORTY-TWO

The smell was the first thing that hit them.

A stench, really, one big enough to almost knock them over as they climbed out of the UTV they'd commandeered from the Hogans' barn.

Nova knew what it was—what it had to be—but didn't say anything as he followed Special Agents McGuire and Bowen, staying a few paces back. Neither had objected to him riding along, at least not verbally, though he'd seen an annoyed look in McGuire's eyes before they started over the hill and past the empty cabin for another two miles until they reached this spot.

McGuire lifted the tail of his tie to hold to his nose and mouth.

"Christ."

The pit was maybe twenty feet across, twenty feet deep. It had been dug by some mechanical digger long ago for what Nova figured was this very purpose.

There wasn't any smoke issuing from the pit, but the acrid stench was enough to confirm a fire had raged here earlier. Maybe earlier today or sometime late last night.

Down in the pit were skeletons.

Most of the remains had become ash, but a few pieces—the outline of a skull in particular—made it explicit they were human remains.

"The girls," Nova said quietly.

The two agents turned to look at him.

Bowen said, "What was that?"

"The guy at the cabin told me Blake and his dad had been sending him girls. He made it pretty clear he was having sex with them. My guess is they were put here."

McGuire asked, "What makes you say that?"

"Blake Hogan refuses to acknowledge the guy. Even your agent told me nobody had seen him. My guess is they wanted to guarantee there were no witnesses to whoever he is. In fact…"

But Nova didn't say anything more, glancing again down into the pit.

The undercover agent, Dean Roberts, was likely included with the other remains.

McGuire addressed the agent who'd found the pit and was lingering off to the side.

"ETA?"

The agent said, "A team is coming ASAP. But I still don't have an exact ETA."

"Call them again. Tell them I need them here now. We need to determine how many bodies are down there and whether one of them is—"

McGuire cut himself off, shaking his head.

"Just get them here."

Then he turned back to Nova and Agent Bowen, and sighed.

"Let's go see this cabin."

They found two agents inside the cabin, wearing baggies on their shoes, snapping photos of every item.

Nova and McGuire and Bowen put pairs of baggies on their feet so they could move through the cabin. Living area, kitchen, massive bedroom. Even with the windows open, the place stank of sex.

McGuire asked one of the agents, "Did either of you open the windows?"

One of the agents paused with his camera in hand, and shook his head.

"No, sir. The windows were already open when we got here."

Airing the place out. Blake Hogan or whoever had no doubt done that as soon as their guest had departed.

But where had he gone?

Hands on his hips, gazing once more around the cabin, Agent McGuire nodded and glanced at his partner.

"I think it's time we have a chat with Mr. Hogan."

George Murphy was still sitting in one of the chairs outside the barn when they returned.

As the agents headed into the house, Nova broke away and strode over to the mechanic.

"How are you holding up?"

George was still staring out at the helicopter in the field. He didn't look at Nova but shrugged.

Nova said, "Why don't you go home?"

George's face slowly swiveled toward him. His eyes were wide, his face gaunt.

"Home? What home? You mean that shitty apartment I've been living in? That … that's not home."

Nova said nothing.

"I thought I was going to die. I've never really thought that a day in my life, not once. But today ... I honestly believed I was going to die."

Nova offered up a small smile.

"You get used to it."

George slowly shook his head, staring back out at the field.

"My ex-wife told me that once. How she thought she was going to die when I got into one of my drunken rages. I hadn't believed her at the time—I just thought she was overreacting—but now ... now I get what she meant. And, Jesus, it shouldn't take almost getting killed by a bunch of assholes with guns to see that, but here I am."

"Maybe you should tell her that."

"What?"

"That you're sorry. That you're a different man. You could maybe see your daughter."

George, shaking his head again: "Nah, it's a lost cause. I'm never going to see Nina again."

A young female agent approached them.

"Mr. Murphy? We have a car ready to take you home."

George groaned as he stood from the chair. He looked at Nova, nodded once, and then followed the agent to an idling car.

Nova watched them go. He waited until the car had disappeared down the long drive before he headed toward the house.

The two FBI agents and Chief Master Sergeant Howard exited the side door as he reached the house, all three looking frustrated.

Nova said, "He still stonewalling you?"

"Just keeps saying *lawyer*, again and again," McGuire said. "But you're right—something big is happening very soon."

"How do you know?"

"Because when we asked him, that little shit got this smile

on his face for only a second before he asked again for a lawyer."

Nova closed his eyes, took a deep breath. But all he saw were the skeletal remains in that pit. The bodies as they were thrown onto the bed of ashes. The kerosene that was poured onto the bodies before a match was lit and tossed down below.

Opening his eyes, he asked, "How badly do you want to know what Blake Hogan is hiding?"

McGuire said, "Pretty goddamn bad, but at this point our hands are tied."

Nova gazed out over the large field. The sun was already starting to dip toward the horizon, purple shadows stretching across the helicopter.

"You're right," he said. "Your hands are tied. But not mine."

FORTY-THREE

Blake Hogan stayed silent as Nova marched him through the kitchen and out the side door, but once he realized where they were headed, he suddenly spoke up.

"Where are we going?"

Silent, Nova propelled him forward, gripping his arm. Blake, his hands bound behind his back, twisted to look at him.

"Where are you taking me?"

Nova said nothing.

"I want my lawyer! Do you hear me? Lawyer!"

They reached the Pave Hawk, the massive rotor blades looming over them. Nova pushed Blake toward the open side door.

"Get in."

Blake spun around, his eyes going wide.

"What the fuck are you doing?"

Nova drew his FNX-45, aimed it right at the man's face.

"I'm not going to tell you again."

Blake's wide eyes shifted all around the property, frantic.

"Where is everybody? Where's Jimmy? Where'd all the agents go?"

Nova cocked the pistol's hammer back.

"Move."

Blake glared back at him, shaking his head.

"You're not going to do anything to me."

Nova smacked him across the face with the pistol, then stowed the gun in his waistband as he hefted Blake up into the helo and slammed him into one of the troop seats.

Nova jumped in after him, grabbing a headset and fitting it over Blake's ears.

"How do those feel?"

Sitting awkward with his hands bound behind his back, Blake Hogan sneered at him.

"I'm going to sue you for every penny you have."

Slipping on a headset of his own, Nova said, "Good thing then I'm not worth much."

He drew the FNX-45 again, leaned over toward the two pilots who'd watched, stunned, this entire time, and put the barrel to the one pilot's head.

"Get us up in the air."

The pilot stammered, "I'm not—"

"Now!"

Within seconds the Sikorsky's engine had fired up, the rotor blades starting to turn. The whole aircraft beginning to tremble in anticipation.

Blake Hogan shouted, "You can't do this to me!"

Nova glanced back at him.

"Why not? It's a free country."

The helicopter began to take flight, its 16,000-pound frame rising steadily into the air.

Nova said, "Do you know what Veronica told me about you? That you would rather die than end up in a wheelchair like your old man."

Blake's face had gone pale as he stared out the open door. They were already one thousand feet in the air and rising, the sun a fat slab of reddish orange on the horizon.

"You can't do this to me."

"Says who?"

"I demand to speak to my lawyer!"

"And I demand to know who the guy was staying in the cabin."

"Go to hell."

The Pave Hawk kept rising, now two thousand feet in the air.

One of the pilots asked, "Now what?"

Nova said, "Take us to the burn pit."

Panic in Blake Hogan's eyes.

"You can't do this to me!"

"Again, says who?"

"You're FBI! Or ATF! Or whatever agency! There are rules you have to follow!"

Nova laughed.

"Like I told you, I don't work for anyone. I'm just a guy who came to this town to fish."

Blake stared out over the trees as they flew. There was still enough light to see the ground below them. He attempted to scoot his body closer toward the center but Nova swung his pistol around to aim it at him.

"Stop right there."

"You going to shoot me?"

"Maybe. Depends on what you tell me."

"I'm not telling you anything!"

Nova glanced down below them. They'd already passed over the cabin and the shooting range and would soon reach the burn pit.

Stepping closer to Blake, Nova grabbed one of the safety

straps and looped it around his waist, pulled the strap taut to make sure it was secure.

Blake Hogan's eyes went even wider.

"What are you doing?"

Securing the FNX-45 in his waistband again, Nova leaned forward.

"What do you think?"

Blake saw where Nova was heading with this, and blurted, "I can't tell you where he is!"

"Why not?"

"That's how we set it up. We leave it entirely to him. Just like the others before him."

"What others?"

"Just others! We haven't done it too many times in the past! Only when the market needs some juice!"

The Pave Hawk began to slow. Nova peered over the edge and saw they'd arrived at the burn pit. The pilots, as they'd been instructed before Nova brought Blake Hogan out of the house, hovered the helo right above it.

Nova asked the pilots, "What's our latitude?"

The one answered, "About five thousand feet."

Nova smiled at Blake, and tilted his head toward the side.

"That's quite a drop, isn't it?"

"His name's Darrell! Darrell Pritchard!"

"Where did Darrell go?"

"I don't know! Finlay left with him hours ago!"

Sensing that the man was still withholding information, Nova made sure his own body was secure before grabbing Blake by his shirt and jerking him toward the open door.

"Where did they go?"

"I swear, I don't know! Nobody does!"

"Bullshit. I spoke to Darrell. He told me you signed off on the target."

"Yes, but the location of the target is entirely up to him."

"How do we get in contact with Finlay?"

"You can't. And besides, he's just transporting Darrell. He's probably already dropped him off by now."

"Why? What is Darrell going to do?"

Something changed in Blake Hogan's face, the fear suddenly vanishing. He smiled at Nova, all at once confident.

"You're not going to drop me."

Nova jerked the man's body out even more from his seat, so that most of his torso was now in the air. The only thing holding him in place was Nova's grip on his shirt.

"Let's hope this isn't some cheap-ass fabric for your sake."

"He's going to kill people! Okay? That's what the others have done in the past."

"Where?"

"I told you, I don't know! We always leave it up to them. They pick the location. We just make sure they have a good time before we send them off."

"And then what? How is that putting juice into the market?"

"How do you think? Mass shootings happen in this country all the time. People become numb to them. But every once in a while, there's a big mass shooting—something that shocks the system."

"Are you trying to tell me all the major mass shootings in the past were your doing?"

"No! Most of them were deranged racists killing Black and brown people. There's almost always a political bent to the killings. But those are predictable—they cause the same back and forth in the media for a few days before fading away."

"So that isn't the case here?"

Blake Hogan shook his head, his eyes still wide as the rotor blades spun above him.

"We keep an eye on certain guys who visit the message board."

"You mean Bullet Country."

"Yes! We keep an eye on those guys who mostly keep to themselves. Who don't post much on social media, or if they do, they don't obviously lean left or right."

"Why?"

"Because it creates more confusion when they go and kill a bunch of people! The left or the right can't point at the other side. And the killing … it's always so large that Congress announces they'll pass some major gun legislation. It usually peters out after a week or two, but there's still the worry that the government is going to confiscate guns, so—"

Nova finished the thought, suddenly feeling numb inside.

"So that way people buy a shitload of guns. And the stock prices of the gun manufacturers skyrocket."

He paused, thinking about it, and shook his head.

"Wait—are you telling me this whole thing is just a scam to make money?"

"*Money?* We're not talking about a couple thousand dollars. *Millions* are at stake here. *Hundreds* of millions in some cases."

Nova finally saw it, the whole goddamned picture vivid as though in Technicolor, but it didn't make him happy. Besides still feeling numb, it caused the rage inside of him to bubble even more.

"Why did you kill all those girls?"

"Why do you think? They saw Darrell. They could ID him. So they needed to go away."

"Is the FBI agent's body down there too?"

Blake Hogan just sneered up at him, silent.

"Last chance—what's the target?"

Blake cackled, hysterical.

"I'm never going to tell you! You can threaten me all you want—you're not going to drop me! You don't have the balls! But it doesn't matter! By tomorrow, I'll be hundreds of millions of dollars richer! I'll hire every lawyer in this country to sue you for all the—"

But the rest of the man's words faded as his shirt slipped through Nova's fingers. Blake Hogan fell, his arms and legs flailing, straight down to the burn pit where he had disposed of God knew how many bodies, leaving the headset to dangle in the air where his own body had been only moments ago.

Nova leaned out far enough to watch Blake land smack in the middle of the burn pit, then he stepped back and, his expression deadpan, shrugged at the pilots.

"Whoops."

FORTY-FOUR

"What the hell was that?"

As soon the helicopter landed and Nova's feet were back on the ground, Special Agents McGuire and Bowen hurried over. McGuire accosted him, nearly shoving him over.

"You said you were only going to scare him! Not drop him out of a fucking helicopter!"

"It was an accident."

"Bullshit."

"He slipped."

"I should place you under arrest."

Nova held out his arms, wrists together.

"Then do it. Otherwise, you heard what Blake said. This Darrell Pritchard is going to kill a lot of people."

Howard approached them, his face solemn.

"Do we know if Blake still alive?"

McGuire said, "I've got agents headed back out there to check. But my guess is no."

"I think we're focusing on the wrong thing here," Nova said. "We need to find Darrell Pritchard *now*."

Howard said, "Mr. Bartkowski, this isn't one of the black op missions you're so used to doing. Every man and woman here has the rule of law to follow."

He cleared his throat, turning to the two agents.

"My people and I are leaving. Do you have any objection, Agent McGuire?"

McGuire shook his head, waving them off, and they moved away from the Pave Hawk as Howard and his men loaded into the helo. As soon as it rose into the air and started north, Nova turned back to McGuire and Bowen.

"Darrell Pritchard," he repeated. "Have you run the name yet?"

McGuire issued an irritated sigh and motioned Nova toward the barn, where inside three tables had been set up with laptops.

"We've run the name. In the country there are just over two hundred fifty Darrell Pritchards. Based on your description, we eliminated those under the age of twenty and those over fifty. Plus those that aren't Caucasian. That leaves us with under one hundred Darrell Pritchards."

The agent gestured at a chair, and Nova sank into it, his muscles still wired from being in the helicopter.

"All right, let's see them."

McGuire clicked on a file that brought up photographs, most likely taken from the DMV database. Three headshots filled the screen, and with the click of a mouse, another three headshots replaced them.

As Nova started clicking through, scanning each face, he said, "We should also search for Finlay, since Blake said the man is transporting him."

McGuire said, "Is Finlay his first name or last?"

Still staring at the screen, Nova shook his head.

"I have no clue."

"Transporting," Agent Bowen said. "Why did Blake say transporting and not driving?"

The question caused Nova to pause. Staring at the screen at the three headshots, he was thinking about last night, he and George in the garage with their flashlight beams slicing the dark and the heavy smell of oil in the air.

He twisted in his seat to look back at McGuire and Bowen.

"Your agents at the dealership—did they find a box truck in the garage?"

McGuire said, "What are you talking about?"

Nova pulled his phone from his pocket, searched his photos until he found the one he'd taken last night.

"This box truck was in the garage last night. And here"—he swiped to another photo—"is the car inside that box truck."

Bowen turned away immediately, slipping her own phone out and making a call. Then she turned back, shaking her head.

"That truck isn't anywhere on site."

Nova nodded and handed her the phone with the photo showing the box truck's license plate.

"Then that's our target right now. Find that truck."

Three minutes later Nova clicked the mouse again, returning to the previous page.

He leaned forward, squinting, and then pointed his finger at the headshot on the left.

"That's him."

McGuire stepped forward, tilting his head down to get a better look at the screen. Then he called for another one of his agents standing nearby.

"Run a background check on this one." Then, to his other agents: "Any word yet on the box truck?"

McGuire had a team coordinating with another team reviewing highway cameras for the past several hours, trying to ascertain when the truck had left the dealership and in which direction it had gone.

Everyone was working frantically, knowing that there was a chance they were already too late. That at any minute they'd receive a call notifying them of another mass shooting, one on more of a massive scale than usual. Twenty, thirty, forty people dead, if not more. Countless injured.

"I've got his car," shouted one of the agents. "A 2011 silver Honda Accord."

The same one Nova had found inside the box truck. The car which had been backed in so he couldn't see the plate, but at least he'd gotten a photo of the front of the car, which he now showed to McGuire as confirmation.

McGuire shouted to his team, "That's him! I want every piece of intel on this guy now!"

As the agents got to work, Nova stood up to stretch his legs. He stepped outside into the twilight. He breathed in the fresh air, clearing his lungs. Staring out at the distant peaks and the faint sunlight fading behind them.

Special Agent McGuire stepped up next to Nova, his arms crossed.

"I want to apologize."

"Don't worry about it."

"No, I do. I came in too hot. Plus, I'm fucking pissed about losing my agents."

"That's understandable."

"I appreciate everything you've done so far, despite what happened to Blake Hogan."

"He was going to keep stonewalling you."

"Still, it wasn't right what you did."

Nova turned to look at him.

"If it saves lives, it was."

"And if it doesn't save lives—if we're too late?"

Behind them, one of the agents shouted, "We found the truck!"

FORTY-FIVE

At just after one o'clock that afternoon—not long after Nova was sitting with Veronica Chapman in the Yellow Bird Cafe—the unmarked box truck departed Hogan Auto and turned right onto I-90.

The interstate eventually curved and took the box truck south, down into Wyoming, where it merged onto I-25 and kept going south.

All the way through the rest of the state and then into Colorado, where the techs had determined it had just passed through Colorado Springs.

Special Agent McGuire and the other agents worked the phones while Nova stood back and watched them.

A debate ensued on whether to have the Colorado State Patrol pull over the truck, but it was decided that they didn't want to risk spooking the driver, at least not yet.

But they managed to get the nearest SWAT team on the road, with someone in an undercover car to trail the box truck three car lengths back to give the team in the barn a real-time visual.

As they watched the surveillance feed, McGuire said, "What intel do we have so far on our suspect?"

Agent Bowen said, glancing down at her phone, "Darrell Pritchard. Forty-two years old. Lives in Greencastle, Indiana. Never married. Only child. His father passed away five years ago. His mother is disabled."

"Occupation?"

"He works in construction. Makes almost eighty thousand dollars a year. He doesn't appear to be in any debt."

"Political leaning?"

"As far as we can tell, there isn't one. He's registered as an Independent. He has a Facebook page but doesn't post any political content on it. We're trying to dig further, but so far we're not coming up with much."

"That's by design," Nova said.

The two agents turned to look at him.

McGuire asked, "What are you talking about?"

"You heard what Blake Hogan said. They purposely try to find people who don't lean one way or another politically."

Agent Bowen nodded.

"Because that way it creates more confusion. One side can't easily point and try to blame the other."

McGuire turned back to the monitor and the live video of the box truck. It was headed past Pueblo now, which put it almost ten hours away from their location.

Agent Bowen said, "What do you want to do?"

McGuire folded his arms over his chest, watching the monitor. He was quiet for a moment, thinking, then turned back to the rest of the team.

"On the one hand, I'm curious to learn the target. The other hand, we can't afford to take the chance of losing any lives."

He glanced back at the monitor, and nodded.

"Take it down."

They watched as a half-dozen vehicles converged on the box truck.

The truck was directed to pull over, and it complied without hesitation, its taillights glowing red on the monitor as it halted on the side of the highway.

Agents swarmed the truck, weapons ready.

The driver's door opened, and the man Finlay held his hands up, his expression filled with pure confusion.

"What's going on?" he asked, anxious. "What did I do wrong?"

One of the agents shouted that there was a padlock on the rear door. Another agent hurried over with a pair of bolt cutters. One snip and the padlock crashed to the ground.

The roll-top door was pushed open to reveal—

Agent McGuire whispered, "What the hell?"

Empty. The entire rear of the box truck was empty.

The man refused to answer questions and only asked for a lawyer. Leaning on his crutches beside the truck, casted leg in front of him, watching in amusement as the other agents scrambled to figure out what had happened.

In the barn, the techs worked furiously to backtrack through the video feeds.

There isn't always a set distance between highway cameras. Much of it depends on the route of each highway, plus the exits and entrances to those highways.

McGuire said, "The truck had to turn off at some point. Maybe to get gas or something. Find it!"

Agent Bowen and the other agents got to work, but then she paused.

"What if it's a decoy?"

"What do you mean?"

"The box truck. What if it's a decoy and Darrell Pritchard left in his car in the other direction?"

Silence for a moment as they all considered it.

Nova said, "You have the make and model and the plate number, don't you? Can't you search the cameras for the car?"

"It's not that simple," McGuire said. "We can send out the info, yes, but the idea was to keep this low profile for the time being. But maybe now we don't have a choice."

"Sir?"

It was one of the agents, sitting at one of the tables. The light from her computer monitor shined off her glasses as she waved over Agent McGuire.

"I found where the box truck exited."

Everyone shifted over to watch her monitor. The agent had backtracked through the highway camera footage and determined that the box truck had gotten off at an exit just past Denver. From there the agent followed the box truck to a gas station, where Finlay filled up the tank and then climbed back into the truck. But instead of returning to the highway, he made a slight detour. The truck disappeared behind a car wash. Almost ten minutes passed before it reappeared and headed back to the highway.

McGuire said, "Any way we can get a shot of the back of the building?"

The agent shook her head.

"Most likely the car wash has a security feed. We'll need to contact the company who owns it to get that footage, assuming they save any of it. But look."

A silver Honda Accord appeared from behind the car wash. The left turn signal blinked on as it slowed to pull out onto the street. The car was halted just long enough to give the camera a good view of the driver.

Despite the low quality and the distance, Nova recognized the man immediately.

"That's him."

It took a bit longer for the agents to access the local traffic cams, but once they did, they were able to track the Accord as it worked its way west. Down one street and then another. Pausing at stop signs and red lights. Never going faster than any of the other vehicles. Just one car among a million others on the road.

It moved in a circuitous route, going east and then west, north and then south, and after twenty minutes they lost the car entirely.

Agent McGuire muttered, "You're shitting me."

One of the agents said, "We're searching nearby traffic cams now, but so far no sign of the suspect."

Agent Bowen had stepped away to take a call, but now she returned.

"The plane's waiting."

McGuire checked his watch, then something on his phone, then gazed around at the other agents before nodding.

"Find the suspect as soon as you can. Keep me posted. I expect to know where he is by the time we land."

McGuire and Bowen headed out of the barn, straight for one of the cars. They only paused when they realized Nova was following them.

Agent McGuire didn't bother to try to hide the irritation in his voice when he said, "What do you think you're doing?"

"I'm coming with you."

"The hell you are."

"You have a picture of the suspect and a profile that so far seems pretty slim. I've interacted with the man. I know the sound of his voice. I know how he carries himself, how he walks. If you want to find this guy and keep people alive, I'm coming with you."

McGuire's jaw flexed as he shared a glance with Agent Bowen. He clearly didn't like it, but he didn't see any other option.

"Fine. But you're only coming along in a consulting capacity. Got it?"

Nova nodded.

"Good," McGuire said. "Now let's go."

FORTY-SIX

Darrell Pritchard liked structure.

He liked having a work schedule, to know when the day started and when it ended.

He liked making a grocery list, to know exactly what he needed and in which aisles of the store he could find those items.

He liked calling his mother every evening around six, like clockwork.

He liked the familiar sound of her voice. The lilting tone every time she laughed. The pedestrian nature of her stories and gripes. Sure, sometimes she got on his nerves, but it was all fine because she was his mother and he loved her more than anything else in the world.

Darrell knew she wouldn't understand when word got out. Especially when the lamestream media started bending the truth and tried to paint him as some kind of monster.

On the one hand, he knew what he planned to do wasn't right.

On the other hand, he knew it was something that had to be done.

Mr. Hogan had said as much. How every once in a while the country needed a good shock to its system. To remind everybody the true cost of freedom. People become lax in their every day lives, cogs in one giant machine that never stops moving. What people need, most of all, is to open their eyes. To see clearly. To understand.

Some of the greatest men in history had been villainized at one point. That's what someone had posted on the Bullet Country board a while back. The person had listed off a bunch of names that Darrell couldn't remember now, but he remembered thinking how true it was, that sometimes you have to make choices that don't seem popular at the time but which later turn out to be the only choices there are.

Darrell had been dreaming about this day for months now, ever since Mr. Hogan had reached out to him privately and started talking to him off the boards.

About what kind of target he envisioned.

The statement he could make to the country—to the world —when he initiated his plan.

Mr. Hogan had been impressed when Darrell told him the target, but he'd maintained that he should not know the location. Nobody should. Not even Finlay, who had somehow broken his leg and who'd helped Darrell up into the back of the truck with his gear before closing the big roll-top door and enveloping him in darkness.

He'd left his phone back at home. By now it had more than likely lost all its power. So no way for the government to track him anymore.

It felt almost freeing, the knowledge that Big Brother no longer knew where he was on the grid.

Still, when one of the girls had shown up, she had a phone on her, a burner she admitted she wasn't supposed to bring along but that she had a daughter at home who was probably too young to be by herself and so the girl needed the phone in case there was an emergency.

Darrell had slipped the phone from the girl's bag and kept it hidden, because he realized that he wanted to commemorate the occasion once everything was said and done.

He knew the Hogans would disapprove, and while he respected them immensely and was grateful for everything they had given him, he also felt he could add some extra ... well, *pizzazz* to the main event.

Live-streaming what he planned on social media for the whole world to see?

Talk about a shock to the system!

The reason he was never vocal online about his political leanings—or his moral leanings, for that matter—was because he didn't want the government to know more about him than they already did.

Why so many fools posted about what was going through their heads on different websites always amazed him. He supposed it was so that they could get the validation of likes and shares and whatever else, but didn't they realize they were putting a bull's-eye on their own backs, letting the government know exactly who they were and what they thought and how they felt?

No, Darrell was too smart for that. Even at work he was careful not to get involved in what used to be called "water cooler talk," especially when it came to politics.

It was something Mr. Hogan said he'd noticed, Darrell's commitment to keeping to himself, which had given Darrell this once-in-a-lifetime opportunity.

And he sure as hell wasn't going to spoil it.

But they had left earlier than anticipated. Why, Darrell didn't know—it was never explained to him—but the plan had been for them to leave after midnight and instead they had left twelve hours earlier, and that really messed everything up.

Mr. Hogan had said it shouldn't be a problem. That Darrell could change the location. That the main thing was the number of victims.

But didn't Mr. Hogan understand Darrell had a vision? That his plan was something he'd been dreaming about for years? That now that he was so close to accomplishing what he had set out to do, he couldn't just change his plan midstream?

No, that wasn't going to happen. No way. No how.

So riding in the back of the box truck, in the complete dark, Darrell had used the girl's phone to search for a place to hide out for a while. A place that wasn't near any main throughway in case the authorities somehow got wind of what was going on.

That's why after Finlay had dropped him off behind the car wash and went on his way, Darrell had confirmed the location on the phone and then headed there.

He'd found a dozen potential spots using the girl's phone, and it was the fourth house for rent that seemed to be the right fit. Completely dark, nobody home at all. No security markings anywhere on the property. No motion sensors on the garage to bring on the lights once someone pulled into the driveway.

Even better, the garage was located down a dark alleyway.

He killed the lights as he eased down the alley and then, keeping the engine running, stepped out to check the garage door.

It opened without any trouble, and what was better, the garage itself was empty.

Almost like it was destined to be.

Darrell had backed into the garage and closed the door, once more enveloping him in darkness.

Now, still in darkness, he checked the time on the girl's phone.

Three o'clock in the morning.

He had at least another six hours to go before it was time to leave and get himself in position.

Another seven hours to go until it was showtime.

In the musty dark of a stranger's garage, Darrell Pritchard smiled.

FORTY-SEVEN

They landed at Centennial Airport at five o'clock that morning.

The sky was still dark, with just a glimmer of light glowing on the horizon. Nova figured they would head north to the Denver field office but instead they climbed into an unmarked sedan—Bowen behind the wheel, McGuire in the passenger seat, with Nova in the back—and headed west.

McGuire had been on his phone for most of the hour-and-a-half flight, after they'd already driven almost an hour to reach Billings to board the plane. If any updates had come in, he hadn't bothered to share them, and even now he seemed agitated as he stared at his phone.

Nova said, "Where are we headed?"

Bowen glanced at him in the rearview mirror as she merged onto a highway.

"Last known sighting was near Holcomb. We've got agents scouring the entire area, plus agents searching security feeds for a ten-mile radius, but so far he hasn't popped up."

"So then he ditched the car."

"Most likely. The problem is"—she threw a cautious glance at her partner—"we haven't even found his vehicle yet."

McGuire, still staring down at his phone: "But it's definitely still out there somewhere."

"How about a door-to-door sweep?"

McGuire glanced up to gaze out his window, as though considering it, before he shook his head.

"Too risky. Might spook him."

"Agent McGuire, with all due respect, he might already be in place with a couple of those M4A1s, just waiting to cut down a crowd."

The agent twisted around in his seat, his eyes glowing with irritation from the passing streetlights.

"Don't you think I fucking know that? Christ, I shouldn't have bothered bringing you along. Shut the fuck up and let us work."

They met up with a few other agents in a King Soopers parking lot.

Someone had brought coffee, but it was so strong and acidic that Nova almost spit it out.

He stood off to the side and listened to the agents discuss possible targets. Malls, schools, hospitals, even churches—by this point pretty much every location had been a target of a mass shooting in the last decade.

Finally, when it was determined they couldn't stand around and wait any longer, everyone got back into their cars.

Nova asked, "What about the local PD?"

McGuire shook his head as he stared again out his window.

"We can't trust the local cops with this."

"It's more eyes."

"More eyes, sure, but can we trust them to keep their traps shut? The last thing we need is someone leaking this to the media. That would create a firestorm."

Six o'clock bled into seven o'clock, and still no updates.

School buses began to populate the streets, with groups of kids—ages ranging anywhere from six to eighteen—leaving their homes and walking to school or bus stops.

Nova watched them as they slid by, feeling something tight in the base of his stomach.

There was something on the edge of his memory, something he wanted to grasp but was too far out of reach. Maybe because he was exhausted—he'd been up for more than twenty-four hours with hardly anything to eat, and he hadn't bothered to try to doze on the plane.

Agent McGuire's phone buzzed, and he practically yelped in triumph.

"We found the car!"

The Accord was parked behind a Lutheran church.

As it was Friday, the parking lot was mostly deserted, with only a handful of vehicles belonging to staff. None of them claimed to have seen anything when questioned. They admitted that sometimes people parked in the lot, but they never made much of a fuss about it as long as there were enough spaces for church services on Sunday.

Twenty minutes earlier, one of the agents searching the traffic cams spotted the Accord. It seemed to have come out of nowhere. They tracked it for two miles, turning down one street after another, until it came to the church.

Behind the church was a rather large cemetery. Dew-speckled grass, dotted with grave markers, shimmered in the low light. It was believed Darrell Pritchard had set out through there. The agents were busy going back through traffic cam footage, attempting to ascertain where he'd come from and where he was headed.

The morning sun was rising steadily, brightening the already pale sky. The sounds of the waking neighborhood—traffic on the street, a distant lawn mower, a trio of barking dogs—pushed in on them from every direction.

And Nova stood off to the side, as he felt like he'd been doing for the past twelve hours, running through everything that had taken place the past couple of days.

Especially his brief interaction with Darrell Pritchard.

The energy in the man's eyes when he told Nova that he already had his target in mind.

Then the quiet somberness when he—

"Fuck."

Everyone turned to look at him.

Nova said, "I know what the target is."

McGuire stepped closer, phone in hand, brow knitted. "What is it?"

"An elementary school."

FORTY-EIGHT

They pulled up a map of their location on a tablet, and as soon as the surrounding landmarks came into focus, Agent Bowen sucked in a breath.

"Oh my God."

The Lutheran church sat in the middle of an orbit of educational facilities: one state college and two elementary schools.

"Christ," Nova said. "There isn't even a mile between the two schools."

McGuire said, "We can't rule out the state college either. In theory, the security there isn't as tight. He could walk into any of the buildings and open fire. With the elementary schools, he'd stick out too much during his approach."

Nova slowly shook his head, shifting his focus from one elementary school to the other.

North Holcomb Elementary.

Thomas Jefferson Elementary.

"He doesn't have to approach."

"What do you mean?"

"Something he said to me seemed off at the time. About

when he was a kid and went out to play for recess. He said he hated it. He said he realized he liked to have structure, and that recess was chaos."

A heavy silence fell over the group.

Nova looked up at McGuire.

"You have to contact the schools. Lock them down. Do whatever it takes. Just make sure none of the kids go outside for any reason."

Agent McGuire was nodding, staring down at the tablet and the two tiny dots signifying the schools.

"I'll call them now. I'll call the superintendent too. But if the kids *don't* come out for recess, that might tip him off that we're on to him."

"I know," Nova said. "That's why we need to find him first."

As Agent McGuire stepped away to make calls, Agent Bowen moved closer to stare down at the tablet.

"We need to figure out where a shooter would have the best view of the playground."

Nova reached out, tracing his finger along the various routes connecting the two schools.

"We should do a drive-by, scope out each location."

"I don't know," Agent Bowen said, glancing over at the unmarked sedan.

"I didn't mean in that. That thing screams police. We need something a bit more ... pedestrian."

He turned his attention to the handful of vehicles in the lot beside the church. Two cars, one SUV, one minivan. Among the four, only one stuck out.

"Agent Bowen, if you would be so kind as to follow me."

He led her around the side of the church and up the steps

to enter through the front door. The lights were dim, the air stale.

Agent Bowen whispered, "What are we doing?"

"It's better if you drive so I can focus on the locations around the schools. Plus, it might be better cover—two people in a car, a man and woman."

"If I drove what?"

They came to the office. Nova knocked quietly. Four faces swiveled up from desks to peer at him.

Nova put on his best smile.

"Who owns the VW Beetle outside?"

A woman in her sixties with a puff of white hair on her head raised her tiny hand, hesitant.

Nova, smiling even harder: "I was hoping you could do us a favor."

Agent Bowen drove normally, staying with the rest of the traffic as they approached North Holcomb Elementary.

Nova had his window down, his arm resting on the sill. Wearing sunglasses and a Rockies cap that he'd borrowed from one of the men at the church. Led Zeppelin on the radio for background noise, singing about coming from the land of the ice and snow.

The American flag in front of the school was at half-mast, curled around the pole.

Residential houses clustered around the school, most of them single story.

A dentist's office on the east corner across the street, facing the playground.

Nova said, "Keep going."

As Agent Bowen turned onto a side street to head in the other direction, she glanced at him.

"You said Agent Roberts saved your life."

"He did. He was a good man. Did you know him?"

Her sunglasses made it impossible to read her eyes. Agent Bowen's jaw flexed as she stared out the windshield. Her voice, low and focused.

"We're almost there."

Thomas Jefferson Elementary was a bit larger than North Holcomb. The playground where the students presumably had recess was larger too—about half the size of a football field— with what looked to be brand-new playground equipment.

But the thing that caught Nova's attention was the hospital across the street.

And the parking garage currently under construction.

One glance, that's all it took, but it was enough to cause every muscle in Nova's shoulders to tense.

Because a portion of the garage looked out across the street, directly at the playground.

"Let's head back."

"You sure?"

Nova nodded slowly, his gaze focused on the street ahead of them.

"I think I know where he is."

FORTY-NINE

Agent McGuire didn't like it.

Standing behind the church, he glared at Nova, his arms crossed, his head tilted as he measured his options.

"You took off without alerting me."

Nova said, "You were busy."

McGuire shot an irritated glance at Bowen, then rubbed at the stubble on his chin.

"I've already contacted the principals as well as the superintendent. They'll keep the kids inside until we give them the green light that everything is fine. They're going to say it's a standard lockdown drill. Now, tell me again why you think Darrell Pritchard is in the parking garage structure."

"We did recon on both schools. The parking garage across from Thomas Jefferson has the highest sight advantage of the playground."

"But as far as we know Pritchard isn't a sniper."

"He doesn't need to be. The distance between the playground and the parking garage is less than a hundred yards. With a playground full of kids, all he needs to do is open fire."

"Did you spot him?"

"No."

"Then how can you be so confident that's where he is?"

Nova hesitated.

"Because that's where I'd set up if I were him."

McGuire rubbed his chin again, staring down at the tablet in front of him. They were standing around the unmarked sedan in the shade.

To one of his agents: "How far out is SWAT?"

"Twenty minutes."

McGuire nodded slowly, thinking it over.

"Then we wait."

Nova said, "Not a good idea."

"Excuse me?"

"We're only five minutes away."

"SWAT will take care of it."

"They'll kill him."

"So?"

"He doesn't deserve to die."

"Are you defending this psycho all of a sudden?"

"He's been manipulated into doing this. All his life he's been fed one continuous line of bullshit."

"That isn't our problem, Mr. Bartkowski. Our focus is on saving lives."

"Exactly. So let me try to talk to him first."

"Why?"

"I've met with him. He thinks I work for the Hogans."

"The Hogans may have already told him that isn't the case."

"Either way, I've spoken to this man. I've looked him in the eye. I think … I can talk him down."

"You don't sound certain."

"Because I'm not. But it's worth a try. In the meantime, SWAT can set up a perimeter. If I fail—if Pritchard kills me—they can come in guns blazing."

McGuire stared at Nova, again assessing the options on the table.

"Howard said you do special work for the government."

"I used to."

"You get fired?"

"I quit."

"Why's that?"

"It's none of your business."

McGuire grinned, shook his head, released a heavy breath.

"We don't even know if the school is the target."

Nova said, "That's true."

"He could be in the hospital right this minute, readying to open fire in the emergency department."

"That's true too. Did you contact them?"

"I spoke to the director about our concerns. He wanted to initiate a lockdown, but I told him that would cause even more panic."

"What about security?"

"I told him to put them on high alert."

"Time's wasting, Agent McGuire."

The man glanced at Agent Bowen and his other agents before he stared at Nova again, his eyes narrowing as he came to a decision.

"Fine. But I'm going to take you there myself. You've got one shot, Mr. Bartkowski. Don't mess it up."

FIFTY

Principal Timothy Jacobs stepped out of his office and surveyed his three secretaries. Each of them at their desks, eyes on their computers, as they worked in silence.

He asked, "Where's Peter?"

The resource officer.

Stacey said, "I believe he's checking on the exit doors again. Do you want me to call him?"

"No, I'll find him."

Jacobs started toward the door leading into the hallway but paused, turned back around. Forced a smile.

"Everything's going to be okay. This is all just a precaution. We've gone through this before during our drills."

Each of the secretaries nodded at him, though it was clear none of them felt at ease with the situation.

"I'll be back," Jacobs said. "If any further calls come in from the FBI, please have them forwarded to my cell."

As soon as the door closed, all three women released a breath. Their chairs squeaked as they turned toward each other.

Stacey: "I can't believe this is happening."

Louisa: "Tim is right—it might not be anything."

Elizabeth: "Jeanette's at North Holcomb."

Her voice cracked when she said this, eliciting sympathetic expressions from both women. But that was it. Stacey's kids were all grown, one of them still in college, while Louisa had recently gotten married and didn't have any kids, at least not yet.

They didn't understand what Elizabeth was going through. Even if Jeanette was her stepdaughter, she was still her daughter, no matter what.

"I … I need to use the restroom."

Elizabeth stood from her chair, her Samsung phone in hand, ready to march toward the private unisex bathroom at the end of the office hallway.

Stacey said, "Please leave your phone."

Elizabeth turned slowly, her mouth partly open.

"What did you say?"

"Please leave your phone at your desk."

"I … I wasn't going to—"

"I know. But you heard what Tim said. The FBI is handling this. They hope to have everything taken care of as soon as possible. The last thing we need is for word to get out and for people to panic."

Elizabeth's mouth was a tight line as she stood trembling. There was so much emotion in her voice that she was surprised the words came out coherently.

"But Jeanette—"

Stacey cut her off, rising from her chair, her hand extended with an open palm as she calmly stepped toward her.

"Will be safe. All the students will be safe. As will the staff. As long as we stay calm and think clearly."

Elizabeth slowly breathed in through her nose, released the air through her mouth.

Stacey was right—Stacey was always right—but it still didn't mean Elizabeth had to like it.

Keeping her eyes on the older woman, Elizabeth gingerly set the phone on her desk.

"There. Happy now?"

Stacey nodded but didn't sit back down. Instead, she motioned toward the hallway.

"Okay, let's go."

"What?"

"I'll walk you to the restroom."

"Why? It's like fifteen feet away."

Stacey didn't say anything, and Elizabeth felt her shoulders sag. Even if she had no intention of stopping in one of the other offices to make a call from a landline, it was clear Stacey didn't trust her.

"Fine," she mumbled, turning and stalking down the hallway to the bathroom, Stacey calmly following three paces behind.

Louisa watched them go, holding her breath. As soon as they were out of sight, she scrambled to grab her phone from the drawer.

She'd debated sending an email—not from her school account, of course not—but worried about even using her private email on the school computer.

Would they be able to determine later if something happened?

She didn't think anything would happen—the FBI was taking care of it, just like Stacey said, and Stacey was always right—but still, she couldn't *not* tell her sister.

Her sister who had two children here at the school.

One in the second grade, one in the fourth.

She texted,

> We just initiated lockdown.

At once the gray dancing dots showed up on the other side

of the screen, her sister always with her phone within arm's reach, a true addict.

Y?

Louisa hesitated, glancing toward the hallway. Part of her knew she'd already stepped over a line. But another part loved her nephew and niece as if they were her own children and would do anything to protect them.

Even if it meant leaking the news to her sister.

Even if it meant her sister would probably post it to Facebook and Instagram and anyplace else that would make it go viral.

Louisa knew that she shouldn't—that she should put her phone back in the drawer, focus on her work—but she couldn't help herself as she typed and sent the one-word response.

Shooter.

FIFTY-ONE

They parked on the other side of the hospital, in a cramped lot with only a few open spaces. Before they left the church they had already geared up—both wearing Kevlar vests—and checked their weapons, so as soon as McGuire parked, they immediately headed toward the parking garage.

Nova had been allowed to bring along his FNX-45, which he had secured in a holster clipped to his belt.

He also had a radio in his ear, which kept him in communication with Agent McGuire and the SWAT team as they got into position. Agent Bowen and the other agents had stayed back at the church.

While the garage was under construction, it didn't appear active today. Equipment loomed all over the place—a crane, two backhoes, one dump truck—protected by a chain-link fence.

Nova quickly found an opening and slipped through and headed for the stairs.

As soon as he was in the stairwell, he had his pistol out, held at the ready.

He stared up toward the top of the five stories but didn't see or hear anything.

His voice, a whisper for the radio: "I'm in the stairwell and headed up now."

He knew McGuire would stay back until Nova had made visual contact. The SWAT team would wait for McGuire's command. If Nova couldn't talk Darrell Pritchard down—or Darrell opened fire—the team would rush in and eliminate the threat.

On the second level he leaned out, the barrel of his pistol swinging left and right. He slowly moved about the space, staying close to the concrete pillars for cover, but didn't spot any sign of Darrell on this level.

Returning to the stairwell, he whispered, "Nothing on the second level. Headed up to third."

Same thing on the third level, though it was easier to scan as it was still very much under construction. At a glance he could tell that Darrell Pritchard wasn't here.

"Nothing on the third level. Headed up to fourth."

This was where he found Darrell. Hunched over in the corner, his back against a pillar, his face tilted just enough to see up over the wall at the school grounds across the way.

Two Springfield Armory Saint M-Lok rifles on the ground beside him.

Nova knew each mag held thirty 5.56mm rounds.

Besides the two mags already loaded on the rifles, a dozen other mags were lined up like soldiers ready to go into battle.

Nova felt his grip on the pistol tighten. Part of him wanted to aim for the man's head, squeeze off a round. All it would take was one shot. Just one bullet to end this man's life and ensure that he wasn't a threat to anyone ever again.

Nova whispered, "Found him."

McGuire's voice through the earpiece: "What level?"

"Four."

Nova briefly wondered about the SWAT team's location. The brilliance of Darrell's position was that he had the high ground for at least a mile. Much too far for a sniper to accurately take him out, at least as long as he kept cover.

He wasn't sure if that had been planned or was pure dumb luck. It didn't matter. Right now, Darrell Pritchard had no target. The students were in school and would not be leaving until the administration was given the green light.

Taking shallow breaths, Nova moved silently. One slow, steady step in front of the other. Making sure he didn't make any noise. All the concrete around them would make the slightest sound ring out, and he couldn't risk spooking Darrell.

In his peripheral vision, he saw the school. The plain brick building that looked like any other school in the country. The playground closest to the parking garage. The grass like a sheet of emerald in the bright sun.

The sound of screeching tires drew his attention.

A BMW had halted in front of the main doors, and a woman popped out, racing up the steps and jabbing her finger on the bell, then banging her fist against the glass door.

Nova swung his gaze back toward Darrell Pritchard.

His head had come up as he watched the woman. Slowly reaching for one of the AR-15s.

Another car screeched into the school's main parking lot.

A man jumped out of a Lexus and raced up the steps to the front doors. He spoke briefly to the woman, then began banging on the glass too, both he and the woman shouting.

Nova was aware of other cars now streaming into the parking lot—where the hell had they come from?—but he kept his focus on Darrell Pritchard.

Because the man had the rifle in his hands now. Positioning the buttstock against his shoulder. One hand on the grip, his other on the handguard. Uncurling his body so that he could get into the proper stance.

Nova said, "Darrell."

The man jumped in surprise, no doubt already wired, and hopped to his feet, swinging the rifle's barrel at Nova.

But he saw that Nova already had a bead on him, and hesitated.

"You," he whispered, his voice tight. "Did … did Mr. Hogan send you?"

So Darrell still thought Nova worked for the Hogans. He could use that.

"He did, Darrell. Mr. Hogan wanted me to track you down and tell you the plan's off."

The two men were standing less than forty feet apart, which was more than enough distance for Nova to see the flicker of disappointment flash across the man's face.

But then Darrell Pritchard shook his head, his eyes hardening.

"That's a lie. Mr. Hogan would never do that. I don't care what you guys say."

For a brief second, Nova wasn't sure what the man meant. Did he say *guys*? Then he sensed a presence behind him and tilted his head just enough to spy Special Agent James McGuire standing there, his agency-issued Glock in hand.

Aimed straight at Nova.

The agent said, quiet and cool, "Don't worry, Darrell. Just stick to the plan. You're doing great."

FIFTY-TWO

More vehicles arrived at the school, creating a bottleneck.

A chorus of horns sounded out, accompanied by a tempo of raised voices shouting and screaming that they needed their children *now* as fists banged against the glass doors.

Keeping his gun trained on Nova, Special Agent McGuire released a breath.

"Guess the cat's out of the bag. Just as well. I had to contact the schools, Darrell. I tried stalling as long as possible, but I had no choice. They're all on lockdown. So there's no chance you'll get any of those kids. But maybe ... maybe instead you can open fire on the parents. Then again, they're not as close as the playground. Maybe if you head down to the other corner you'll have a better shot. Or maybe you can head straight there, let loose on the crowd on ground level. But SWAT is already getting into position, so whatever you decide to do, you best hurry."

Darrell's eyes were wide as they shifted back and forth between Nova and the FBI agent.

"Who ... who the hell *are* you?"

"I'm your guardian angel, Darrell. Now hurry up—you don't have much time left."

Darrell hesitated, still not sure what to do, before he started to crouch down to collect the other rifle.

Nova said, "They're manipulating you, Darrell."

The man paused again, a shadow of a frown crossing his face.

"What?"

"Ignore him," McGuire said. "Just act like he's not even here."

Darrell coughed out a laugh.

"Yeah, but he's holding a gun on me!"

"And I'm holding a gun on him. It'll be fine."

Nova said, "I don't think you honestly know what you're doing, Darrell. That's why I wanted to try to talk you out of this. But either way, I can't let you kill anyone."

"Shut up," Agent McGuire growled. Then to Darrell: "Move your ass!"

Darrell jumped again, spooked, and crouched once more to grab the other rifle and the spare magazines.

Keeping his eyes on Darrell, Nova said, "You're not going to shoot me, Agent McGuire."

"Is that so?"

"Hard for you to explain, isn't it? I'm still not sure how you expect to get away with this."

"It's simple, really," McGuire said as he shifted the Glock to his left hand and slipped a SIG from his waistband. "You'll be killed by what they'll later believe is one of Darrell's guns. He'll be killed by my gun. But not until he does what he came here to do."

Nova tilted his chin toward Darrell, who was still watching them with wide eyes.

"Is that what you signed up for, Darrell?"

Darrell started to open his mouth, but McGuire cut him off.

"Of course it is. Darrell's a true patriot, just like me."

Nova said, "It makes sense now how the Hogans knew about the undercover agents in the house on Mottley Lane. I'm guessing you gave them up."

"Heller and Barton had started questioning whether I'd been passing on their full reports. Blake had had the house bugged while they were out so we could keep tabs on them. We overheard them talking about going above my head. We couldn't let that happen, especially when we were so close to the end."

"And Agent Roberts?"

"The Hogans knew he was undercover from day one. That's why they kept him on a short leash."

Across the street, the parents had become frenzied. The sound of glass breaking as two fathers kicked in one of the windows by the door. The crowd pulsing forward, one giant blob.

McGuire said, "Fucking move, Darrell!"

Jumping at the intensity in the agent's voice, Darrell started nodding as he began to collect his gear.

Nova said, "They're using you, Darrell."

Darrell hesitated once again.

"What do you mean?"

McGuire said to Nova, "Shut up."

"They want to spike the stock prices for a bunch of gun manufacturers. That's all this is about, Darrell—money. It's got nothing to do with freedom or being a true patriot or the Constitution or whatever nonsense they put in your head."

Darrell's wide eyes shifted to the FBI agent.

"Is ... is that true?"

"Don't listen to him. He's trying to fuck with your head."

Nova smiled—he couldn't help himself.

McGuire said, "What's so funny?"

"You've been talking this entire time while we're on comms."

"Is that what you think? Have you heard anyone else since you came up here?"

Nova's smile began to fade.

"I'm carrying an RF jammer," McGuire said. "Turned it on right as I started up the steps. As far as everyone will be concerned once this is all over, it belongs to Darrell."

A radio frequency jammer. That made sense. And it wasn't good news for Nova.

"Enough screwing around, Darrell. Either you're a true patriot, or you're a pussy. Now which is it?"

Darrell seemed to brace himself. He nodded, a quick up and down, and grabbed the other rifle and strapped it over his shoulder and bent again to scoop up as many spare magazines as he could carry.

Still watching Darrell, still training his pistol on him, Nova said, "So what's your deal in all of this, Agent McGuire? Are you in this for the money too?"

"It doesn't matter if I am. The only thing that matters is that I'm a patriot."

"No," said a voice directly behind Nova, in the stairwell, "you're a traitor."

In Nova's peripheral vision he saw Agent McGuire jerk his head to the left—and in the same instant Nova twisted around, shooting McGuire in the side of the head as the man fired off a round at the new arrival.

Agent Bowen stood in the stairwell, her Glock trained on McGuire, pieces of cinderblock beside her head spraying up from the round's impact.

She didn't even flinch.

Nova said to her, "You okay?"

"Yes."

He swung back toward Darrell, who still had both rifles strapped over his shoulders, the magazines in his hands.

"Slowly, Darrell, put everything on the ground."

Darrell's eyes somehow managed to grow even wider. He stared back at Nova, before glancing out at the school.

"This … this wasn't how it was supposed to be. It was supposed to be beautiful."

"Killing children is beautiful?"

He shook his head slowly, his expression full of sorrow.

"People like you will never understand."

Nova took a slow step toward him.

"How about you explain it to me later?"

Darrell continued to shake his head.

"I gave Mr. Hogan my word I wouldn't be taken alive. And a true patriot never breaks his word."

The magazines clattered to the ground as he reached behind his waist, pulled out a Kimber 1911, placed it under his chin, and pulled the trigger.

FIFTY-THREE

"How did you know?"

Agent Bowen had finished with the SWAT leader and the Special Agent in Charge of the Denver field office to give them a briefing on what went down. Allegations of one of their own being bent was damaging enough, but at least Bowen had the audio evidence to back it up, having recorded everything on her phone as she came up the stairwell behind McGuire.

She looked at Nova for a moment, measuring him, before she sighed.

"That Agent McGuire was crooked? I've had my suspicions for a while now. Just the feeling that something was ... off."

"And what made you follow us here and into the garage?"

"For starters, he wasn't following protocol. For as long as I've known him, James has always played everything by the book. Granted, the situation was time sensitive, but still ..."

Nova said, "That wasn't all."

Agent Bowen looked off to the ambulances stationed across the street at the school. More than one parent had been injured as they attempted to force their way into the building to rescue their children.

"*Where's Jimmy?*"

Her voice was soft, almost reflective, and it took Nova a moment before he realized where he'd heard the question before.

"Blake Hogan said that. Right before I got him in the helicopter."

Agent Bowen nodded slowly, still staring out at the school. In addition to the ambulances were several police cars, officers moving about trying to restore order.

"I felt my heart stop when I heard him say that. We were all hiding in the barn, and I looked to see if anybody else had caught it, but as far as I could tell nobody did."

"So that clued you in."

Agent Bowen nodded again, still seemingly lost in thought. Then she blinked, and looked at him.

"We were at Quantico together. Agent Roberts and me. We were good friends. Well, we were more than good friends. We sort of had an on-again, off-again thing going."

"I'm sorry for your loss."

She smiled the kind of smile a person makes when they don't want to cry.

"He was a good agent. A good man. He will be missed dearly. As will agents Heller and Barton."

Nova asked, "So what happens now?"

Agent Bowen almost coughed out a laugh.

"You mean besides a shitload of paperwork and an investigation from the Justice Department? We'll get you back to Remington soon, if that's what you're asking."

"Any chance I can be kept out of the official record?"

Her expression told him he shouldn't have even bothered to ask such a ridiculous question.

"Fine," he said. "Then can you at least keep my name from any official media reports?"

Another sigh.

"That's really not my call …"

"If you have to give the media anybody, how about George Murphy?"

"You mean the mechanic?"

"If it wasn't for him, none of this would have happened. A bunch of kids would probably be dead. The man's a hero."

Agent Bowen bit her lip, considering it.

"I'll see what I can do." Then her tone turned sardonic: "Is there anything else I can help you with?"

Nova slipped his phone from his pocket.

"There is one thing …"

Agent Bowen stared at the photo on the screen. She read what was there, then read it again, before frowning at him.

"Where did you get this?"

Nova told her.

"Jesus Christ," Bowen muttered. "And she sent her son along with you?"

"Yes."

Agent Bowen shook her head again.

"That reminds me. The boy's father—the other mechanic?"

Nova felt his heart rate suddenly tick up.

"What about him?"

"One of the agents in Remington called with an update."

Nova swallowed.

"Did he pass away?"

"Who—the other mechanic? No, he didn't. In fact, he's awake now. Woke up late last night, actually."

"Oh. Well, I'm glad to hear that."

"Yes," Agent Bowen said, watching him carefully again. "But that's not the only reason the agent called."

"What's the other reason?"

"Apparently he's asking to speak to you."

FIFTY-FOUR

Mandy Schaffer was sitting on a bench fifty feet from the hospital entrance. A single sodium arc lamp directly above, spotlighting her in the growing dusk.

Despite the No Smoking signs posted everywhere, she was leaning forward on the bench, cigarette pinched between two fingers, eyes focused on her phone as she scrolled with her thumb.

Mandy didn't notice Nova until he was standing right in front of her.

"Oh!" Her hand holding the cell phone went to her chest as she laughed. "You scared me."

The parking lot was surprisingly quiet for early evening, as though it was just the two of them on a movie set.

Nova said, "I heard your husband is awake."

"He is! Alex is so happy. His arm is broken, but he thinks it's cool that he gets to wear a cast."

Nova stared down at her. Aware of the world around them. Insects off in the distance making their insect noises and traffic a mile away on the interstate zooming back and forth and a jet somewhere above them in the thickening evening sky.

"How did you know to find us on Herron Road?"

The confusion on her face—it looked genuine enough, he had to give her that.

"What do you mean? That's where you told me the two of you were going to fish."

"No, I told you we were going to fish at the end of Patterson Road."

Silence. A strand of smoke curled up from the cigarette tip.

The confusion still on her face, though she tried to smile, tried to play it off.

"No, you didn't. You said Herron Road."

"I didn't, Mandy."

"Well, anyway, I did go down Patterson Road first. But I didn't see your truck. So I figured maybe I heard you wrong and went to check Herron Road. Wait—if you said you were going to be on Patterson Road, why'd you end up parked at the end of Herron Road?"

"Because," he said, holding her gaze, "I wanted to test a theory."

Uncomfortable now. Those green eyes scanning the parking lot again, anxious.

"What are you talking about?"

Nova already had his phone in hand. He opened the screen, showed her the photo he already had ready to go.

She stared at it. Her eyes narrowing just the tiniest bit. Trying her hardest not to make any reaction.

"What … what is that?"

"Mandy."

"I've never … I've never seen that before."

"And why would you assume I'd think you had seen it before?"

Silence again. That forced, crooked smile of someone who knows they've been caught.

Nova said, "Is it because this is a photo I took of your phone?"

That's when Agent Bowen climbed out of the sedan parked ten spaces away. And Deputy Jamie Bennett—who'd already confirmed that he'd had no idea what Veronica Chapman had been up to—stepped around the corner.

The cigarette fell from her fingers, hitting the sidewalk with a spark of ash.

"When you took Alex upstairs to change his shirt, you left your phone on the table. I got curious. Fact is, I had a feeling, and I've learned to trust my gut. It didn't take long at all to find the encrypted messaging app you had hidden in a folder. And, well …"

Nova glanced at his phone. At the photo he'd taken a minute before Mandy and her son returned to the kitchen. Alex going straight for the phone and whining that the game had restarted. Nova at the sink, spraying off the dishes, deciding how he wanted to move forward.

The text exchange:

CHRIS

Do you think you can do it?

I think so yes

Try to get him alone. Maybe suggest he take Alex fishing.

I don't want Alex in any danger!!!

He won't be. The boys will make sure to keep him safe.

OK

I love you babe.

Love u 2 🙂

Nova said, "You told Alex to say he needed to go pee at ten o'clock, didn't you? That's why he kept asking what time it was. So that way he wouldn't be there when they came to kill me."

Mandy's eyes darted around the parking lot again, at the FBI agent and sheriff's deputy standing nearby. Then those eyes narrowed on Nova.

"You hurt him real bad."

"No, I didn't. One of Blake's men dropped him."

"I'm not talking about Alex. I'm talking about Chris. You broke his leg."

"And Chris and his buddy almost killed your husband. Not that you care about any of that, since Chris Finlay is the actual father of your son."

In the light of the sodium arc lamp Nova watched a single tear trail down Mandy Schaffer's cheek.

"I couldn't raise Alex on my own."

Her voice, a low, trembling whisper.

"Ed had always been nice to me. I thought, well, maybe he could do for the time being. But then when Chris got out, he expected me to leave Ed and start over with him. I kept telling him that things had changed, that I loved Ed now and that Alex did too, but Chris wouldn't hear it. He … he eventually wore me down. Made me realize Alex and I should be with him. But I couldn't leave Ed. Not just abandon him like that. It didn't seem fair. And Chris … Chris was getting impatient, so I guess he and BJ went to tell Ed he should get lost, and that's when …"

More tears. Mandy wiped at them with the back of her hand, trying to say more, but Nova had heard enough.

He nodded at Agent Bowen and Deputy Bennett, just once, and then headed directly for the hospital entrance. He didn't bother glancing back as the two moved forward to take Mandy Schaffer into custody.

FIFTY-FIVE

George Murphy was waiting for him when the elevator opened on the third floor.

"Did Mandy just get arrested?"

Nova stepped into the bright artificial light. The sterileness in the air made his stomach churn.

"How are you feeling?"

"What? My nose?"

George unconsciously touched the bandage still on his face, winced.

"It's okay, I guess. I broke my nose back in high school so I've been through it before. Hey, did you know Ed is awake? I've been hanging out in his room, even though they say only family members should be there. Alex is in there too. Mandy went out to get a cigarette, and she was gone for a while, so I glanced out the window when I was getting a soda."

He hefted the Mountain Dew in his hand as though Nova hadn't noticed the bright green bottle.

"So what's going on? Have you been up at the Hogans' this entire time?"

"I stopped by to see your boss."

"Oh yeah? I'm sure he'll be happy to see you. But what about Mandy—is she really under arrest?"

Nova didn't know what all to tell the man, but he felt he deserved the truth.

"She is."

"For what?"

"It's not my place to say."

"Damn. Little Alex is gonna be devastated. But at least his dad's awake now, so maybe that evens things out?"

They started down the hallway, their boots squeaking on the linoleum, George one step ahead as he led Nova to his father's room.

"George, I want to thank you again for saving my life."

George waved it away with his free hand, shrugging.

"It was nothing. But ... do you think I should still move on? I mean, do you think it's still dangerous?"

"I don't know. There might be people in town who feel loyal to the Hogans. If they find out you were involved—even peripherally—they might not take it well."

George's shoulders slumped, only a fraction.

"I never thought about it like that. Maybe you're right. Maybe I should move on. But not before Ed's back on his feet. He needs somebody to keep the shop going."

"Have you given any more thought to going back home?"

That slowed George's pace. He halted, turning to look at Nova. Or not look at him—George's eyes were downcast, shifting back and forth.

"Like I told you, I don't think that's a good idea. I walked out on my family. I don't think they'd want me back."

"You won't know unless you try."

"They've gotta hate me by this point. Especially Nina."

Nova wasn't going to tell George how he'd already spoken to Agent Bowen, asking her to make sure the local news in George's hometown mentioned how he'd been involved in helping the FBI break its case. It would be a small mention, barely a blip, but hopefully word would get around to the right people and make George's homecoming—if that's what he decided—a bit easier.

"You won't know until you know," Nova said, clapping George gently on his shoulder.

George, his eyes still downcast, nodded again.

"I suppose you're right."

Then he shook his head, as if waking himself up.

"Here we are. What … what should I tell Ed about Mandy?"

"Nothing. The police will do that in a bit."

George nodded, steeling himself, then smiled wide as he pushed open the door.

"Ed! Look who I ran into. It's the guy I was telling you about. His name is—"

Nova cut him off.

"Hello," he said to the man in the hospital bed.

Ed Schaffer's gray eyes zeroed in on him. Staring for a beat too long. Then he blinked and shifted on the bed to address Alex sitting in the chair beside him.

"Son, do you mind stepping out to give me a minute with this gentleman? Maybe George will get you something from the vending machine."

Alex, whose focus was on a tablet (even with his arm in a cast, he handled it like a pro), nodded and jumped off the chair. He leaned up and hugged his dad around the neck, Ed smiling and gently patting him on the back. Alex dashed to George, waving briefly at Nova, before disappearing out into the hallway. Then, before Nova realized it, the door fell shut, and it was just Nova and the man who had walked out on him and his mother nearly two decades ago.

FIFTY-SIX

Almost immediately the chaos of the day washed over him, a giant wave ready to knock him off his feet.

Nova had only a few hours to rest on his way back to Montana, but he'd been too wired, going over everything in his mind that he wanted to say to the man he hated most in life. But now that he was standing here in this hospital room, facing the man in question, all he wanted to do was lay down and close his eyes.

His father watched him for several seconds, maybe waiting for Nova to speak. When it became clear Nova wasn't going to say anything, he shifted again on the bed and cleared his throat.

"I don't remember much about that day. I was going about my work as usual when those two showed up. Everything happened so fast. And then you ... you came out of nowhere."

The voice didn't sound at all as Nova remembered it. It had aged, yes, but there was a softness to it that he didn't recognize.

"I'm still not sure how I ended up in Remington. But I guess in some ways, places choose you. I was on the road with no idea where I was headed, and I stopped off in town, and I just ... stayed."

One of the machines beside the bed made a soft clicking sound, and another machine emitted a slow and steady beep ... beep ... beep.

"When I came to town the garage was abandoned. That's how I managed to buy it. Paid nickels on the dollar. But the place was a mess, and it took a long time to get everything set up, and then before I realized it, I was running a mechanic shop in the middle of nowhere."

His father broke a smile, offered up a soft chuckle.

"Wasn't the greatest business decision in the world, was it? It took a while before people started to trust me, what with me being an outsider and all. But time passed, and everything seemed to be going well. Then one night I was out at the bar, minding my own business, when Mandy comes up and places her hand on my back."

He shifted on the bed again to readjust himself, wincing at the pain or maybe the memory.

"Remington's so tiny everybody knows each other more than they probably should. And I knew she'd been going with a guy, one of Blake Hogan's men. But that man had just been sent to prison, from what I heard. And then suddenly she shows up in the bar, and there are a dozen other guys much younger and better looking than myself, but she comes and puts her hand on my back."

Shaking his head again, still wincing.

"I'm not a complete idiot. I know Alex isn't my son. At least not biologically. And it isn't that he was born roughly eight months after that night at the bar. The fact is ... well, I had a vasectomy almost twenty years ago."

He paused, watching Nova for some reaction, a simple acknowledgment. But when Nova remained silent, his father shifted his gaze toward the window and the darkness beyond.

"Once upon a time, I was a different man. Younger, yes, but also angrier. More bullheaded. More ... selfish. Right out of high school I got together with this girl. I thought she was an angel, she was so beautiful."

Pausing again, his gaze now dropping to his lap, staring into a distant past.

"She got pregnant, and we decided to have the baby. I was scared out of my mind. I was eighteen years old—what did I know about being a father? What did the girl I loved know about being a mother? But we made it work, the best we knew how. We were kids ourselves, but we did our best to raise a kid. But the more time that went by, the more ... I guess you'd call it resentment started to build. Every time I looked at that kid, I saw a life that I was being denied, and that resentment grew and grew until I couldn't take it anymore. I drank hard, and I became an angry drunk, just like my old man. I tried to connect at times with the boy, tried to be a true father to him, but ... I wasn't cut out for it."

One of the machines beside the bed made that soft clicking sound again.

"Then the girl I loved got sick. Cancer—it's always cancer, isn't it? By that point, my boy was in high school. I don't want to say he and I had drifted apart because that assumes we had ever been close to begin with. And ... I don't know, all that resentment, all that anger, all that fear, suddenly burst out of me, and I did the most cowardly thing imaginable. I ran away. Just upped and packed my things and walked out the door."

Those gray eyes, staring into that distant past, focused on Nova again.

"I'm a piece of shit—no question about it. Soon, I'd regretted what I'd done. I went back, but it was too late—the girl I loved had passed away, and our son ... was gone. Joined the military, from what I heard. I thought about reaching out to him but knew I shouldn't bother, that he no doubt hated me with every fiber in his body."

He shifted again, wincing once more.

"That's why I'd gotten the vasectomy. Some men just aren't cut out to be fathers—I had come to realize that, to accept that, and I was at peace with that. I never wanted to have that responsibility again. But then Mandy came along that night and put her hand on my back. And then eight months later Alex was born. And I realized I couldn't abandon those two like I had before, even if the boy wasn't my own. So I stayed. And…I made it work. Not that it's been perfect or anything, but I made it work. Alex may not be my biological son, but that doesn't mean I'm not his father."

Even from across the room Nova could see the tears forming in the corner of the man's eyes.

"I'm not a religious man, but I've found myself praying from time to time. I don't ask God for forgiveness, because I don't believe I deserve it. But I've prayed to one day see the boy again, the one I walked out on so long ago. I've always figured he turned out right. Because he had more of his mother in him than his father. His mother was a strong woman—smart and caring—while his old man … well, look at me."

A smile that lasted only a second or two before fading.

"I've prayed to one day see the boy again to tell him just how sorry I am. Not that it would matter. Not that I would expect the boy to forgive me. That's not something I'd ask of him, anyway, because I don't deserve it. Because, well, like I said, I'm a piece of shit. But I know for a fact that my boy isn't. I know that he's strong and smart and caring, just like his mother."

The door behind Nova clicked open. Alex charged inside, a small bag of Cheetos in hand, and hopped onto the chair beside his father.

"So," said the man in the hospital bed, smiling again,

"thank you. Thank you for showing up when you did. Thank you for saving my life. And not just my life, but ..."

And he tilted his head toward the boy in the chair beside him, little Alex having already immersed himself with the tablet.

Nova stared ahead, seeing his father but not seeing him. Instead, seeing his mother sitting on the ground with her back against the tree so long ago. The midafternoon sun soaking her in a golden hue. A light breeze blowing through, causing several strands of the hair from her wig to shiver.

There's an anger in you, isn't there? I can see it. It's been building for most of your life. I don't blame you—not after what all you've been through—but you can't let the anger control you. Because once the anger controls you ...

She'd tilted her head, just slightly to look up at him, and he saw his reflection in the sunglasses, a boy who thought he was a man but who didn't know the first thing about life.

You're lost.

Nova sensed George Murphy out in the hallway, wanting to talk to him. He sensed his father in the bed, wanting a response.

Very soon he would leave this hospital room. He would ride the elevator down to the first floor, go out to his truck where his things were already packed. And from there? Nova had no idea where he would end up, but he would keep driving until he got there. Even if it took days. Even if it took weeks. He would drive until he sensed that wherever he landed was home.

But that was then, and this was now, and Nova kept standing by the door, silent, feeling that rage bubbling deep inside of him.

He closed his eyes, took a deep breath, and said the only words he could think to say.

"You're welcome."

CODA

ONE YEAR LATER

He'd built the cabin from scratch.

It had just the right amount of space for him and his few belongings. No TV. No computer. No cell phone. Nothing to connect him with the outside world.

And it wasn't like the outside world was right outside his door. No, this was a dead zone—no cell service whatsoever—and the closest town was ten miles away, the same type of town as Remington: nothing more than a dot on the map.

His internal clock woke him at the same time every morning. Seven a.m., as the sun was rising and firing its light through the cluster of Douglas firs and Sitka spruces and western hemlocks.

He lit the portable stove to boil water for coffee as he brushed his teeth in the makeshift sink. Then he dressed and poured himself coffee and stepped out onto the porch.

His truck was parked in front of the cabin. Beyond it, a half-mile rutted drive that led to a secondary road that after four miles led to the highway. The turnoff to get to the cabin was so hidden that nobody would spot it unless they were looking.

There was a small river a quarter mile away, headed north. Most mornings he hiked there with his gear to fish. Over the past year, he'd become an expert, and now the fly-casting technique had become second nature.

But the truth was he was getting sick of eating fish for almost every meal. Maybe he'd take the day and drive to the nearest Walmart, which was over an hour away. Stock up on items he couldn't get at the general store in town.

A sudden noise caught his attention, and he felt the muscles in his back tighten as he realized a vehicle was headed up the rutted drive.

Slipping into the cabin, he set the coffee on the table and grabbed the FNX-45 hanging near the door. Already locked and loaded, he stuffed it into the rear waistband of his jeans as he stepped back out onto the porch.

A Kia Sorento trundled up the drive, taking it easy, going maybe five miles per hour. The morning sunlight glinted off the windshield, but still Nova could make out only one occupant, the driver.

His muscles loosened a bit, knowing that if somebody was coming for him, they wouldn't be doing it so noticeably.

He waited until the crossover halted behind his truck and the driver got out, the only sound now the engine ticking and the creak of the door.

"Wow, I didn't think there'd be anything back here."

The kid was young, maybe nineteen years old. Wearing jeans and a vintage T-shirt, baseball cap on backward.

"Are you Nova?"

The kid didn't wait for an answer, ducking back inside the car. Nova felt his muscles tense again, his fingers flexing to grab for his pistol. But then the kid leaned back out, a small box in his hands.

He started forward, flashing a hesitant smile.

"Sorry that it's already opened. But the dude told me I

should charge it on my way here. He was adamant about that, saying you wouldn't have any power."

The kid leaned to the left, squinting at the cabin.

"Damn, dude, you really don't have any power in this place, do you?"

Nova said, "Who told you to come here?"

The kid, shrugging: "No idea what his name is. He hit me up on the app."

"What app?"

"Postmates, dude. It's what I do part-time for some extra scratch."

"And you were told to come here."

"Yeah."

"And to bring that box."

The kid grinned, hefting the unmarked box.

"I had to go to a special electronics store to pick this up. Dude had already called ahead and paid for it. Honestly, I thought I was getting pranked or something, that there was no way this was real, but here you are."

"How far did you come?"

"Seattle, dude! It took me, like, four hours to get here. But the guy's paying me ridiculous money, so I couldn't pass it up. Hey, we're real close to the Canadian border, aren't we?"

Nova said nothing.

"Yeah, anyway, here you go."

The kid held out the box. Nova stared at it for a beat, not wanting to take it. Because he knew taking it would leaving this quiet solitude he'd become accustomed to these many long months. He'd need to return to the world of artificial lights, to the crush of people too wrapped up in their own petty lives to see the bigger picture.

He almost told the kid no, sorry, you've got the wrong guy, have a nice drive back.

Almost.

Nova took the box, already knowing exactly what was inside it.

"Cool," the kid said when he realized Nova wasn't going to say anything else. "Well, nice meeting you. I dig your cabin. Your beard's cool too. You've got a real Rocky Mountain Man thing going."

The kid waited, maybe hoping for Nova to return his grin, but when he realized Nova had no intention of doing so, he quickly retreated to the Sorento.

Nova waited until the vehicle was out of sight before opening the box.

A black satellite phone slid out into his hand. Already powered on. Its battery fully charged.

He peeked inside the box but didn't see anything else. No number to call. No other directions.

Nova dialed a number he knew by heart. After two rings, a voicemail picked up.

"Thank you for calling Scout Dry Cleaners. Our normal business hours are Monday through Friday, seven a.m to seven p.m., and on Saturday eight a.m. to three p.m. We are closed Sundays."

Beep.

"It's me. I'm assuming you sent the kid. And I'm assuming you'll see the number to call back on your end."

The phone buzzed a minute later.

Atticus Caine said, "Good morning."

Nova said nothing.

"You certainly don't make it easy to get in touch with you. I had no choice but to send the young man. I'm glad you didn't shoot him."

"Who says I didn't?"

"You never struck me as the type of person to live off the grid."

"Everybody is full of surprises."

"Don't you get lonely?"

"Not really. My first month here, I got a senior dog from the shelter. He'd been there two years, and everyone kept passing him by."

"It's nice that you adopted him. What's his name?"

"His name was Charlie."

"Was?"

"He passed away three months ago. Cancer. He'd been slowing down, so I took him in to see the vet. Had he been in a proper home earlier, maybe they would have caught it in time. As it was, I had to put him down. He was in too much pain."

"I'm sorry."

"He was a good dog. He loved roaming all over the woods. Anyway, what did she do this time?"

"Who?"

"You know who. I'm assuming you did all this because Holly Lin's gotten into trouble."

"She killed two men."

"Yeah, well, that's what she was trained to do. Only, I'd thought she'd retired from all of that."

"She did."

"So then what happened?"

"I need you to head down to Methow Valley State Airport. James is flying in on a private jet. From there, you'll both head to Alden, Texas."

"Hold up. Who says I'm going anywhere? I haven't seen or heard from Holly in almost a year. The same with you."

"You've gone off the grid, Nova. How exactly is anyone supposed to be in contact with you?"

"Whatever. I'm retired. I'm sorry that Holly got into a sticky situation, but that's on her."

Silence. It stretched for five seconds. Ten.

"You're right," Atticus said. "Evidently I've made a mistake. My apologies. The beard suits you, by the way."

Nova's eyes scanned the forest, as though Atticus would be sitting among the trees in his electric wheelchair.

A smile in Atticus's voice: "Just because you've been off the grid doesn't mean I haven't kept tabs on you. Regardless, I'll let you go. Do what you want with the phone."

Nova closed his eyes, sucked in a silent breath.

"Wait," he said. "What happened, exactly?"

"For whatever reason, Holly killed two ICE agents."

"Christ."

"My theory, at least as of right now, is that somebody set her up."

"What makes you say that?"

"Two U.S. Marshals transporting her to San Antonio for arraignment were ambushed. Both of them were killed as well."

Nova felt a spike of adrenaline shoot through his body.

"And Holly?"

Atticus said, "She's missing."

www.ingramcontent.com/pod-product-compliance
Lightning Source LLC
Chambersburg PA
CBHW021207250626
47155CB00008B/2709